"I thought of you every second the month past." He advanced across the carpet, immune to the sense of danger terrifying her. "I counted the hours. . . ."

"No, Robbie," she gasped, retreating. "Don't say that, don't pretend everything is fine when it isn't. It's terrifyingly *not* fine." She glanced fearfully at the draped windows as though they might be seen through the heavy velvet. "You have to leave *right* now!"

He shook his head. "Sorry. I'm staying."

She found her retreat arrested by the wall and pressed her palms against the cherrywood wainscoting. Robbie Carre was much too close, and the memories and implications of that closeness made her tremble. "Please, Robbie, just leave."

"I can't. I wish I could."

His fingers curled over her silk-covered shoulders and pulled her to him. Black leather and lilac silk glided against each other in the smallest of undulations—invitation, enticement, potent memory in the exquisite drifting impulse.

He murmured deep in his throat, half groan, half sigh. "A month's too long."

To Please a Lady

SUSAN JOHNSON

Bantam Books

NEW YORK   TORONTO   LONDON   SYDNEY   AUCKLAND

TO PLEASE A LADY
A Bantam Book / October 1999

All rights reserved.
Copyright © 1999 by Susan Johnson.
Cover art copyright © 1999 by Alan Ayers.

ISBN 0-553-57866-9

Published simultaneously in the United States and Canada

Bantam Books are published by Bantam Books, a division of Random
House, Inc. Its trademark, consisting of the words "Bantam Books"
and the portrayal of a rooster, is Registered in U.S. Patent and Trademark Office and in other countries. Marca Registrada. Bantam
Books, 1540 Broadway, New York, New York 10036.

PRINTED IN THE UNITED STATES OF AMERICA
OPM   10   9   8   7   6   5   4   3   2   1

Dear Reader,

Robbie Carre appeared in my consciousness, like so many of my heroes, in a flashing visual image—in this case, riding across a windswept field beside the infamous Harold Godfrey in *Outlaw*. He immediately engaged my interest, reminding me of the beautiful young men so vividly portrayed by the Renaissance painters, their wildness and restless energy only partially restrained.

But Johnnie Carre's presence was so powerful in *Outlaw*, Robbie didn't step out of the background until the closing chapters when the Carres were about to be exiled. I hadn't planned on him walking into Roxane's room the night before they sailed; he took the initiative. And while Roxane tried to resist, his seductive skills were already legendary.

Robbie Carre's back now, disregarding his fugitive status, intent on wooing and winning his lady.

I hope you enjoy his particular hot-blooded style of courtship.

Best,

Susan Johnson

To Please a Lady

Chapter 1

*R*OBBIE CARRE IS BACK."

"So I've heard. The question is where?"

The two men spoke in undertones, their words lost in the sounds of music, conversation, and laughter swirling around them. Guests of honor at the evening soiree, they'd found a rare moment of privacy in the crowded ballroom, but both men cautiously scanned the room as they spoke. Robbie Carre had friends everywhere.

"He'll come for her. There's no doubt," the Duke of Queensberry murmured. A thin, swarthy man of middle age, he had the natural look of a conspirator.

"She's unrivaled." The words, husky, low, palpably lustful, were uttered by the Duke of Argyll, the new commissioner who'd come from London to bring Scotland to heel.

Queensberry wondered if their hostess would be able to thwart the young man's predatory instincts. "I hear she's in love," he maliciously noted.

"So?" Argyll shot Queensberry an insolent look.

"So you might wish to cultivate your seductive skills. The Countess of Kilmarnock is no ingénue. Twice widowed and with her pick of suitors, from the

Indies to the poles, she might prove a formidable challenge."

"Then the prize will be that much sweeter," Argyll said, his gray gaze following Roxane Forrestor's twirling progress across the ballroom.

*M*AY KILMARNOCK'S WRETCHED FAMILY ROT IN hell!" Slamming the bedroom door behind her so hard the paintings quivered on the silk-hung walls, Roxane stalked across the rich Turkey carpet, pulling her tiara from her coiffed head. "They have their damned nerve!" She flung the diamond headpiece across the room with such fury it bounced twice before coming to rest.

"Could I be of some help?" a deep voice drawled.

Spinning around, she scrutinized the shadowed reaches of her large bedchamber. The indolent voice was familiar, and a sudden stark fear gripped her senses.

"Lord God, you can't *be* here!" she exclaimed, shock and horror in her tone, her eyes tracing the dim outlines of the young man lounging on her gilded chair, her frustration and anger dissipating before the horrendous jeopardy of his position in Edinburgh. "The house is awash with your enemies!"

As if to punctuate her exclamation, the melodious strains of violins drifted in through the opened windows from the floor below, numerous voices joining in on the chorus of the familiar Scottish ballad of Muirland Willie.

"Like Muirland Willie I've come for you," Robbie said, his pose utterly still, his dark eyes traveling slowly down the countess's fashionably attired form. "Do you know how long it's been?"

"Not long enough. You're insane, Robbie." She glanced back at him in her swift passage to the windows. "They'll hang you if they find you here!" Shutting a window, she pulled the green velvet drapes closed, then moved to a second window. "You have to leave."

"I thought I might keep you company tonight." He rose from the chair, all grace and languid power.

"No! Don't even think that." Her words ended on a hushed vibrato, for he'd walked from the shadows, tall, lean, beautiful, his hair lying in waves on his shoulders, the auburn curls striking against the pure black leather of his jack.

"I can't do this, Robbie," she whispered, moving away, as though putting distance between them could allay her clamorous heartbeat. How beautiful he looked—breathtaking, dressed in leather like some pagan warrior, taller than she remembered, broader as if he'd grown in the month of their separation, the powerful intensity of his youth dazzling.

"I thought of you every second the month past." He advanced across the carpet, immune to the sense of danger terrifying her. "I counted the hours. . . ."

"No, Robbie," she gasped, retreating, the faint music reminding her of the hundreds of guests below, many of them dangerous. "Don't say that, don't pretend everything is fine when it isn't. It's terrifyingly *not* fine." She glanced fearfully at the draped windows as though they might be seen through the heavy velvet. "You have to leave *right* now!"

He shook his head so faintly his long hair barely

rippled in the candlelight. "Sorry," he murmured, moving toward her, "I'm staying."

"Than one of us has to be sensible," she sharply replied, the way she might speak to a recalcitrant child. "In any event, I have to go back downstairs or I'll be missed. I'm hosting this political soiree," she went on, trying to maintain her composure against his inexorable advance.

"Is the reptile Queensberry still as charming as ever?" The outlawed young Earl of Greenlaw's words were casual, as though he wasn't a mere floor away from his mortal enemy.

"Yes, no—" She moved back a step, then another. "Lord, Robbie, you know what he's like."

"Filled with gentle malice. Smiling while he shoves his knife into your heart." He took note of the short distance between the countess's back and the wall. "We'll have to see what we can do to curb his arrogance."

"Not we, Robbie," she corrected him. Finding her retreat arrested, she pressed her palms into the cherry-wood wainscoting and tried to hold herself steady against the violent beating of her heart. Robbie Carre's tall, rawboned body was much too close, and the memories and implications of that closeness made her tremble. "Please, Robbie, just leave." Her voice was taut with emotion.

"I can't. I wish I could." He stood very still, his expression grave. "But the last month was the longest of my life."

"Please, Robbie, be sensible. In a few years you'll forget this ever happened."

"Us, you mean?"

"There can't be any us, Robbie. Do you want me to begin listing all the reasons? The very first one is that my five children are in peril if I'm seen with you." Her brows came together in apprehension. "And the other thousand after that don't matter."

"Go, then." All suave charm and indulgence, he shifted slightly so his body no longer curbed her departure. "We'll talk about this later."

"There's no later, Robbie Don't you understand?" Her in-laws from her first marriage to Jamie Low had given warning they intended to protect their four grandchildren from the taint of the Carres. The Erskines, the family of her second husband, Kilmarnock, had practically threatened to have her thrown into the Tolbooth if she spoke one word to any of the Carres. They wanted nothing to blemish the chance of Kilmarnock's only issue, Angus, being given an English peerage.

"We'll make certain no one sees us together."

"This isn't sport, Robbie. The Erskines are rabid Queensberry supporters. They'd like nothing better than to see your whole family drawn and quartered in their castle courtyard."

"Why would they suspect that I've returned?"

"Because you're a hotheaded Carre."

"Hot-blooded, more like," he said with a grin. "How soon can you rid yourself of your guests?"

"Robbie!" she wailed. "Listen!"

"Darling, darling," he soothed her, gently brushing her mouth with his fingertip. "I've heard every word. Now go be a gracious hostess to all the treacherous cutthroats downstairs, and I'll be here when you return. No one knows I'm in the country." He leaned forward so his breath was warm on her mouth, then his lips met hers in a delicate, restrained caress, a butterfly kiss of politesse and affection. "So you're safe, your children are safe." His bronzed fingers curled over her silk-covered shoulders, pulled her close. "There now, that's better." His arousal was blatant against her belly, black leather and lilac silk gliding against each other in the smallest of undulations—invitation, enticement, potent memory in the exquisite drifting impulse. He murmured deep in his throat—half groan, half sigh, paradise regained after months in the wilderness. As he leaned into her soft, voluptuous body, his kiss subtly changed, deepened, his mouth slowly forcing hers open, his tongue gently exploring, tasting, sliding far into her mouth, prelude to the more tantalizing offer of his virile body hard against hers.

A scorching heat ignited deep within her, her response immediate, extreme, so fierce with memory and need she moaned, a soft, low, animal sound that gave voice to the urgent desire burning through her senses.

"A month's too long," he whispered, rubbing against her, crushing a handful of skirt in his hand and lifting it up.

Panicked at the sensation of cool air on her thighs, she twisted her mouth away, swiftly brought her hands up to push him away. "No! Please, Robbie, no."

Immune to her pleas, he recaptured her mouth, the pressure of her hands insignificant against his strength. Like a man intent on claiming what was his, he branded her with a demanding, possessive kiss that burned away reason, brought the throbbing between her thighs to fever pitch, made her forget everything but reckless desire.

They were both breathless when he finally released her. With his erection straining his black leather breeches, it required a deep breath to master his rash impulses. "Go now," he whispered. "But don't be gone too long."

Shivering, she clung to him, fear and longing a chaos in her brain, the feel of him tantalizing, his body toned, hard, exquisitely tempting—like his arousal. And knowing how he could make her feel, how insatiable his sexual appetite and stamina, she wondered if she was capable of leaving him.

But she'd survived as a widow in a man's world because she rarely let impulse overwhelm the practical considerations of her life. Inhaling to steady her dizzying susceptibilities, cautioning herself against succumbing to reckless urges, she lifted her head from his chest and gazed up into his dark eyes. "Darling Robbie, if I allow this, I put my children in jeopardy. No matter how much I want to make love to you, I can't."

"Do you think I came from Holland only for that? I wouldn't have to go so far for sex."

"I understand," she acknowledged. "But how can there by anything more with the limitations curtailing me? And you shouldn't have written, not with Queensberry's spies everywhere."

He took a half-step back, scrutinizing her with an inquisitor's fierce regard, all the grace and charm stripped from his face. "The letter was sent through Roxburgh. Are you saying he's suspect now? I think you found someone new." His voice took on a rough, flinty edge. "That's what I think."

"You're wrong," she responded coolly. "Everyone's suspect since the bribes from London have escalated.

And I've slept alone the last month, if you must know."

His smile was instant, unutterably warm, like a brilliant ray of sunshine after a storm. "Alone? For me? I'm honored."

"Don't be presumptuous," she retorted, testy after his accusations, not inclined to allow him such simplistic guidelines of right and wrong. "I've been busy trying to keep my in-laws' clutches off my children since you left for Holland. It didn't give me time to invite any men into my bed."

"I'm just arrived in Edinburgh, the spies haven't sent in their reports yet." Indulgent to her temper now that his jealousy was assuaged, he repressed his smile of satisfaction. "So your children are safe."

"For how long?" Determined to resist his dangerous temptations, she moved away.

He could have stopped her but he let her go, half turning to follow her progress.

"Don't be here when I return," she quietly ordered, reserve in her tone, the Countess of Kilmarnock speaking now. "I *can't* see you."

He didn't reply beyond the merest inclination of his head, but he'd felt what she'd felt when they'd kissed.

As if reading his thoughts, she spun around and faced him, her hands clenched at her sides. "Damn you, Robbie, you can't have everything you want."

"But then I don't want everything," he murmured. "I only want you."

Snatching up her tiara from the carpet, she swung the glittering diamond headpiece in the curve of her fingers, disturbed, agitated, out of temper with her conflicting needs, with the impertinent young man smiling at her. "This isn't a game, Robbie." Vexation showed in her violet gaze. "I'm not available—for a score of reasons you wouldn't understand."

"I understand perfectly. I'll take care of them all."

"If you're not hung first."

"We'll have our estates back by fall," he replied, undisturbed by the menace in her words. "You worry too much."

"And you don't worry enough." Setting the tiara on her titian curls, she glanced in her dressing table mirror and adjusted the glittering ornament minutely, "I have my children to consider, not just my carnal urges. I'm sorry," she briskly added, as if her bracing tone would strengthen her resolve. "I can't become involved with you." Turning from the mirror, she twitched the folds of her skirt into order, looked at the young Earl of Greenlaw for a breath-held moment, and then, in a swish of lilac silk, walked from the room.

Chapter 2

MOVING SWIFTLY DOWN THE CARPETED HALL-way, she could hear her heart beating like a drum, the sound echoing in her ears, the heated flush on her face indication of her dread, lust, pleasure at seeing Robbie again. He'd come back to her as he said he would, she thought—and so quickly. An irrepressible smile appeared on her mouth at such charming, ardent impetuousness.

She'd missed him the past month, really missed him.

Which several of her friends had noticed. Not that they understood whose absence was affecting her, but they realized she'd lost interest in the usual crowd of men hovering around her.

Unfortunately, with Roxburgh's defection, her Er-skine mother-in-law had been apprised of Robbie's correspondence with her, and the gulf between her wishes and reality was vast.

Catching a glimpse of herself in a passing mirror, she came to an abrupt standstill. The image in the glass was that of a young girl giddy in love—glowing skin, sparkling eyes, breathless with passion. Her bosom rose and fell in fevered cadence, and the throbbing between her legs had only marginally diminished. A shame love was impossible, not to say dangerous, she reflected, making a small moue of disappointment. Although, even ruthless politics could be overlooked, Robbie was still much, much too young to love.

"There you are," an abrasive, female voice declared.

Spinning around, Roxane took note of her Erskine mother-in-law mounting the stairs, her thin, narrow face bright red with the exertion of the long climb.

"Argyll . . . is asking . . . for you," the elderly matron gasped, resting on a stair to catch her breath. "I should think . . . you'd know better . . . than to leave . . . your guests unattended."

Roxane often wondered how the old woman maintained life in her withered body; simmering bile no doubt. "I needed a moment of quiet."

"Kindly remember . . . where your duty lies." The Dowager Countess Kilmarnock's voice was like acid. "Kilmarnock's son needs court patronage . . . and Queensberry and Argyll are critical to . . . that patronage."

"I'm well aware of that, Agnes. And if I hadn't been, your constant reminders have engraved it on my liver."

"I told Kilmarnock he was making a mistake marrying you, but he wouldn't listen," she snapped, rude as always about her son's marriage. "Now you will do your duty to the Erskines and my grandson, or I'll see that Angus is taken from you and raised in a God-fearing home."

"Except for my marriage settlement, of course, which disallows that," Roxane coolly returned. But she was bluffing and she knew it; the Erskines had enough influence in court to make the outcome of any legal fight uncertain.

"I don't think you'd care to put that scrap of paper to the test," the old lady tartly noted. "Now, remember, Argyll likes docile women."

"Meaning—" A barely repressed fury trembled in the single word.

"Meaning I expect you to be docile, my haughty daughter-in-law." The dowager's voice was cold as ice. "In any way that's necessary."

How easy it would be to push her down the stairs, Roxane thought, the fleeting impulse quickly overcome by the moral strictures of a lifetime. But it was damned tempting; she wondered if the old bag of bones would explode in a puff of dust on impact. "I'll be polite to Argyll, but my duty to the Erskines ceases at that point. I hope we're clear on the definition of politeness. And if you don't like it, I'd be happy to tell the young duke that you're pimping in your old age."

"I wouldn't suggest you take me on, young lady. And don't think pimping in a thousand different forms hasn't contributed to many an aristocratic fortune. I'll be watching you, so make sure you're suitably gracious to the queen's new commissioner."

Checkmated again, Roxane bitterly noted—her frequent position since the discovery of Robbie's letter. But she didn't have to give the old dragon the satisfaction of thinking she'd won the argument. "I'll consider it," Roxane casually replied, moving down the stairs. "But I wouldn't press my luck right now, Agnes. If a woman your age tripped and fell down these stairs, who knows what might break."

There was satisfaction in seeing the old witch clutch the banister with both hands. Roxane allowed herself a small smile of triumph, even while chastising herself for such wickedness.

But she wasn't allowed her minor victory for long. Within minutes after entering the drawing room, she found herself face-to-face with the Duke of Argyll, her smiling mother-in-law at his side.

"The duke tells me your brother Colter served him well as ADC in Holland." The dowager countess lightly tapped her fan on the duke's arm and offered him a warm smile, then returned her gaze to Roxane. "I'm sure you have a number of questions you'd like to ask him about Colter. Kilmarnock always said you two were so close, my dear." She looked past Roxane. "Ah, I see Lady Frances waving at me," she mendaciously went on. "I beg your leave, Argyll, but I'm sure Roxane will entertain you in my absence."

As the duke bowed over the old woman's hand, Agnes cast Roxane a gloating look.

"She's not very subtle," Roxane said as her mother-in-law walked away. "And Colter and I have agreed to disagree since he left to serve Marlborough."

"A patriot, and so beautiful," John Campbell murmured, gazing down on his hostess with the eyes of a predator. "The queen's court holds no appeal for you?"

"I don't need her money."

"A direct cut." His smile was gracious. "I should be offended."

"Please do, and release me from my mother-in-law's designs."

"But then my designs would be curtailed as well."

"Your wife doesn't mind?" Roxane lightly queried.

"I've never asked her."

"I see."

A small pause ensued while the young duke took in the full glory of the flame-haired woman before him. The reigning beauty of her time was even more dazzling at close range. "Should I ask you directly?" he said, thinking she fairly glowed with sensual allure.

"I'd rather you didn't."

"But if I should?"

"I would be forced to be evasive, my lord."

He smiled. Already a brigadier general at twenty-five, he understood tactical offense better than most. "The Parliament should be in session most of the summer. Do you like to sail?"

"Only with friends."

"Then we must become friends," he cordially said. "I hear the Erskines are hoping for an English earldom."

"And I'm the means to that peerage?" she sardonically observed.

He shrugged, his epaulets shimmering with the movement. "Let's just say that, as commissioner, I have enormous latitude in . . . a variety of areas, peerages included." His smile was open, warm. "I'm sure we can come to some agreement."

"I prefer keeping my distance from the entire Erskine family."

"You don't want an earldom for your son?"

"Not if the price is my independence."

"I could easily discourage Agnes's involvement," he

perceptively replied, his voice solicitous. "Would you like her sent to the country?"

Roxane smiled faintly. "You amaze me, my lord, with the extent of your powers. The queen was generous."

"I was under no illusions as to my value to the court when I bargained for this commissionership."

"You have carte blanche?"

"Very nearly. Certainly enough to send Agnes to her country estate if you but give me leave." Innuendo was prominent in his words.

"You tempt me, Argyll, if for no other reason than to nonplus my malicious mother-in-law."

"I'm at your service, my dear Roxane, in whatever capacity you wish. Just say the word."

She understood, in her few minutes of conversation with the young head of the Campbell clan, how he'd accomplished the remarkable feat of not only bringing Queensberry back into the government against the queen's wishes, but also gaining the broad powers he'd been granted by Her Majesty, Queen Anne. He was remarkably charming, and willing to do whatever was necessary to obtain his objectives. While a political novice, he was neither naive nor inexperienced in the art of diplomacy. His offer of liberation from the grating control of her mother-in-law was extremely persuasive.

"I'll consider it, my lord," she smoothly returned, her own arts of persuasion and politesse honed to a fine pitch after years of adroitly evading advances from powerful men familiar with having their way.

"Could I interest you in a country dance, my lady,

while you're considering my proposal?" He was content with the progress of his campaign. It was May, and the long Parliamentary sessions would continue through the summer and early fall. He needn't rush. The enchanting Roxane's resistance would eventually succumb to his persuasion.

Chapter 3

"YOU'RE SMILING," DOUGLAS COUTTS SAID, ASSessing the presumptuous young man who'd risked his life to return to Scotland. "You must have seen her already."

"I have, and she's as bonnie as ever." Robbie beckoned the man in the doorway into the study of the Carre apartment. Lounging in shirtsleeves and breeches, his leather jack discarded, he had neither the pose nor look of a harried outlaw. "Roxie's hosting Queensberry and Argyll tonight for her nasty Erskine in-laws, as it turns out. I considered two bullets through the drawing room windows," he cheerfully said, "but the bastards kept moving and the grounds were crawling with guards."

"You're quite rash to have even shown yourself in the gardens." Coutts sat down across from Robbie, near the grate where a small fire kept away the chill of the spring evening. "Both Argyll and Queensberry move about only with a full complement of Highland guards and swordsmen."[1]

"Evidence of the great esteem with which they're regarded," Robbie drawled, leaning forward to offer his guest a glass of whiskey.

"The reprisals would be severe should they be

assassinated," the Carre family lawyer cautioned. "That threat keeps them alive more than the guards. So don't be reckless"—he smiled faintly, raising the glass to his mouth—"and make the lovely Roxie a widow for the third time."

"Amen to that." Robbie lifted his glass to the man who was coordinating the Carres' defense against the treasonous charges brought against them. "Although she's being skittish at the moment."

"With good reason," Coutts said, in acknowledgement of the fluid state of political alliances. "Be careful. I wouldn't doubt that the Erskines have put informers in her household."

"I'm always careful"—Robbie winked—"or at least well armed. Now tell me of the latest maneuvers in the courts and Privy Council concerning our case."

"You brought the documents I requested?"

"A full saddlebag." Robbie slipped down into a more comfortable sprawl and gazed at his visitor from under his long dark lashes. "Every account of every merchant and burgess in Scotland, along with letters pleading for the release of their funds." The men faced financial ruin, their bills of exchange unrecoverable from their accounts held by the Carres' bank in Rotterdam.

"Even Queensberry is affected, you know," Coutts observed with a half smile. "He invested heavily in the last cargo of wine from Bordeaux."

"Not enough to repay his confiscation of our properties, though," Robbie gruffly replied. "Personally, I'd prefer he repay us with his blood."

"You'll hurt him more by beggaring him, my lord. His vanity is his greatest vice."

"As is Argyll's. I hear he's sold himself dear to the English court."

"And he got what he asked for. His commissionership is a case of *pis aller*. All the other experienced political magnates are unacceptable to either the court or Parliament. We'll see what he can do."

"It depends on how much money the queen is willing to spend to buy votes."

"Unlike last session, rumor has it the money is going to be forthcoming this time. Godolphin ordered Seafield to move on arrears of salaries and gratifications."

"Then I see Scotland sold away." A deep scowl gave indication of Robbie's resentment. "Are there any patriots left who can't be bought?"

"Fewer than last session. The court is systematically recruiting those most necessitous. William Seton the younger, of Pitmedden, was bought for a hundred pounds a year."

"So everyone has become suspect, Roxburgh a case in point."

"Agreed. You see how little it takes for some. They're also creating new peerages with an extravagant largesse to bolster the court's interests."

"*Merde*," Robbie softly swore, gazing into the remnants of the whiskey in his glass. "It's damned depressing."

"Gossip is Hamilton himself has sold out."

Robbie's lashes slowly lifted and his eyes were much too cynical for his years. "He's always strapped for cash. I heard his agents in London were trying to negotiate a deal for him. It seems," he said with a small sigh, "even the great patriot Hamilton has his price."[2]

"The Carre integrity is more easily maintained." Coutts was as aware as anyone of what it took to afford to be a patriot. "Your family assets, once regained, will maintain the Carres in opulence. You needn't feel the pressures others do."

"I know. Our shipping fleet generates more than enough wealth. And the new tobacco depots in the American colonies are proving lucrative."

"Exactly. So you have no need of English money. Even your case before the Privy Council should be settled with a minimum of expense," he noted with the frugality of a Scottish lawyer. "Paying for the Privy Council's cooperation is unnecessary when you already hold the wealth of much of Scotland in your Dutch banks."

Robbie glanced at the clock on the mantel. Sliding upright in his chair, he set his glass aside. "Use the Carre money to buy what loyalty you can, and let me know how I can best help. This apartment is secure; the servants are loyal. Any message you wish to leave will be relayed to me." Rising, he moved to a chest set against a wall. "Take the back way when you leave. Holmes will guide you through the passages." Sliding a key from his pocket, he unlocked the painted chest, took out the saddlebags he'd brought from The Hague, and carried them over to Coutts. "I'm not certain exactly where I'll be. It depends on the countess's degree of apprehension."

"And on the Erskines' threats."

"I suppose," Robbie brusquely retorted. "Damn their mercenary hides. Leave a message with Holmes, should you need me to twist arms or cajole those wavering in their loyalty to Scotland. And I'll keep in contact with you."

"Be cautious, Robbie. Your death would be very profitable to Queensberry."

A flashing smile graced the Earl of Greenlaw's handsome face. "I have no intention of dying, now that I'm back with Roxie." A wicked gleam shone in his eyes. "Or at least not in the conventional sense. Wish me good fortune with my reluctant lover."

"I don't doubt your good fortune with the countess. The Erskines, on the other hand, may prove formidable opponents. Watch your back. They're lying scoundrels, submissive to Queensberry's every whim."

"So long as they stay out of Roxie's bed, I don't expect to see them." He paused. "I'll get in touch with you tomorrow in case you have any questions about the documents I brought. I bid you good night now. Roxie's soiree should be over soon."

"Take care, Robbie," Coutts cautioned. Robbie Carre was still eighteen and though long a full-grown man, gifted and capable, he didn't have the experience of a devious schemer like Queensberry.

"I'm armed to the teeth, Douglas, and the Edinburgh streets at night will offer obscurity," he assured his friend. "Let me know if you have any further word from Johnnie. My brother talked of coming over, although I discouraged him. Elizabeth's still uncertain. Their son is not a month old." He looped his sword baldric over his shoulder and quickly tested the draw of his weapon, the Toledo blade sliding in and out of the scabbard like silk on silk. Picking up his two pistols, he jammed them through his belt, checked the dirk tucked into his boot, and, straightening, tipped his head in adieu. "I'll see you tomorrow."

The door opened and closed so quickly he seemed to disappear before Coutts's eyes.

A moment later the lawyer heaved himself out of his chair with a sigh, offering up a silent prayer for Robbie Carre's safety. England was playing a dangerous game to neutralize Scotland's independence. Human life was being sold cheaply, and utterly ruthless men were making the bargains.

I THOUGHT I MIGHT HAVE TO SHARE YOUR BED with Argyll tonight," Robbie sardonically murmured as Roxane entered her bedroom suite an hour later. He was leaning against the wall very near the door, his arms folded across his chest, but his dark eyes held none of the languidness of his pose.

"He followed me upstairs. I didn't invite him. And you shouldn't have listened if it bothered you." She took note of his challenging gaze and went on, with a challenging look of her own. "Furthermore, after spending the entire evening resisting the duke's advances, I'm not in the mood for any more male possessiveness. You're not supposed to be here in any event." She moved away, walking toward her dressing table.

"He's married, you know."

"Like your Mrs. Barrett. And don't say that was different."

He pushed away from the wall. "Very well . . . although it was."

Her acerbic moue was visible in the mirror over the mantel. "Don't remind me of male hypocrisy. I'm not currently disposed to listen. Kilmarnock's mother, by the way, is serving as pimp for Erskine interests. I've been instructed to be gracious to Argyll in any manner he chooses."

"Fuck that."

"My sentiments exactly." She kicked off her slippers, sending them across the room in her fury.

"Should I stay out of your way?" Robbie teased, his jealousy mollified by her response to the duke. He stopped in the middle of the room as if in wait for her answer, still fully armed—an incongruous sight in the silken bedchamber, a dark specter against the celadon damask and gilded furniture.

"You'd better. You're not on Agnes's list of useful paramours." She unclasped one diamond earring from her ear and tossed it on her dressing table. "As if I give a damn about the Erskines anyway. Kilmarnock was an unmitigated ass, and I more than paid my dues to that family by living with him for two years."

"My condolences."

"I should have received soldiers' wages for surviving that family for so long." She tossed the second earring on the tabletop and, turning around, smiled at him for the first time that evening. "I thought about pushing Agnes down the stairs a few hours ago." Her expression was cheerful. "You may not want to associate with a reprobate like me."

"You aren't the only one who's considered ways to put Agnes Erskine in her grave. Don't they say the good die young?"

"No doubt the saying was coined with her in mind. Help me with this necklace." She turned her back to him.

"With pleasure. I brought you something that will go equally well with that gown."

She glanced over her shoulder. "You shouldn't have." She smiled. "Actually, you shouldn't be here at all."

"I know. That's why I didn't come out and punch Argyll. I was being circumspect—for you, for your children . . . for the Carres, for God and country." He grinned. "Why is this all so damned complicated?" he murmured, stripping his gloves off.

His fingers were warm on her skin as he unclasped her diamond necklace, his delicate touch evoking sensations of lust out of all proportion to the circumstances.

"Put mine on instead." Dropping the necklace on the dressing table, he pushed her gently toward the bed.

She glanced at him again, and his smile obliterated the entirety of her durance vile that evening. "Will I like it?" One brow arched flirtatiously, an undercurrent of seduction in her voice.

"Definitely." Even Johnnie, known for his largesse, had questioned the extravagance of his brother's purchase. Roxane's gasp brought a grin to his face. "All the best diamonds go through Rotterdam. . . ."

"This must be *all* the diamonds in Rotterdam," she breathlessly intoned, awestruck.

A wide collar of diamonds with a graduated fringe of larger diamonds, centered with a huge square-cut emerald, glittered on the bedcover. No fewer than two thousand diamonds made up the elaborate necklace.

"The emerald detaches for a brooch if you wish,

as does the central portion for a tiara. It's very functional."

"Everyone will know you're back in town if I wear this."

"Then wear it just for me until our court case is settled."

"It's too much, Robbie. I'd feel beholden."

"Think of it as a gift from Queensberry, then. We're holding a great deal of his funds in our banks in Holland. Try it on."

She hesitated still, the costly necklace not some bagatelle that could be casually accepted from a lover. "I'm not sure."

"Should I give it to Mrs. Barrett?" he teased.

"Probably not." She grinned. "Her husband would kill her for it, or more likely she'd divorce him to marry you."

"A terrifying prospect," Robbie playfully observed.

"She didn't capture your heart, then."

He shook his head. "My heart was already taken by a scandalously beautiful widow."

"She was a stopgap, you're saying."

"A way of passing the time until I could engage your interest."

"And now that you have, the risks are horrendous," she gravely replied, the light suddenly gone from her eyes.

"I'll lock the door."

"Don't be casual about this." Her violet gaze held his with a piercing regard. "You're talking about my children."

"I'm not going to jeopardize your children by being

here tonight. I'll leave before first light. All I want to do is hold you," he said. "I came here because I couldn't live without you another moment, and I'm not leaving tonight unless Argyll's Highlanders come and take me away."

"I don't allow peremptory men in my life anymore."

"I'll try to be more submissive," he lightly murmured, pulling his pistols from his belt.

"Put those back." Alarm echoed in her words. "You really can't stay." But her voice trailed away at the end, the strength of his large hands on the pistol grips riveting.

He looked up from the bureau where he was depositing his handguns. "Just for an hour or so. Why don't you lock the door."

She was in her stocking feet, her white silk-covered toes peaking out from beneath the lilac hem of her gown; in her hesitant pose, she had the look of an uncertain maiden. Bereft of jewels, clad in a simple, unornamented gown, she looked fifteen, and for a moment he wished he could have met her before all the other men.

But as quickly he discarded the romantical notion, too long a man of the world to concern himself with virginity. He loved her, not her past or her future, not her fame or repute.

"Or I could lock the door," he gently added, slipping his baldric over his head.

His words seemed to reach her at last. "I always forget how watching you makes me tremble. Why can't I remember that?"

"You've forgotten what it is to love someone."

Laying his sword beside his pistols, he slid the buckles free on his jack. "It's been too long."

His fingers were tanned, long and slender, brushed with a light dusting of russet hairs on the knuckles, the red-gold hair swirling upward over his hand to slide under the wristband of his black linen shirt. A fragment of his powerful wrist became visible as he slid the heavy jack from his shoulders.

Stretching, he luxuriated in the freedom from the weight of the guilted armor, and as if mesmerized, her gaze traveled from his fingertips to his muscled arms and his hard lean torso, then down over the sleek black leather of his breeches clinging to his powerful thighs, to the dusty toes of his black riding boots.

"I'm pleased you came back," she said.

His arms dropped to his sides, his hands swinging gently for a moment. "I know."

"Tell me love is enough."

"It's everything," he said, his voice velvet soft.

"It's been so long . . ."

"You begin believing it doesn't exist."

"I tried to talk myself out of you."

He smiled. "I could tell."

"Don't be so smug." The corners of her mouth curved upward, a lush intimacy in her voice. "You're too young to know everything."

"I've been on my own for a long time, darling. Johnnie wasn't exactly a model of circumspect behavior after our father died. So I know more than you think."

"Can you blot Agnes from my life?" Grinning like a young girl, she teased him.

"I can do anything you want."

"That Carre assurance," she whispered, taking in the full beauty of his strong, bonny body.

"One learns to fashion the world to one's liking. And why not? Life's short."

"Not *too* short, I hope." A minute terror quivered in her words.

"Let me rephrase that," he diplomatically asserted, moving toward her. "One learns to take what one wants. Period."

"The freebooter Carres."

"It's a tradition on the Borders. We're born and bred to the practice."

"And you want me."

"Very much." He spoke in the merest whisper, but authority impregnated the quiet words.

How much of her independence was at stake? she wondered. "Would you take me against my will?"

He stopped just short of her, careful not to touch her. "I might wish to but, no, I wouldn't. Don't let the likes of Agnes Erskine turn you away from me, though. She was a corrupt and vicious woman long before you and I were born."

"More than you and me, it's about my children right now." A gravity underscored her words.

"Have them taken out of the country for safety. Don't you trust Jamie's sister Amelia?"

Her expression immediately brightened, her small frown disappeared. "I adore you."

"Problem solved?"

"Maybe." She sighed with a new-felt optimism. "Just maybe . . ."

"I'll have Coutts send someone to talk to her." A

small army of Carre retainers was at his command.
"Someone neutral."

"Is there anyone neutral left in these times of
tainted principles and dishonest men?"

"We'll find someone." His confidence was always a
source of wonder to her. As if he could do anything.
His presence in Edinburgh was evidence enough of his
competence; every authority in Scotland was on
watch for the outlawed Carres.

"In the morning," she offered, her voice tantalizing.

He shut his eyes briefly, a smile already forming on
his mouth before his eyes opened once again. "Don't
move." He held his hand up for a moment, the words
of welcome he'd been waiting to hear sweet in his ears.
"I'll lock the door."

When he returned, he saw her waiting exactly
where he'd left her, but her arms were opened wide
and her smile was the lush, seductive one he'd yearned
for during the lonely weeks past.

"I've been dreaming of this a very long time," he
said on a suffocated breath, taking her in his arms.

"And I feel helpless, when I never have before."

"Helpless in love," he whispered. "I know."

She nodded, gazing up at him, tears shining in her
eyes. "You should go. I should make you go. But all I
can think of is wanton desire. This is insanity, Robbie,
with Agnes Erskine and her servants here—none of
whom I can trust—and Queensberry and Argyll in
town with their armies of swordsmen."

"Hush, darling." Pulling her closer, he slid his hands
down her back. "After a month without you all I want
to do is feel you . . . everywhere. To hell with everything else."

"The danger—"

His mouth covered hers, obliterating the rest of her sentence, and the last remnants of her prudence died in a sigh.

He was blatantly aroused, ardent, his hard, lean body so flagrantly aphrodisiac that lust spiked through her, jolted her senses. He was all muscle and sinew beneath the soft linen of his shirt, the broad expanse of his back under her roving hands triggering sweet memory. She'd know him in the dark, she thought, sliding her palms down his sleek body, a flaring heat responding to the familiar feel of him, as though his audacious sexuality had been forever seared on her senses.

Knowing her reluctance, greedy for her after a celibate month, single-minded, he wooed her with kisses and whispered promises of pleasure, reminding her of all he could do to her, of how he could make her feel, how long he could sustain her pleasure. He almost lost control at that point, his memory keen, but disciplining his impulses with an iron will, he coaxed and petted and caressed until she was panting, breathless with need.

"You seem ready," he teased, nibbling on her bottom lip, moving his hips gently against hers.

"A month's a long time." She reached for the buttons on his breeches, so irrepressibly aroused she was drenching wet, throbbing with desire.

"A novel experience for you?"

Her gaze flickered upward. "Unheard of."

"Then we'll have to make this a memorable night." A carnal heat flared in his eyes.

"I have a feeling it will be." She slid her palm down

the leather stretched taut over his erection, and closed her fingers around his rigid length. "I'm glad I decided to keep you."

About to speak, he changed his mind. This wasn't the time to take issue with who was keeping whom. The blood of a reiver ran true in his veins, and whether the Countess of Kilmarnock knew it or not, she was his, now, tomorrow—always.

A door slammed downstairs and Roxane trembled. "Oh, lord, Robbie, I don't know if I can do this. You should go . . . you should."

"I will," he murmured, reaching down to unfasten another button on his breeches.

She tried to push him away. "What if they find you here?"

He pulled back marginally in response, but instead of leaving he slid his hand between her thighs. "Or they could find me *here*." He pressed his palm firmly against her mons, his middle finger sliding in her pulsing slit.

She moaned, inundated by a heady, feverish heat.

"It won't take long." Quickly pushing her skirt aside, he slipped two fingers inside her drenched, sleek cleft, stroking the throbbing flesh with such exquisite tenderness, she thought she'd die of longing.

A rivulet of pearly fluid oozed down his palm. "I'll make you climax before I go." His voice was fragrant with lust as he plunged his fingers deeper, touching her to the quick. Her thighs tightened around his hand and she squirmed restlessly, wildly aroused, her fears obliterated by an intoxicating madness that overlooked sense and sensibility, that brought her trembling under his hands.

Easing in a third finger, he forced her incited tissue wider and tantalizingly stroked the aching, moist flesh while she melted around his hand and felt the first stirrings of orgasm. Her irrepressible small cry vibrated in the room before he could muffle her mouth with his.

And as the riveting swell flowed in wave after sensational wave, violent, explosive, he leaned into her climax and inhaled the ecstasy of her breathless sighs.

After the turbulence stilled, he kissed away her last small gasps and lifting her into his arms, carried her to the bed. Pushing the diamond necklace aside, he placed her on the embroidered coverlet. Still blissfully aglow, she gazed up at him though half-lowered lashes and languidly murmured, "I've really missed you."

"I know." His smile was indulgent. Sitting down beside her, he ran his palm over her silken thigh, stroked upward to the heated, damp verge of auburn curls. "We won't have to rush this time." He leaned over, his long, silken hair framing her face, blending with hers, and kissed her lightly. "You always were impatient," he whispered, untying the laces of her gown, his fingers scented with her smell. She lay docile under his hands, content, sated, while he eased the lilac silk away along with her lacy petticoats, slipped the ties of her furbelows free, pulled off the fine linen of her chemise. Then tracing a delicate finger over the bounteous soft curves of her breasts he said, "Don't go away."

Unbuttoning his cuffs, he pulled off his shirt, tossed it aside, and reached down to take off his boots.

She touched his back, so close and tempting, her fingers splaying down his muscles—supple and lithe beneath his bronzed skin, the firm, toned perfection of his body lure to her senses.

Turning his head, he smiled at her. "Touch me all you want—anywhere at all."

"I intend to."

"Then my trip was definitely worthwhile." He kicked his boots aside.

"I thought you didn't come for sex," she purred.

"Did I say that?" He stood to slip his breeches down and turned, revealing the full extent of his erection.

She drew in an admiring breath as he stepped out of his pants. "And then again, I'm not opposed," she murmured, anticipation in the hush of her voice.

He smiled broadly. "Good, because sex with you is high on my list of priorities."

"You definitely intrigue me, my lord," she coquettishly whispered.

"How convenient, since I'm planning on making love to you most of the night."

"Really? And if I were to refuse?"

"Perhaps I could persuade you." Taking his erection lightly in his hand, he slid his fingers lazily down and up, once, twice, three times, his penis swelling larger, longer, the veins pulsing with blood, the rampant head gleaming waist high.

"Oh, yes, " she breathed, savoring the sight.

"Does that mean I can have my way with you?" he said, cheeky and brash.

She laughed.

He climbed into bed and, lowering his body over hers, he spread her thighs apart with a gentle pressure of his hands and settled between her legs—skin to naked skin. "Now then, Countess," he whispered, his words husky and low, tilting her chin up with one finger, "it's my turn."

The sound of footsteps in the hallway suddenly intruded into the quiet of the room and Roxane stiffened under his hands.

"You're going to die over this," she warned him.

"But willingly, darling. Hush." And moving slightly forward, he placed his erection against her vulva.

Stifling her urgent longing, forcing herself to a prudence he was ignoring, she pushed at his chest. "It's too dangerous," she whispered.

He brushed her hands aside, guided the swollen crest of his arousal just inside her pulsing cleft, and said on a soft sigh, "I know . . ."

Fortuitously, the footsteps died away, for hot-blooded temptation burned through her senses, all feeling suddenly converging on the hot, needy core of her body, and enraptured, heedless to peril, she moved her hips to ease him in more fully.

Pushing forward another small distance, he smiled down at her, his hair brushing her face. "Changed your mind?" He flicked his hair back behind his ears with a quick, fluid gesture—much practiced, she jealously thought, wishing for a moment she could be blasé about him, as she was with so many of her suitors.

"Maybe," she equivocated, uncomfortable with her insatiable need, with his knowing smile.

"Maybe you'd rather have Argyll. You were enticing the hell out of him not long ago."

"I was trying not to."

"And not succeeding from the sounds of it."

"You're jealous, too." Her smile was lush, gratified.

"He can't have you, just remember that," he whispered, his violent need for possession adding dimension to his erection, an unconstrained fierceness to his sudden plunging descent. She gasped. Opened wide, invaded so deeply, she shivered at the acute, riveting rapture.

"Tell me there's no one else." His voice was heated, peremptory as his strong, young body arched hard into her, impaling her.

"No, never," she breathed, wanton desire raging in her mind.

Appeased, he slid back a fraction, his fingers sliding under her bottom, holding her, before he forced himself deeper again, filled her to the mouth of her womb. "How does it feel when someone really loves you?"

"It feels heavenly"—she moaned as he moved inside her— "unspeakably sweet . . ."

"I can make you feel like this all night," he whispered, withdrawing marginally, penetrating again. "All week, if you want."

And she knew he could. His body was a fine-tuned instrument for making love, well-practiced, accomplished, indefatigable.

"How darling you are," she lightly said, jealousy underscoring the flippancy.

"Don't do that."

"What?"

"Use that practiced tone—like a courtesan," he growled.

"And yet you tell me how practiced you are."

"Men are."

"So are women."

"You can't be anymore," he brusquely ordered. "Agree or I won't let you come."

"Yes, yes," she quickly agreed and she could feel as well as see his sudden smile.

"I could get you to say anything right now, couldn't I?"

"Yes."

"No matter what I'd ask."

She laughed. "Yes."

"To have this."

"To have you."

"You can't talk to Argyll."

"I don't want to."

"You can't dance with him."

"Be realistic."

"I don't have to be realistic at the moment, do I?" He moved his lower body in perfect, long strokes, his lush, slow rhythm of thrust and withdrawal impossible to resist.

"This reality will definitely do," she purred, holding his lean hips, pulling him closer so she could feel him inside her with more flagrant intensity, wanting to absorb him body and soul—his sweet whiskey taste and sandalwood scent, the fragile transience of his wildness and youth and love.

"I'm going to come in you now."

She should have said no, she should have seen that he used a French *lettre*.[3] She shouldn't be so derelict. And yet she only sighed and held him close and wanted him inside her forever.

He waited, though, because he was indulgent in all things to her, because he was back in Scotland for this, for her, for these feelings. Only when her climax began peaking did he allow his own release.

And they came together in an endless, hot, ravishing orgasm that left them damp with sweat, panting.

Catching his breath, he whispered, "You're mine forever, blythsome lass . . . for all eternity. . . ."

She smiled up at him, her heart beating wildly. "Always, always my bonny, braw lad." And she lay breathless and content, no longer unsure.

While he'd known without question he was here to stay.

They made love that night for hours more, as though making up for lost time, for the weeks of their deprivation, reveling in the feel and scent and taste of each other, exploring the limits of desire, delighting in the new, fresh enchantment of their love.

But at last she said, "Enough," already half-asleep in his arms, and he gratified her because he was home and she was his once more.

He dozed off, too, after a time, although his rest was light, a reiver's style of repose. He knew better than to actually sleep.

Chapter 4

───◆◆◆───

$\mathcal{N}$EAR DAWN, WHEN THE SKY WAS STILL DARK but the stars were fading, Robbie lifted his head minutely and listened. A second later, he woke Roxane and put a finger to her mouth, then rolled away and sat up. He was reaching for his weapons hanging from the headboard when the crash of an ax blade splintered the door.

Queensberry's intelligence system had improved, Robbie thought, leaping to his feet, snatching up his pistols in a blur of movement, searching the darkness for intruders.

None.

Yet.

As if in emphasis of their precarious safety, another ax stroke cracked into the door.

Grabbing his breeches from the chair, he quickly stepped into them while gauging the strength of the door against the assault. It looked as though the thick oak would make their attackers sweat before giving way, he decided. Swiftly buckling his belt, he slid his pistols into place and leaning over the bed, murmured, "There isn't much time. Go into the dressing room so you won't be hurt."

A shrill voice exhorting the attackers to more speed screeched above the sound of battering axes.

Swinging her legs over the side of the bed, Roxane came to her feet as though galvanized by the sound of her mother-in-law's commands. "No one's getting hurt, least of all you, so don't take that well-bred, chivalrous tone with me." She shrugged into her dressing gown. "As if I'm going to play docile maiden while they shoot you dead. Now get out of here!" she ordered, throwing his shirt at him, picking up his boots and holding them out.

"If there are only a few, I can handle them." He calmly slid his shirt on as though men with axes weren't hacking her door to pieces. Pulling his boots on, he listened to the raucous tumult for a moment. "I've plenty of ammunition."

"Don't even think of staying," she heatedly said. "That old harridan is shrieking for your blood. If you don't go, she'll *have* it! Damn her anyway—this is *my* house. I'm going to wring her scrawny neck."

"You might need help for that." Robbie reached over to loop the ties of her robe into a bow at her waist.

"I prefer not having you killed tonight because of me." Irritably, she brushed his hands aside, taking exception to his reckless disregard for his safety. "Go!" She shoved him hard with the flat of her hand. "*Right now!*"

The assault on the door increased in a rising crescendo of sound, additional reserves augmenting the cacophony of male voices shouting orders, Agnes's screeches and squawks escalating to earsplitting proportions, the thunderous crash of axes ripping into wood reverberating through the room.

"Please, Robbie!" She was desperate for him to go. "Don't even consider some damnable male code of honor that tells you to stay. No one's going to hurt me. They want you. And consider," she said in what she hoped was a reasonable voice that would encourage him to be reasonable, too, "I've been taking care of myself since you were in leading strings."

"Perhaps it's time you had someone taking care of you."

"It might help if you were alive for that," she tartly replied.

"You're sure?" The axes had settled into a workmanlike rhythm.

She glared at him. "Keep up this bloody conversation and I'll see you on the gallows."

"It doesn't seem right . . ."

The destruction of the door had reached a point where the hinges were creaking, beginning to pull away from the door frame.

He was recklessly considering taking on the attackers; she could see it in his eyes.

"If you stay, I'll shoot you myself," she furiously whispered. "You're putting my children at risk."

The predaceous look vanished from his eyes. "Lord, I forgot." He pulled his jack from the bedpost. "Forgive my selfishness. Leave a message for Holmes at Steil's Tavern if you need anything. Take one of these." He offered her a pistol. "Just in case you need to shoot anyone besides me," he added with a teasing smile.

"I will *not* be getting in touch with you. I never saw you before in my life. I don't need that—Oh, very well," she finally agreed, taking the pistol so he'd leave. "For the love of God, go!"

He looked at her for a another moment, clearly indecisive.

"I want you alive, Robbie." Tears glistened in her eyes. "Please."

He pulled her into his arms and kissed her with unbearable sweetness. And then with an achingly beautiful smile, he turned away and disappeared into the dressing room.

SECONDS LATER THE BEDROOM DOOR BURST OPEN and when the attackers entered, stepping over the splintered debris, their lanterns held high, they found the Countess of Kilmarnock, silent and poised, holding a pistol.

Numerous male gasps resonated in the sudden silence, the troopers arrested in the doorway.

The stuff of legends filled their eyes.

Edinburgh's reigning beauty stood before them, bewitching in dishabille. Her long red hair was loose on her shoulders, tousled; her cheeks were flushed, her voluptuous form conspicuous beneath the pale silk of her robe, the overlapping neckline askew, offering a partial glimpse of one breast.

"What's the meaning of this intrusion?" Roxane stood straight and tall, her arm was steady as a rock, the pistol cocked.

"There's no need to shoot anyone," Queensberry gently said, moving forward through the throng, his gaze focused on the weapon.

Shoving her way through the host of troopers, the dowager sharply said, "Where is he?"

"Isn't it past your bedtime, Agnes?" Roxane met her mother-in-law's gelid stare with her own.

"I know he's in here. Have her tell you where he is," the dowager ordered, turning her beady eyes on Queensberry.

"We'd like to check your apartments." Queensberry signaled one of his men to hold Agnes back. Returning his gaze to Roxane's weapon, he courteously added, "If you don't mind."

"I'm quite alone. Agnes hears things at her age."

"If we might just look, for our peace of mind," the duke replied. "Reports of a—" he paused, searching for the least provocative word "—stranger in the neighborhood alarmed us."

Roxane's brows rose delicately. "So you broke down my door?"

"We were told that he—that is, someone was in your room."

"Have you taken on the role of chaperon for me, James?"

"I would never presume," he murmured, his gaze sweeping the shambles of her bed. "But in these times of political unrest everyone suffers inconveniences."

"I want my door repaired," she curtly said. "And an apology."

"Of course." He wondered if Agnes was becoming senile; this episode was quickly turning into a farce. But just as he was about to apologize, he saw a pair of men's gloves partially concealed beneath the bed. Walking over, he plucked them from their shelter. "Yours?" He examined the black suede gloves, the padded backs designed to guard against sword blades.

"Not that I recall." Her heart was racing, but she forced her voice into a moderate tone.

"I told you." Agnes cackled. "Hear things, indeed."

Ignoring Agnes's outburst, Queensberry smoothly said, "Some friend's gloves, no doubt."

"No doubt." She took care not to avoid his eyes.

Queensberry lifted the gloves to his nose and delicately sniffed. "Citron and sandalwood. From the Levant." He sighed. "I'm afraid my men are obliged to search if given cause." He waved the gloves. "You understand."

"If you must." She lowered the pistol, considering sufficient time had elapsed for Robbie's escape.

Queensberry ordered his men into the suite.

"They'll find your young lover," Agnes said with delight, "and you can watch him hang."

"You're hallucinating, Agnes. There's no one here but me."

"The Carre whelp writes the most passionate love letters," she mocked. "He was pining for you most dreadful."

The old witch was still dressed in her ball gown, so she'd been spying instead of sleeping. "Last I heard," Roxane casually replied, not about to trade insults with Agnes "he was in Holland."

Short moments later, Queensberry returned from the dressing room, his troopers following him. "No sign of him."

"Check the bedclothes. You'll find evidence he was here, and that should put my slut of a daughter-in-law in the Tolbooth—for harboring a felon."

"If anyone touches my bed, I'll put a bullet through your head Agnes . . . with pleasure." Roxane raised the pistol. "Be my guest, Queensberry," she dulcetly went on.

The dowager countess blanched, her mouth opening and shutting without any audible utterance. And for a breath-held moment a tremulous silence prevailed.

"I'm a very good shot," Roxane noted.

"Now, Roxie, don't do anything foolish. There's no need to check your bed. If you say you were alone, I'm quite ready to accept your word." With the young Carre gone, there was no point in belaboring her credibility. Whether there was stains on the bedclothes scarcely mattered without the young earl in custody. Better to wait until he visited the beautiful Roxie again—as he most certainly would, the Carres' libidinous impulses being what they were.

A gunshot suddenly exploded outside, then another and another. Roxane visibly paled.

"I knew he was here!" Agnes crowed, a flush of color returning to her face.

"Excuse me, my dear." Queensberry addressed Roxane with a feigned courtesy as a new flurry of gunshots exploded outside. "They must have found the intruder on your grounds." He executed a brief bow as he passed her. "Never fear, my men will dispatch him."

It took every ounce of willpower she possessed to appear composed. "How convenient you were here."

"A fortuitous circumstance," he silkily replied, already contemplating the length of time before he could legally hang Robbie Carre and eliminate another threat to his appropriated properties. "I hope you'll be able to sleep after our disturbing entrance."

"I'm sure I will," she said, as mendaciously polite as he.

"They're going to hang him—or drown him and save the cost of the rope," her mother-in-law gloated, the two women alone now.

"I can still shoot you, Agnes. Perhaps I have even more reason now." Roxane aimed the pistol once more at the malevolent woman. "And Queensberry and his men aren't here to protect you."

Seconds later, Roxane found herself alone, her mother-in-law having sensibly retreated, the sound of her running feet a minor solace in the vast terror of the moment. Sinking into a nearby chair, Roxane trembled uncontrollably, fearful for Robbie's safety, terrified he might have been hurt. Pray to God he was safe. Pray to any God who would protect him. Or was it too late? Had those gunshots already proved fatal? She couldn't bring herself to go downstairs to discover the truth. Instead she desperately prayed that he be delivered from his enemies.

He shouldn't have come back to Scotland. She shouldn't have allowed him to stay tonight, she reflected, chastising herself for her lack of restraint. Oh, Lord, should he die, she was to blame—unbearable thought. Gripping his pistol, she held on to it as though it were her lifeline to sanity and hope, her last link to him.

ROBBIE WAS A STREET AWAY, BLOODIED, BRUISED, out of breath, running hard, still prey to the pursuit behind him. He'd been hanging from the third-floor dressing room window, about to drop on the roof below, when he'd been sighted by Queensberry's men. The first shots had missed him; he'd dropped too quickly. But the jump from the second floor roof to the ridgepole of the adjacent building was such a deadly distance, he'd hesitated a second too long and his pursuers had had time to sight their muskets. The shot he'd taken had brought him briefly to his knees, but driven by necessity, he'd come to his feet and leaped. Managing to grab a scrambling handhold on the ridgepole by sheer luck and grit, he'd heaved himself over the top of the roof and then out of sight. Gasping for breath, he'd rested against the cool slate. Gingerly moving his wounded arm, he tested its reliability and range of motion. If the bleeding didn't worsen, it should function adequately. Not daring to linger with a score of troopers on his trail, he slid down the roof tiles to a decorative parapet and, easing himself over the edge, dropped to the porch roof. The impact jarred his wounded arm, the corrosive agony bringing a beading of sweat to his brow, and he lay utterly still for a breathless moment until the worst of the torment receded. Drawing in a sustaining breath before swinging from the lead rain trough to the ground, he landed with a muffled grunt of pain.

His arm was bleeding heavily now, but after years of carouse he knew the streets of Edinburgh better than most and with luck, he'd reach his lodgings before his strength faltered. Cautiously moving through the courtyard gates, he sprinted across the open thoroughfare and into a dark alley that gave him protection. But eventually he was forced to cross a more conspicuous thoroughfare, and when he did, Queensberry's scouts caught sight of him. After that they were in full cry.

With his bleeding wound leaving an easily identifi-
able trail, it was imperative he staunch the blood flow
before coming within range of his lodgings.

Scanning the street ahead for refuge, he slipped
through the open door of an alehouse a half block distant, entering a low-ceilinged room dim with smoke,
flickering lamps casting only a desultory light over the
rough interior. Scrutinizing the occupants with a quick
glance as he moved toward the bar, he met only blank,
suspicious stares. But the crisis required taking risks,
and approaching the barkeep he murmured, "A hundred pounds for your shirt and deliverance from
Queensberry's men." With the duke universally de-
spised in Scotland, he hoped for, if not aid, a minimum
of hindrance. "Is there a back door?"

The man gazed at him for a moment. "Back there,"
he gruffly muttered, indicating a shadowed corridor
with a nod of his head. Motioning a serving wench to
take his place behind the bar, he followed Robbie.

"I need some kind of bandage for this," Robbie
noted, handing him a purse. "I'm leaving a trail for
Queensberry's men."

"The bastard should be hung for a traitor," the barkeep growled, jerking his rough shirt over his head and
handing it to Robbie.

"Amen to that." Robbie wrapped the garment
around his arm. "Tie this for me," he murmured, indicating the makeshift bandage. "And take care if the
troopers come in to question you."

"Ain't no one in here going to give the court's
troopers naught for answers. And I dinna' want no
money for helping someone escape from the likes of

that blackguard Queensberry," he said, slipping the purse back into Robbie's jack.

Grinning, Robbie put out his hand. "Then I'm in your debt. Robbie Carre, at your service—if I get out of this alive."

"You're a rash young buck to be back in town," the burly barman declared. Edinburgh was a small town; everyone knew of the outlawed Carres and Queensberry's rapacious appropriation of their estates.

"I missed my lady."

The man chuckled as he jerked the knot tight on the bandage. "Cunt can do that to ye. Now begone so ye can fuck her anither day."

Robbie's arm was throbbing violently now, a stabbing pain pulsing through his shoulder and across his chest. Taking a deep breath, he inhaled the stench of ale and smoke, the pungent air like a brisk jolt to his senses. "My thanks," he gravely said.

"Fuckin' over Queensberry's a pleasure, me laird. Watch that first step in the dark, sair," he added, guiding Robbie down the dark corridor with a hand on his arm.

Moments later Robbie was warily moving down a silent, shadowed alley, his nostrils flaring like a dog on the scent, as if he could smell Queensberry's men on the night air. But regardless of the two-score troopers who had spread out to search him down, he made his way through circuitous byways, stealthily traversing narrow mews, silent courtyards, and shadowed streets he'd known from childhood, until he was within the safety of the stables behind his Edinburgh apartments.

He waited there for a lengthy interval, not wishing

to carry disaster to those inside should Queensberry's men be near. But after a considerable time, when no sign of pursuit was evident, when the first light of dawn clarified his view of the alley devoid of troopers, he slipped through the stable doorway into the walled yard and entered the back door of his lodgings.

Chapter 5

"ᖱOR YOUR OWN SAFETY," QUEENSBERRY WAS saying sometime later, seated on a chair in Roxane's boudoir, "I'd suggest you stay within the confines of your house until further notice."

"Am I under arrest?" She'd dressed in the interval when Queensberry had left to pursue Robbie, and she faced him now in a simple gown of brown serge. Any other woman would have been undistinguished in such a plain garment, but Roxane's pale skin glowed, her titian-colored hair framed her face in a riot of lush curls, and her seductive violet eyes were never anything but graphically sensual, while her sumptuous body would have dazzled in sackcloth.

"You're simply detained for your own security until we find—er—"

"Robbie Carre? Does the name stick in your throat, James? I didn't realize you had scruples."

Her gaze flashed with heated indignation that made him briefly fantasize about another kind of heated ardor. If he didn't know with certainty she'd be repulsed, he would have bluntly propositioned her. But the lovely Roxane had been able to indulge her own fancy in bedmates from a very young age, her flagrant sensuality bringing every man with breath in his body under her spell. Independent now, financially secure, assured of her allure, she was beyond his reach. A considerable irritation to a man of his wealth and power. "Scruples are much overrated, my dear. As you should know, with your unwise choice of lovers."

"I choose my lovers for their sexual expertise, not for the size of their purse. Which puts you out of the running, now, doesn't it."

"Take care your rudeness doesn't jeopardize your future, my dear."

"Fortunately I have a new protector in Argyll. His interest should be sufficient defense against your threats. Or do you have the queen's ear again?" she inquired, her disrespect oversweet.

He rose with a small sigh, fatigued in the early morning hours, frustrated by his lack of success in capturing the young Carre, not inclined to exchange insults with a woman. "A word of caution, my dear. I always prevail in the end, which Argyll will discover soon enough. Our young general's a tyro in this game he's playing. So I'd suggest you remain in your house, until I give you leave. Is that clear?"

"We'll see if your orders are clear to the duke as well," she smoothly replied. "I have a feeling we'll be meeting tonight at Catherine's soiree."

"Then I wish Argyll his pleasure of you, if that's your bargain. Remember he knows how to negotiate for what he wants, my dear. As evidenced by my presence in Scotland once again, over even the queen's most vociferous protests. So don't sell yourself too cheaply, or your darling young Carre lover will have to call out Argyll to uphold your honor." He bowed, his smile wicked with the truth of his words. "You could do worse than Argyll, though," he gently added. "At least he won't end up on the gallows."

He walked from the room, leaving in his wake the cruel reality of his threats. Queensberry knew better than most how to expose a person's vulnerabilities. It was his greatest talent.

Later that morning, he met with the Duke of Argyll, apprising him of the previous night's events.

"You should have notified me before you attacked the countess," Argyll coolly observed. "You overstepped your bounds."

"Time was of the essence, my Lord Commissioner, after Agnes Erskine sent her message to me. Even with our expeditious action, the rogue escaped."

"Are you sure he was there?"

"The countess was holding one of his pistols. The Carres have a penchant for Venetian niello-work on their weapons—a distinguished mark of their ownership. And he left his gloves." Queensberry tossed the fringed gauntlets on the table between them. "Florentine, as you see. Nothing but the best for the Carres."

"Then it's a shame you didn't have enough troops surrounding the house." The duke raised one disdainful brow. "Your lack of military experience proved your undoing. But then politics is hardly a suitable training ground for tactical skirmishes."

Swallowing the humiliating rebuff without argument, since he needed Argyll's cooperation, Queensberry continued his flattery unabated. "I fully defer to your battlefield experience, my lord, but do you not think it useful to institute a full-scale search for

Carre?" Leaning forward in his chair, he obsequiously smiled. "His capture would be a fine feather in your bonnet, my Lord Commissioner."

"I doubt Robbie Carre's capture will influence union negotiations," the duke briskly countered, staring down his prominent nose with barely concealed temper. Argyll knew full well why Queensberry wanted the Carres dead. But that personal fight had nothing to do with his orders from Queen Anne and her ministers. "I prefer not devoting my troopers to extraneous duties. They have better things to do." His voice was crisp with finality.

"Yes, my lord," Queensberry murmured, masking his fury. Was Argyll deliberately thwarting him, or simply disinclined to offend the lovely Countess of Kilmarnock? "Under the circumstances though, my lord, considering Carre might return to—er—visit the countess, I thought it expedient to put her under house detention." Queensberry needed to make sure the duke was aware of his rival's flourishing relationship with Roxane.

"You did what?" Argyll's voice snapped with authority. He allowed no abridgement to his prerogatives as commissioner—a nonnegotiable point in his bargain with the queen.

"I considered it prudent, my lord." It grated on Queensberry to have to acquiesce to a man without political experience, a man decades younger than himself. But he concealed his anger behind a sycophantic smile. "At least until you could make your own determination, my lord." He dipped his head with deferential grace.

"I have no intention of turning this country into a patrolled camp, Queensberry. The queen's wishes and my mission will be accomplished with a degree more subtlety. And if you have a personal vendetta against the Carres, kindly fulfill it without the use of the queen's resources. Do we understand each other?"

"Yes, my lord." While his words were moderate, Queensberry's jaw was set hard against the duke's insult.

"I'll call on the countess and apologize for your actions," Argyll said, sensible of Queensberry's wrath, but unmoved by the scheming machinations of an artful politician. "In the future, see that you confer with me before ordering any . . . attacks. Good day." Motioning for a footman to refill his coffee cup, he turned to the papers on his desk.

He'd been dismissed like a nonentity, Queensberry fumed, rising from his chair. Already planning his revenge as he descended the stairway of the duke's quarters in Holyrood Palace, he determined to track down Robbie Carre with or without Argyll's sanction or aid. The commissioner would do well to pick his enemies with more caution, he reflected. Damn his haughty insolence.

Standing outside on the porch for a moment, he surveyed the bustling Royal Mile with an unseeing gaze, contemplating how best to outmaneuver the queen's commissioner. Despite Argyll's stellar reputation as a victorious soldier, once the union between England and Scotland was sealed, the young generalissimo would no longer be needed by the queen or her ministers.

And after Argyll was returned to some remote battlefield, he, Queensberry, would be the one left to rule Scotland

In the meantime, he must tread softly.

𝓡OXANE WAS UPSTAIRS IN THE NURSERY WITH HER children when she received word of the Duke of Argyll's visit. He'd arrived much too early for a social call—a fact noted by Agnes, peering through her bedroom window, and by Roxane, who wondered at his motive.

"Have him shown into the nursery," she directed the servant who delivered the news of his presence. She preferred receiving him in the midst of her children; whatever his intent, the nursery would curtail all but impersonal conversation.

But her heart was beating wildly by the time he entered the large sunny room at the top of the house, because there was the possibility he might be bringing news of Robbie's capture. If he were malicious like Queensberry and had hied himself over at this early hour to torture her, please, she prayed, at least let Robbie be alive. There was hope if he was alive.

When the duke arrived on the fourth floor, he stood in the doorway for a brief moment, his gaze sweeping the room, searching for his hostess. Fearful she might embarrass herself by trembling in anxiety, she'd not risen to greet him.

Spying her surrounded by her children, he courteously bowed. "I've come to apologize for Queensberry's discourtesies," he politely said. "And to offer amends for his unmitigated offense to your privacy."

Her smile instantly rivaled the most glorious sunrise. A profound joy infused her spirits. There was reason to hope; he'd not said Robbie was dead.

"How kind of you, John," she graciously replied, rising from her chair, more than willing to be courteous now. If Argyll were intent on defending her from Queensberry, that additional advantage couldn't be overlooked. But, careful to maintain a level of reserve, she deliberately included her children in his visit. "Do come and meet my children."

From thirteen-year-old Jeanne to five-year-old Angus, each of her five children made their bow to the queen's commissioner. The duke was charming, asking each a personal question, listening with interest to their answers. Neither at a loss for conversation nor uncomfortable in the nursery, he maintained small talk about the amusements he'd enjoyed as a child until her young brood warmed to him and began to chatter. When, after a time, it seemed as though he intended to stay, Roxane invited him to join them in their breakfast.

"I'd like that," he said without hesitation. "Porridge and bannock cakes are my favorites."

Cynical enough to question such simple tastes in a man of his wealth, nevertheless she offered him a chair at the table with the required politesse. Balancing himself on the small nursery chairs with unexpected ease, he listened to the children's conversation without noticeable boredom, ate with apparent relish, and didn't seem alarmed when Roxane's rambunctious brood took to throwing bannock cakes once their appetites were satisfied.

Taking pity on him when his splendid uniform received two direct hits, she moved with him to a grouping of adult chairs by the windows overlooking the gardens.

"You manage men very well," he said, sitting down.

She smiled faintly as she dropped into the chair with a rustle of petticoats. "It's a matter of practice, my lord. Or survival. So forgive me if I question whether you came here only to apologize for Queensberry."

"Brown serge is remarkably provocative on you," he said with a faint smile. "Does that answer your question? Although, to be blunt, Queensberry has been given his congé in no uncertain terms. I don't expect he'll bother you again."

"And if he does?"

"I'll see that he's punished."

Her brows rose the merest fraction. "Such assurance, my lord."

"The queen is intent on pleasing me."

"And you her."

He leaned back in his chair. "In time, yes."

"When all the bribes are well spent."

He shrugged away her sarcasm. "Scotland will gain as well. But I prefer not talking politics when so many more pleasant topics are available. For instance, do you have need of anything?" His voice went very soft. "Anything at all . . ."

"Am I in detention?" If he wished to be useful, let him be useful.

"Of course not. Queensberry's action was completely unwarranted."

"I thank you, then." Each move in this dance of seduction required finesse.

"Why not thank me by being my guest at Catherine Haddock's dinner party tonight?"

She gazed at him from under half-lowered lashes. "If I were to refuse your offer, would I be detained once again?"

"Certainly not. But your company tonight would be greatly appreciated." His voice was gentle.

She exhaled in the faintest of sighs. "I find it too early in the morning for this amorous sparring." Her violet eyes showed the smallest touch of weariness. "I have no intention of sleeping with you. Do you still wish me to come to Catherine's?"

"Yes, very much," he answered without taking offense. "Any number of women in Edinburgh are willing to sleep with me, if that's all I want."

Her gaze narrowed minutely.

"So cynical, my lady," he said, amusement in his tone.

"The smell of Queensberry puts one's cynical senses on full alert, my lord, and you weren't made commissioner because the queen liked the cut of your coat."

"True. But at least for tonight I promise not to importune you. Fair enough?"

"Your word as a Campbell?" A queen's commissioner was by definition duplicitous.

"My word as a Campbell."

"I'll be ready by nine."

She didn't offer a flirtatious response, nor give him any indication his invitation was pleasing to her. But her frankness, perhaps more than all the deceitful flattery addressed to him now that he was commissioner, intrigued him most.

What would it be like to bed her, he wondered, this woman who spoke and acted with such candor? Would she be equally audacious in her lovemaking? he wondered.

A pleasant thought.

Chapter 6

$\mathcal{T}$HE DOCTOR HAD COME AND GONE AND ROB-
bie's housekeeper was bustling around him, offering
him hot broth and tea, a pillow, a book to read while he
rested in his chair.

"Thank you, no," he graciously replied to each of
her offers. "But I'll have a hot toddy and a steak, and
send Holmes to me, if you would."

"I'm not so sertain ye should be havin' a dram in yer
condition, sair. The doctor dinna' say naught about a
dram."

"My condition is fine, Mrs. Beattie. The bleeding
has stopped, I'm bandaged within an inch of my life"—
he lifted his injured arm slightly to display his sizeable
dressing—"and if I could have some food and drink,
I'd heal that much faster." His mouth quirked in a
boyish smile. "Now be a dear, bring me food and
Holmes."

"If ye promise to sleep a wee bit, at least." Having
helped the doctor remove the musket ball from his
arm, she'd seen the ravaged flesh; he needed rest if he
hoped to heal.

"I promise. *After* I've talked to Holmes."

She nodded, satisfied.

Holmes was sent out on an errand shortly after, and

before Robbie had completely finished his meal, his man had returned.

"Tell me." Robbie motioned him into a chair opposite him at the table.

"Lady Carberry is currently in residence at her town house, although Lord Carberry hasn't come into town yet for the meeting of Parliament."

"David prefers his hunting."

"So it seems. The caddy at Carberry House says he's not apt to appear until the last minute, nor will he stay long."

"I'd like to talk to Amelia myself."

"I wouldn't recommend it, sir. Queensberry's troops are everywhere like muck in the streets. Graham will take your message and cause no comment."

"You spoke to him?"

"He should be here soon."

"Thank you, Holmes, for your efficiency." Robbie's voice held a touch of fatigue. He hadn't slept for several days; his surreptitious arrival on the coast and his subsequent journey to Edinburgh had been accomplished without rest.

Holmes was a family retainer who had inherited his position of steward from his father and grandfather before him, generations of Holmeses having served the Carres. So he was comfortable saying, "You need to sleep, sir. If not for your wound, consider you haven't slept for days "

"As soon as Graham is briefed." A weariness had begun seeping into his bones; even he was forced to recognize it. "I want him to speak to Amelia today."

And when Georgie Graham, a distant relation of

Coutts, arrived, Robbie quickly explained the message he was to carry.

"I want Lady Carberry to take Lady Kilmarnock's children to the country—out of danger. Lady Kilmarnock agrees. I hope Amelia will, too. Don't mention my name. Make it clear to her that the children have been threatened by Agnes Erskine, and ask her to call on Roxane immediately. Time's critical. Queensberry will be both tireless and ruthless in his search, now that he knows I'm back in Scotland."

"Done, sir."

"No questions?"

The young lawyer shook his head and rose. "One, perhaps," he said, picking up his gloves.

Robbie quirked his brows.

"When do you expect to have the library at Goldie-house back?"

Robbie smiled. "You liked the maps particularly, didn't you?"

"Everything, sir, but the map room was superb."

Robbie shifted slightly in his chair, the throbbing in his arm having reached discomfort level. "Douglas probably knows better than anyone, but certainly by fall." He smiled faintly. "If all goes well, we'll have my wedding at Goldiehouse."

"Congratulations, sir."

"A bit premature, perhaps. I'm not sure the countess has gotten used to the idea yet," Robbie said, grinning.

"I'm sure you can persuade her."

Robbie's grin broadened. "I'm working on it."

$\mathscr{A}$ BRIEF TIME LATER, LADY CARBERRY WAS AN-nounced at Kilmarnock House. As soon as she entered the parlor where Roxane was working with her steward on business accounts, the man was dismissed and Roxane suggested they take a stroll in the garden. She spoke of ordinary things while they traveled through the hallways to the outside door. But once they were clear of the house, understanding something was amiss, Amelia quietly said, "We're not going out to admire the flowers, are we?"

"I don't know which of my servants can be trusted." Roxane glanced around to see they were alone. "Robbie's back." At her sister-in-law's shocked expression, she added, "And Queensberry knows, which aggravates the risks."

"I *thought* Robbie Carre might be behind my early-morning visitor." Amelia was careful to keep her voice low.

"Did the messenger *say* Robbie sent him?" Roxane was eager for news of Robbie's condition.

"No, and when I asked, he was evasive. He said he was only asked to relay the message that I was to take your children to the country if you approved, and that you'd know the rest. So I came right over. Now tell me everything."

Roxane could feel the tension drain from her body, her fears for Robbie dissipating. Only he knew of their conversation about Amelia taking her children away, so he must be safe—at least for now. Quickly surveying the windows facing on the garden and seeing no observers, she rapidly related the events of the previous evening.

"Robbie was actually in your bedroom?" her sister-in-law exclaimed, wide-eyed. "Dressed or undressed?" Her green eyes shone bright with curiosity.

Roxane blushed.

"Lord, he's reckless." Amelia cast a sidelong glance at her friend. "Are you happy he's back? Silly question," she added, taking in Roxane's reddening cheeks. "You haven't looked at another man since he left."

"And you don't know how foolish I feel." Roxane grimaced. "He's so young, Melie—not ingenuous or, God knows, innocent, but still embarrassingly *eighteen*," she said, her unease evident. "It's a totally irrational, as though I were insensible to reason instead of eminently practical since Jamie died. But I literally tremble when I see him," she murmured, disbelief and wonder in her tone. "I don't know what to do."

Amelia smiled at her as they walked down a garden path bordered with colorful tulips. "He's a bonny young man, there's no doubt of that. Why not enjoy him?"

"With Queensberry's troops chopping down my door? And the noose already around his neck?"

"Enjoy him later, then, when political events have calmed." The women had been friends from childhood, their exchange of confidences a long-standing pattern.

"Unfortunately, he's not interested in waiting."

"The impulsive Carres." Amelia's dark brows arched in acknowledgement. "They're not exactly models of decorum, are they?"

"I can't say I acted much better last night," Roxane confessed. "I wasn't able to control my feelings when I should have, when the risks were outrageous. But when I'm with him, Melie, I feel the way I did with Jamie, if you don't think me too awful to compare him to your brother. Robbie's reckless and wild, too. Remember how Jamie was—laughing and teasing, capable of taking on the world, never afraid of anything. It seems a lifetime ago, doesn't it," she whispered, her eyes glistening with tears.

"Don't cry, darling." Amelia moved closer to put an arm around Roxane's shoulder. "You deserve happiness, you do," she softly said, hugging her. "Don't cry because you love him. Jamie would want you to be happy."

"If only everything wasn't so entangled in Queensberry's vicious web," Roxane breathed, brushing her tears away.

Taking her friend's hand, Amelia led her to a garden bench out of sight of the house. "At least let me help with the children. David never likes to come into town anyway, and I came only because Mother wanted help with her entertainments. But she detests Queensberry as much as anyone. She'll understand if I return to Longmuir with your children."

"I'd be so relieved to have them away," Roxane affirmed with a grateful smile. "Agnes is awful, ready to betray anyone for Erskine advancement."

"Will she allow the children to leave?"

"She's so set on accommodating Argyll's lust," Roxane said with disgust, "she'd do anything to give me more time with him. When I tell her I'm going with him to Catherine's, she'll hardly notice you're taking the children. She's willing to dine with the devil for an English earldom for Angus."[4]

"Or have *you* dine with the devil."

Roxane curled her nose in distaste. "Tonight, as a matter of fact."

"What *are* you going to do with Argyll?" Amelia gently asked. "He won't be led by the nose for long."

"I already told him I had no intention of sleeping with him."

"And?"

"He was extremely polite."

"And lying."

"Yes. But I won't sleep with him."

"Not even for an English earldom?" Amelia drolly remarked.

"Particularly for such a venal reason. I like my freedom. It grows on one."

"Thanks to Johnnie Carre," Amelia murmured.

"Yes," Roxane replied with a small smile. "He protected me from all the others after Kilmarnock's death. And I did the same for him, with all the marriageable females pursuing him."

"A convenient friendship."

"A pleasant one. And if my press of suitors became uncomfortable, Johnnie would speak to them."

"A diplomatic warning from the Laird of Ravensby is always effective," her friend sardonically observed. "Will Robbie take over that role?"

"Nothing so benign for him, I suspect." Roxane sighed. "He's interested in being more than a lover. Which presents a host of problems for me that he's not inclined to understand. I'm not entirely sure I *want* to marry again," she said with quiet emphasis. "Widowhood is decidedly more liberating. And what does he know of being a father to five children?"

"You mean it won't be possible to simply run away and live on moonbeams and rapture?"

Roxane cast a rueful look at her friend. "Not with schoolmasters, nannies, riding and dancing lessons, and children who want me to spend every minute of the day with them. And to be perfectly honest, I'm not sure the whirlwind force and energy of Robbie Carre won't wreak havoc with my comfortable life."

"Can you be that practical, though, against his irresistible charms? The ladies have been standing in line for him since he was sixteen. I hear he's very, very good," she finished in a playful purr.

"Don't look at me like that." Roxane flushed rosy pink. "And, yes, he's very good, if you must know. But I'm hoping all the serious liabilities might temper my reckless passion, Melie. Or at least make me consider the great, vast differences in our lives. Which is why I'd be so grateful, if you took the children for a short time. Robbie isn't sensible. He doesn't know what the word means. And it's too dangerous for my children, with Queensberry's spies everywhere."

"I can't see Robbie Carre quietly walking away *or* listening to reason."

"That's even more reason for my having to be rational about this relationship. I'm terrified he's going to be *killed* because of me. Do you know he was going to take on all of Queensberry's troopers last night and save me like some chivalrous knight? The only thing that changed his mind was my reminder of the danger to my children."

"I don't suppose a man who returns to Scotland so soon after he's outlawed is by definition cautious."

"Which puts me uncomfortably in the middle of the fight between Queensberry and the Carres," Roxane uneasily noted. "I'd much prefer waiting until the Carre lawsuit is settled, until they're no longer outlawed and under penalty of death. Robbie claims they'll have their estates back by fall. Wouldn't it make more sense to wait?"

"Sense and the Carres?"

"You see," Roxane said on a quiet exhalation. "What am I going to do?"

"Keep Argyll at bay, discourage Robbie from his tempestuous path to destruction, block Agnes's determined efforts to put you in Argyll's bed. And try to keep your sanity," Amelia finished with whimsical sarcasm. "Forgive me, darling, but it's outrageously true."

"And any well-bred lady of quality should be able to carry all that off with scarcely a ripple in her social calendar," Roxane playfully replied, grinning at the monstrous folly of Amelia's proposals. "Which brings to mind Catherine's dinner party tonight. A daunting prospect under the best of circumstances. I don't suppose she's given up her pursuit of Argyll."

"She's as determined as ever to bed him, my dear."

Roxane groaned. "At least my life isn't boring."

"With the exception of Catherine's dinner party tonight," Amelia drolly corrected her.

Roxane chuckled. "I suppose it's better to laugh than cry over this evening's absurdities. Is Haddock out of the way, as usual?" she asked, referring to Catherine's husband.

"In Aberdeen, I hear," Amelia sweetly replied.

"Some things don't change, do they?" Roxane jibed. "Who was she after last time? I forget."

"Dundonald. Don't you remember? She talked of Highland cattle all night, like a drover."

"Oh, God, yes." Roxane laughed. "I still remember her reciting the prices of cattle at Crieff. Thanks, Melie, for reminding me of the humor in all this." She leaned over to kiss her sister-in-law's cheek. "And for listening to my problems."

"Again," her bosom friend sportively replied.

"I believe I've listened to you whine about David's hunting a thousand times or more." Roxane's gaze was cheerful.

"While I've had constantly to untangle your troubles with suitors," Amelia returned in friendly banter.

"Unwanted suitors," Roxane amended.

"Very true . . . but this time it's different, isn't it?" Amelia said, a sudden gravity in her voice.

Roxane nodded, all the myriad complications and dangers abruptly recalled. "I'm afraid it's not a matter of graciously declining a suitor's advances this time. It's horrendously more complex . . . and confusing, to be in love again after all these years." She tried to smile, but her lips quivered and she exhaled in frustration instead. "I shouldn't be so emotional about this. A woman who's buried two husbands should have learned something about self-denial and restraint. I thought I had. I thought I was immune to feelings like this."

"You're still young, Roxie. Why shouldn't you have feelings about someone?"

Her mouth quirked ruefully. "Why couldn't I have picked someone safe and dependable?"

"It sounds as though he picked you, and you've been resisting for a very long time. I'm not sure you can always control the events of your life. Do stay safe from the Queensberrys of the world, but don't give up on love," she gently offered.

"I can't have everything, you're saying," Roxane declared with a faint smile.

"It's a shameless fact of adulthood. Although there are advantages as well . . . like the Robbie Carres of the world loving you," she added with a sparkle in her eyes.

"How you always temper my volatile moods, darling Melie," Roxane gratefully declared, needing her sympathy and kindness. "Thank you . . . and thank you, too, for taking the children away from all the turmoil."

"You've done as much or more for me," her sister-in-law replied, remembering how Roxane had helped her through the tragedy of her child Charlotte's death from smallpox. She'd not been able to get out of bed or stop crying, and Roxane had come to Longmuir for an entire month, taken charge of the household and all the children, and still found time to sit with her and comfort her for hours each day and most of the nights. "Now take care of yourself," she kindly urged, patting Roxane's hand. "And if David and I can be of any more help, just let us know."

Roxane sighed. "I hope I can convince Robbie to go back to Holland." Straightening her shoulders, she gave her sister-in-law a determined look. "As for Argyll, I've handled men like him before."

"I'll offer up a prayer," Amelia lightly said.

Roxane's eyes flashed with amusement. "I might need two prayers, considering the incompetence of Catherine's cook."

∞

THE DINNER PARTY LIVED UP TO ROXANE'S DOUR expectations, Catherine Haddock predictably vicious from the first moment she realized Argyll and Roxane had arrived together. "How wonderful to see you, John," she purred, coming to greet them in a rustle of pink silk, her pale blue eyes snidely appraising Roxane in ivory mousseline and black lace. "You look tired, darling," she nastily murmured. "But then you didn't get much sleep last night, I hear."

"For which Queensberry was justly castigated," Argyll interposed. "Did he mention that?" His gaze traveled across the room to where Queensberry held court in the midst of a throng.

"Of course not, John. It would have ruined his story. Although young Robbie Carre's escape was ruin enough." She turned her taunting glance on Roxane. "Are the Carre brothers the same?" she maliciously inquired.

"Now why would I care to tell you that, Catherine?" Roxane blandly replied. "I can't imagine it would do you any good."

"The boy's such a young cub," their hostess declared, not about to be deflected from her uncharitable mockery. "He must be refreshingly different from his older brother, who's refined debauchery to a fine art."

"Are you actually expecting a response to that?" Roxane casually remarked.

"Oh, dear," Catherine said with an artful moue. "Did I overstep propriety?"

"Since you have no idea what propriety is, Catherine, I can't expect you to recognize it."

"Don't be bitter, darling. A woman your age can't afford to frown. Do *you* find youthful lovers refreshing, John?" she went on, feline and catty, gazing pointedly at Roxane, who was seven years older than she. "They seem to be all the rage."

"I find beauty at any age refreshing," Argyll replied, smiling down at Roxane. "Particularly redheads." He took Roxane's hand. "Would you like a glass of wine, my dear?"

With the commissioner's blunt change of subject, their hostess was forced to postpone her malice. Although Catherine Haddock didn't long curtail her nastiness.

She placed her guests of honor, Argyll and Queensberry, to her left and right at dinner, and despite her effort to exile Roxane to the far end of the table, Argyll insisted she be seated beside him.

Queensberry maintained an affable expression throughout dinner, although that cordiality didn't extend to his chill, shuttered gaze. And his conversation, while civil, required a noticeable effort in the company of his archrival.

With her elderly husband absent in Aberdeen, Catherine Haddock's seduction of Argyll was so obvious and blatant that bets were taken by the guests on the duration of Argyll's resistance. Her voice when she spoke to him was lush with suggestion, her gaze limpid and warm. She took every opportunity to touch his hand or arm as emphasis to her conversation, which weighed heavily in favor of Argyll's most successful battles on the Continent.

During an interval when Argyll was once again

obliged to give his attention to Catherine, Queensberry remarked to Roxane in an undertone, "It's like watching a play, isn't it?" His gaze flickered to his hostess, and when it returned to Roxane, his eyes held a genuine amusement.

"Absolve me from any involvement in this discussion of battles and troop maneuvers," Roxane mildly observed. "I'm here only for dinner."

"You like Catherine's cook?"

"Let's just say there's a certain safety in the guest list."

"In your escort, you mean."

"Did I say that, James?" she sweetly returned.

"The news is all around town," he casually noted. "The young Carre won't be able to hide long."

"You may have your spies, but you don't have loyalty from anyone, particularly the Scottish populace. I'm not so sure you're right."

"Perhaps I only have to watch you," he asserted, his tone sinister and low.

"Do it with discretion, then, because Argyll comes to call. Did your spies tell you? He ate breakfast with us and found some sumptuous lilies, so early in the spring, from someone's hothouse, no doubt. Be careful, James." Her warning was softly put.

"I'm not certain I believe you. You don't look at him the way he looks at you."

"Surely you're not thinking anything so romantical as love is involved? I'm surprised, James. I'd thought you cynical to the bone."

"While you've never struck me as cynical at all, my dear."

"Perhaps we both have something to learn."

"Learn what?" Catherine inquired with excessive sweetness, taking note of Argyll's wandering attention.

"The countess and I were discussing the differences between love and amusement," Queensberry urbanely remarked.

"And between cynicism and romance," Roxane lightly added. "James is uncertain, I think, of the distinction."

"Love—how quaint." Catherine's pale brows arched delicately toward her blond hairline. "Do you believe in love, Argyll?" They'd both married for reasons other than love; she felt sure they'd share a common sympathy.

"I'm beginning to entertain a fascinated interest in the subject," he murmured, turning a charming smile on Roxane. "Tell me, Countess, do you believe in love?"

A sudden hush descended on the table as though everyone's ears had pricked to attention at Argyll's startling query. He was known as a man of eminent practicality and loose morals, while news of Roxane's companion last night had generated the most sensational gossip.

"Of course, I do. Every woman of passion believes in love," Roxane smoothly replied. And while Catherine glowered, purse-lipped, she added, "The dilemma facing both James and myself is finding the right man."

"You must tell me what style of man appeals to you," Argyll declared, as though he were alone with her. Arrogant, he ignored her allusion to Robbie as well as the other guests' avid interest.

"Someone who makes me laugh," Roxane answered.

"I must begin to sharpen my wit, then."

"I didn't know you liked humorous men," Catherine sneered, her eyes ice cold.

"I find, with the independence of widowhood, I prefer amusement to excessive ardor."[5]

"Really," Queensberry interposed, mockery in his tone. "The Carres are known for their excess."

"Do you think so?" Serene and unruffled, she gazed across the table at him. "I've always found them men of enormous refinement."

"You're obsessed with the Carres, Queensberry," Argyll bluntly charged. "Pray overcome your lurid alarm. They're only one family, not the devil's host."

"They can put a personal army in the field as large as your Campbell troops."

"But they won't. They'll see to the return of their estates in court like any sensible man would. I'd suggest you concern yourself with your lawyers' competence first. The Carres haven't lost a lawsuit, as I recall."

Queensberry scowled. "Treason is a serious charge."

"You still have to prove it."

Queensberry had no intention of relying on the law to secure his appropriated Carre properties. But his voice was neutral when he spoke. "I must rely on Scottish justice—like you, John, in your quest for a union treaty."

Both men knew better—bribery and collusion were the means of their ultimate goals. Argyll's gaze went blank. "Then we can both expect success with such high-minded principles at work."

Specious words for men who regarded the cause of justice as incidental to their pursuit of power, and for that precise reason had been chosen as the English court's anointed. Once their work was accomplished, however, the English ministers would decide whether the rewards they'd promised would actually be granted.[6]

It was a dirty game—completely without honor.

Chapter 7

DINNER HAD BEEN ESPECIALLY TEDIOUS, ROXane thought, riding back from Catherine's, but at least Queensberry had been apprised of Argyll's degree of protection. Argyll had importuned, of course, the moment they'd settled into the carriage, and it had taken considerable finesse to curtail his eagerness. He was a large man.

Only Roxane's reminder of his given word as a Campbell finally caused him to release her.

Shifting away, he lounged in the corner, his half smile a flash of white in the flicker of the carriage lamp. "It was a tactical mistake to give you my word."

"But then I wouldn't have gone to dinner with you," Roxane pleasantly replied, readjusting the lace on her décolletage.

"I can see this is going to require a degree of wooing," he drawled, his smile teasing.

"Why bother, when Catherine will oblige without cavil? I'm sure she's still up."

"I'm sure she is. She asked me to come back."

"There, you see—all your carnal urges neatly fulfilled, no wooing required."

"Like any of the servant girls at my headquarters."

He was called Big Red John by all the local maids,

with giggles of delight, she knew. "If you're so well supplied with amorous partners, you don't need my company."

"But I particularly *wish* your company. What is it going to take to entice you?"

She was tired. Catherine's venom had been enervating, her previous night sleepless, Argyll's pursuit unflagging as she'd known it would be. So she spoke more plainly than she might have under different circumstances. "Why don't we say independence for Scotland, reversing the false charges of treason against the Carres, curbing Queensberry's interest in my personal life. None of which you can do."

"Scotland aside, I can do the rest," he said as plainly. "Is that the price for your passion? Tell me—for if it is, we have a bargain."

She was stunned. He'd offered an enormous payment for her amorous friendship, and could he be compelled to perform first on her requirements, the possibilities were astonishing.

"The treason charges are the grossest distortion anyway," he casually noted. "Everyone knows that."

"And yet you'd let Queensberry have their lands."

"His dispute doesn't impinge on my undertakings." He shrugged. "I can't involve myself in every property disagreement in Scotland." Sliding upright from his lounging pose, he moved closer to her. "Why don't I send Agnes away first, as indication of my intense . . . interest," he suggested, his strawberry blond hair pale in the lamplight. "And we'll negotiate the terms of our involvement from there." His smile was close, gratified. "I've been doing this for months, darling, with deal-makers of such wiliness and guile, our bargain will be in contrast the height of benevolence. I see no need to quibble when I want you." He'd spoken to the queen the same way, rumor had it—his demands plain, his wishes unequivocal. He wasn't like Queensberry, who was enigmatic and sly.

He went on. "And if you wish your lover's family safe from prosecution and restored to their titles and lands, well, we're both adults. I don't expect your heart and soul." A faint smile underscored his level of accommodation. "Once our bargain is made, I expect only your loyalty."

"You've been doing this much longer than I," Roxane declared, still astonished. He'd made the offer for her companionship so extravagant he knew she couldn't refuse. But she needed time to digest the tumultuous events, and she needed proof as well of his pledge. Anyone who dealt with the English couldn't be trusted. "I'll have to consider your offer."

"Why don't I see that Agnes is gone by noon," he suggested, cordial and obliging. "We'll be able to discuss this in more congenial surroundings without the Erskines."

"I'm intrigued, naturally," Roxane murmured, "but I'll have to speak to counsel first."

"Speak to whomever you wish. Let young Robbie know," he casually offered. "I don't care whom you tell. Once you've decided, we'll draw up the necessary papers."

"So certain, Argyll?"

"We both know what we want and what we can give. It's manifestly simple, my dear."

Fortunately the carriage came to rest at that point, for her state of mind was highly unsettled. "I'll need some time, of course."

Argyll's smile was especially warm; he understood better than most when negotiations were going his way. "Take whatever time you need." He signaled the footman to open the door. "I'm not unduly impatient."

After alighting, he helped Roxane down and stood for a moment with her hand in his. "Send for me this afternoon. I'll bring a clerk to draw up our agreement. Add the moon and stars if you wish." He grinned—at twenty-five he wasn't yet completely blasé. "You see how eager I am to have you."

"While bartering myself away makes me anxious," she said.

"Think of our alliance as an act of Christian charity, darling. I'm sure the Carres will thank you."

*O*N THE CONTRARY.

When Robbie first read Roxane's note, he crumpled it into a ball and flung it away in disgust—which necessitated a summary smoothing out, in order to reread it and discover if she'd truly written what he thought she'd written.

His second perusal was no better than the first, and he swore under his breath as he scanned the shocking words. Phrases like "for the best, I'm sure you understand, it's a small price to pay" brought his temper to fever pitch.

"Holmes!" he shouted, his voice thundering through the closed door, down the corridor and stairwell, rolling through the kitchen where its explosive fury vibrated the surface of the tea in Mrs. Beattie's teacup. She glanced across at Holmes, who was about to join her in a cup. "I'd say he's naught pleased with the countess's note." She nodded briskly at Holmes. "Ye'd best run."

"The Kilmarnock caddy says the footman overheard Argyll promise her the moon when they alighted from the carriage outside her house," Holmes declared, quickly rising. "Maybe she was tempted."

"I'd say from the sound of his lordship's bellow, she dinna' send him words o' love."

"I WANT COUTTS HERE IMMEDIATELY," ROBBIE SAID when Holmes entered the room. "Damn this confinement when I can't do things for myself. Wait," he added as Holmes turned to go. "Take a note to Lady Carberry, too."

Standing, he dashed off three brief sentences, all couched in the form of commands. Scrawling his name at the end, he handed the folded sheet to Holmes. "Go to Lady Carberry's first, and then find Coutts wherever he is and bring him back to me posthaste."

He paced after that like a caged animal, his frustration and rage so violent even the pain in his arm was forgotten. He moved from wall to wall to wall in a pattern of tethered constraint—retaliation and vengeance racing through his mind.

As if he'd let her sacrifice herself to Argyll to save him or his family. Damn her, the notion was preposterous, that she should be some bloody martyr for them. The time had come to supplant all this refined maneuvering with some brute force, he decided. How many men would he need to intimidate Argyll? Perhaps a few score. He'd have to make it clear to Argyll that Roxane wasn't available.

As he would to Roxane as well—in short order.

Where the hell was Coutts? he silently fumed, beginning to gather weapons for a surreptitious trip across the city. He put on a leather coat to cover and protect his bandaged arm, the required movements making him momentarily light-headed. Leaning against the wall briefly, he let the worst of the agony diminish before lifting his sword baldric over his head and easing it onto his shoulder. At least his sword arm hadn't been injured, he gratefully thought, and even his injured right arm was capable of holding a pistol. But the activity necessitated several shots of brandy to dull the pain, and the bottle was half gone when Coutts appeared.

Robbie thrust the wrinkled note at him. "Read this and tell me what can reasonably or unreasonably be done."

He was fully armed, Coutts noted with alarm, and his anger was palpable. It took some time to read the delicate script on the wrinkled paper. The countess had tried to explain Argyll's offer at some length—her reasons for accepting, how the end was well worth the means, how her lawyers had assured her such an agreement was binding in court. And she tried as well to tell Robbie how much she loved him, although it was clear she'd struggled over the wording—several phrases had been scratched out.

"So?" Robbie curtly declared when Coutts finally finished, glaring at him with a dangerous fire in his eyes.

"You know what I'm going to say as a lawyer," Coutts gently pronounced.

"Fuck, yes. But all the compromising and practical lawyer talk aside, you know Argyll can't be trusted, even if the fact that he wants to bed the woman I love wasn't fucking *unthinkable*.

"How does she imagine I'd allow it?" Robbie went on, his voice harsh with anger, "Or that Argyll would even consider keeping his word? He's faithless to the core, like Queensberry. She's outrageously naive. I'm surprised."

Coutts refrained from mentioning the obvious conclusion that Roxane wasn't naive. It wasn't his place to make judgments on the Countess of Kilmarnock's motives.

"Go and talk to her," Robbie gruffly said, "and explain all the legal reasons for this not being necessary. I'll explain the others to her myself when I see her."

"The countess may not receive me."

"Try." The single word was a command.

"I'd caution you against going out, my lord."

"Thank you for the advice," Robbie said with clipped impatience.

He was planning something, Coutts reflected, recognizing the dismissive retort, the impassioned gleam in his eyes. Johnnie Carre's wild young brother was bent on wreaking vengeance on someone.

He'd have to see that Johnnie was informed as quickly as possible.

ROXANNE RECEIVED COUTTS A SHORT TIME LATER but, harried with the arrangements for her children's leave-taking, she listened only out of courtesy to his calm and valid explanations. At the end she offered her own frank question. "Tell me honestly, Mr. Coutts, can you assure me the Carres will win in court?"

His hesitation was all the answer she needed.

"You see," she gently affirmed. "On the other hand, my way will have Argyll's signature on a document restoring their titles and properties. My counselors have already assured me that should the commissioner sign such an agreement, the contract will stand up in any court in the land. Tell Robbie that."

"He won't care to hear it. He's adamantly opposed to your actions, my lady. I can't express strongly enough his degree of opposition. Even wounded, he's quite likely to do something rash."

Her hand came to her mouth, horror in her gaze. "Wounded? How badly? Tell me . . . tell me the truth." A wave of terror rolled over her; Jamie had died from a putrid battle wound.

"A musket ball in the arm, my lady. He seems to be convalescing . . . in his own way."

"Is he in bed?" she quickly asked, pale and shaken. "Has he seen a doctor? He should be in bed so the wound doesn't fester."

"A doctor has seen him, of course, but he refuses to stay in bed. He's headstrong, my lady, as you know."

"Tell him he *must* stay in bed," she ordered, "and he must have the dressing changed every day and he must eat well—broths and a little meat—and he needs sleep to heal. Tell him I insist." She took a small breath to suppress her overwhelming apprehensions. "How does he look? Is he feverish?" she nervously queried.

Armed for battle wouldn't placate her anxieties,

Coutts decided, so he opted for a less traumatic answer. "The earl doesn't appear much indisposed by his wound, my lady."

"Thank God," she breathed, visibly relieved. "Bring him my prayers." And after a moment of hesitation she added, "And my love as well."

"Yes, my lady, I'll convey your concerns and regards."

"Tell him also," she went on, her smile tentative, "I'll see him again when he and Johnnie are back at Goldiehouse."

Coutts refrained from mentioning she may be seeing him considerably sooner. He'd not been given permission to disclose that information, nor was he entirely sure Robbie would make his way across town undetected by Queensberry's patrols. "I'll tell him, ma'am." He rose from his chair and bowed.

"One more thing," she blurted out, ardent feeling overcoming discretion. "Tell him I haven't forgotten 'The Ballad of Muirland Willie.' "

A SCANT HOUR LATER, AFTER A RUSH OF PACKING by the entire Forrestor household, Roxane conveyed her children, their maids, governesses, and nannies, along with an extra baggage cart, to the Carberrys, whose establishment had undergone a similar burst of activity.[7]

Roxane and her children arrived in the sunny second-floor drawing room where Amelia's children and several of their pets had assembled prior to departure. Two large deerhounds sprawled in the warmth of the sun streaming through the south windows. A parrot greeted everyone coming into the room with a raucous "hip, hip, hooray" and other more indelicate words, while two black cats prowled the sofa backs, nervous in the heightened bustle of packing.

Amelia greeted them, her four children smiling at her side. "I told the children we're in a rush, so they've promised to behave until you bid your good-byes."

Her oldest boy pantomimed locking his mouth with a key, which generated a wave of giggles. But everyone settled down after a moment or so.

"Remember to help Aunt Amelia with the children, darling," Roxane said to her daughter, Jeannie, "and write and tell me what everyone's doing." She kissed and hugged her oldest child.

"I will, Mama. And Auntie says Uncle has three prime new racers he'll let me ride." Her bright smile gave evidence of her pleasure. "When you come out to Longmuir I'll race you."

Roxie beamed, proud of her daughter's equestrian skills. She was reminded of her own youth, when the world was still carefree and untroubled and her greatest pleasure was riding across the moors.

"Uncle David has the best jockey in Scotland from Ayrshire, so we're going to lots of race meets."

"I'm riding, too," her eldest son, James, interposed. "Aunt Melie says I can race one of their horses at the meets."

"Do be careful, darling," Roxane murmured, moving to kiss her twelve-year-old son on his freckled nose. "Some of the jockeys ride for blood."

"Mama." He snorted in disgust. "I'm bigger than most of the jockeys already. I can hold my own."

"I know, dear," she murmured, thinking how quickly he'd grown. In a year, two at the most, he'd be off to university.

She still had her twin sons and Angus to mother for a few more years, she reflected, although the twins at ten were becoming more independent every day. They were ecstatic about going to the country, their excitement barely contained. Andrew and Alex, grinning from ear to ear, had their fishing poles in their hands so she received one-armed hugs from them.

"We're going to fish *every* day," Alex proudly declared.

"And at *night,* too," Andrew added. "Aunt Melie says we can sleep in the crofter hut down by the loch and come to the house only to eat dinner."

"*I'm* fishing, too," her youngest piped up, his small fishing pole clutched in his pudgy fist.

"You boys help Angus," Roxane suggested, bending on one knee to hug her littlest. Unlike her older boys, who were dark like their father, Jamie, Angus looked nothing like Kilmarnock. Instead he had Roxane's red hair and the Forrestor features. She'd always considered God benevolent to disregard the Erskine blood when he'd sent Angus to her.

"He can't sleep with us at night, though," Alex and Andrew said in unison.

"Can too," Angus protested, his lower lip thrust forward in stubborn resistance.

"Can't either," Alex rebutted.

Angus's bottom lip began to tremble.

"Jamie will stay with you one night, won't you, Jamie?" Roxane queried, gathering her five-year-old into her arms, fishing pole and all.

"Angus and I will stay in our own fishing hut," Jamie offered, accommodating his mother's wishes.

"Our *own?*" Angus exclaimed, instantly appeased.

"Now apologize to Angus," Roxane ordered, her gaze on her twins.

"He can stay if he *wants*," Alex relented.

"He can swim with us," Andrew volunteered. "He just cries at night when he's away from the house, that's all."

"I won't cry," Angus promised, confident of his grown-up status in the comfort of his mother's arms.

"Why don't we all stay there occasionally," Amelia proposed. "Being outside at night with plenty of company will be less frightening."

"I don't want to sleep outside," Jeannie protested. "And I know Julia doesn't, either."

"You and your cousin needn't, dear," Amelia replied, knowing how her daughter and Jeannie, so close in age, preferred sitting up and talking all night.

Roxane smiled at her daughter, who at thirteen alternated between her love of active sports and the more feminine pastimes of young womanhood. "Now mind Aunt Melie and Uncle David," she said one last time, "and when I come to Longmuir in a fortnight you can tell me all you've done."

"Don't be away *too* long," Angus pleaded, hugging his mother tightly.

"I'll come as soon as I can, darling." Kissing his plump cheek, she set him down. "Now all of you give me a last kiss until I can see you again."

The four Carberry cousins were impatiently waiting near the door, their deerhounds in hand, and Roxane's final kisses were given in a flurry of childish conversations and thunderous barks.

AFTER THE LAST WAVE AND BLOWN KISS, WHEN the children had all run off to the carriages, Roxane turned to Amelia. "I'm not sure they'll wait for you, so I shan't keep you. I can see myself out."

"Miss Wade can monitor them for a moment," Amelia replied, an odd constraint in her tone. "Before you go, I'd like you to look at a new credenza I bought." Touching Roxane's arm, she signaled her to silence with a finger to her mouth. "It's in David's study."

Roxane glanced at her sister-in-law in puzzlement, but Amelia only moved toward the arched entrance to the room. "I need your advice on how best to use it," she went on in a conversational tone. "You remember that Florentine painted piece at Amluxen's we were both admiring." Brows lifted, she emphatically nodded her head, her black curls bobbing with the vigor of her gesture.

Responding to her obvious pantomime, Roxane said, "Of course I remember," her voice bland, her curiosity piqued.

"I'm using it temporarily for David's books, but I was thinking of moving it into my bedroom and putting my lingerie in it, or I could use it in the dining room for the silver or the delftware. I'm not sure . . . exactly what to do with it, so let me know what you think might be most appropriate . . . or useful." She rambled on, obviously nervous, the pitch of her voice too loud in the quiet of the corridor.

Reaching the study, she opened the door and gestured Roxane in. She quickly followed, shut the door behind them and hastily turned the key in the lock as though the fiends of hell might be breathing down their necks.

"What in the world is going on?" Roxane looked at her friend with misgiving. Queensberry's threats covered a large territory.

"You have a visitor." Amelia glanced from Roxane to a shadowed alcove between two great banks of bookshelves. "And keep your voice down," she ordered, speaking to whomever was concealed there. "The servants might hear."

Receiving no answer, she walked toward a doorway to an adjoining room. "Don't stay long. You're putting everyone at risk." She turned back to Roxane, her mouth set in a hard, tense line. "I'll wait for you in the drawing room." She exited the study, the scraping sound of a key turning in the lock evidence of the degree of danger her visitor posed.

Roxane had first realized the visitor's identity when the faint scent of citron had drifted to her, and torn between fear for Robbie's safety and joy at seeing him, she rushed toward him, an irrepressible excitement racing through her.

"What the bloody *hell* did you think you were doing?"

The quiet savagery in his voice stopped her in her tracks, and when he stepped from the shadows, the violence of his expression shocked her. A vicious, cruel mask overlaid his handsome face. His hand was on his sword hilt as though they were enemies. "Did you think I'd say thank you for your kindness and go on with my life?" he ground out. "Or wait patiently for Argyll's fucking leftovers?"

She'd expected him to be disturbed by her note—she understood jealousy as well as he—but she'd not expected this implacable fury. "I thought it would be a reasonable solution to your difficulties. Argyll assures me he'll nullify the charges of treason against your family."

"He does, does he?" Robbie caustically drawled. "Isn't he the kindest fucking traitor England's sent north lately." His face was so chill, his beautiful eyes had turned cruel. "And he's doing this for me," he silkily murmured, loathing in every word.

"Don't be hateful," she quietly said.

"Do you think I'd want my land and titles back because you spread your legs for him?" he lashed out. "Do you think I could live with that filthy thought?"

"You're acting like an obnoxious child," she tartly rebuked. "And don't talk to me of morals as though you were a faultless and pure Presbyterian virgin." She glared at him, angry that he dared order her life. "No one owns me, least of all you." Her voice shook, because it had taken her years to reach independence and she had no intention of relinquishing it to a jealous eighteen-year-old. "Now, if you'd care to discuss this like an adult instead of insulting me, I'm willing to listen."

His fine mouth curled in derision. "What are we going to talk about? Where you're going to fuck him, how often, the different ways?" He was well beyond reason. His sense of possession was defiled, his hot-tempered fury overwhelming any sense of perspective save his. "All I want to know," he softly growled, "is whether you're actually going to fuck him or not."

Her nostrils flared at his presumption. "When did you become my keeper?"

"You want to fuck him? Is that what you're saying?" His eyes burned into her.

"No."

"Then don't."

"You'll have your lands back, damn you. Can't you understand that?" She bristled. "People do as much every day for less reason."

"People?" he sardonically drawled. "You're neutralizing what you're saying, so it won't be you fucking him. I'll tell you what," he gruffly muttered, "let's neutralize the subject completely. I don't want your help. I don't need it. I won't take it. Is that sufficiently clear? We'll fight them our way."

"And maybe get killed in the bargain," she snapped.

"Better than dying of shame," he snapped back.

"Male notions of shame always amaze me. Killing and slaughter isn't shameful, but this is, my getting your land back with a signed agreement."

"Don't even fucking think of doing this for me," he said in a savage whisper.

"You'd risk your life instead. That's better?"

"It is for me."

"Very well," she declared, her anger as decisive. "Then I have some equally firm judgments. I want you to stay away from me until your lawsuit is settled and the Carres no longer represent a danger to my children."

"That's too long."

"My decision isn't negotiable."

"And if I refuse?"

"You jeopardize my life and the lives of my children. I don't like you doing this to me."

"You're asking too much."

"I'm not asking," she coldly said.

"I could take you away. You couldn't stop me."

"Would you want me like that?"

"I'm like Argyll," he silkily murmured. "I'll take you any way I can get you."

"That offends me."

"But Argyll's wanting you doesn't. His is—what word did you use—reasonable? Fucking him is some benign act of friendship?"

"Regardless of what you think, everything isn't about sex."

"It is with Argyll—make no mistake."

"We would have a legal agreement," she said, clipped and cool.

"You can separate it so neatly?" He inhaled deeply, his feelings not so tidily compartmentalized. He wouldn't allow her to be with Argyll, or any man. "How can I put this to least offend you?" he said, hesitating in his search for the proper phrases. He took another deep breath and blew it out. He couldn't say he wanted to own her body and soul when her eyes were so chill. He said instead, his voice deliberately soft and low, "I love you. Because of that, I'd rather die than let Argyll touch you. I'm sorry if my feelings disturb you. And I thought you loved me, too." He made a disparaging gesture, as though brushing away that misunderstanding. A spasm of pain momentarily tightened his jaw.

She took a step toward him and then stopped, not allowing herself to be so easily assuaged. "You should be in bed with that wound," she quietly said, wishing she were able to take away his pain, wishing she weren't so susceptible to his words of love.

"You should be there with me," he gently replied, the cruelty in his eyes replaced now by tenderness. "We shouldn't be arguing about this stupidity."

How tempting he was, she thought. This the man she loved, now that his anger was gone. "It's not stupid. It's practical, it's—"

He held up a hand to stop her words. "We'll never agree on that not if we argue till doomsday. Come away with me. Your children are safe. We'll go to ground in the Cheviots."

"Argyll would scour the country for us. He's determined."

"He can't have you, and that's final—if you'll forgive my jealousy," he added with a gracious smile. "I'd kill him first."

"The queen and her ministers want their treaty. They'd see you dead for that."

"As good a reason as any to die," he murmured, bred to a code of honor she'd never understand.

"Don't die for me, don't even think it," she whispered, terrified he'd waste his bonny life for her. "I'd much prefer a husband who lives this time."

His dark eyes flared in surprise. "You're marrying me?"

"No, no, I dinna' mean that," she said, lapsing into childhood dialect in her confusion.

"You meant it." His smile shone white against the deep bronze of his skin. "I'll have to see that I'm measured for my wedding clothes," he teased.

"Don't tempt fate, Robbie," she pleaded, "not when

our lives are in such disarray. I shouldn't have said what I said. I don't know why I did, or why I feel the way I do about you," she finished with a soft sigh.

"I'm irresistible." His smile was beguiling, full of grace and charm, an undaunted smile of confidence and hope.

Nor could she disagree with the teasing arrogance of his words.

"Perhaps in better times when we're safe again," he said, humoring her reservations, crossing the small distance between them with an unhurried stride. "When the gods are smiling on us once more." His slender fingers closed on her shoulders when he reached her and, drawing her into his arms, he smiled down at her. "Marry me then."

How optimistic he was, she thought, and she hoped in that part of her brain immune to practicalities that he might be right. She was infatuated or in love or simply moonstruck mad, for all she saw was his bonny beauty and all she wanted to hear were his words of love, as though she were a lovestruck ingenue impressed by a gorgeous, handsome man. And there was no denying he was beautiful beyond words, she thought, smiling up at him, his stark cheekbones muted by the flawless blush of his youth, his dark, long-lashed eyes showy, ostentatious in their beauty, his sensual mouth smiling, tempting her.

"Tell me," he murmured.

She hesitated, for what he was asking wasn't only difficult, but perhaps impossible, and she wasn't an ingenue, not by the farthest stretch. "If it were just me—"

"Say yes," he interrupted.

"I can't."

"I'll make you happy."

"I know."

"It's enough. Don't you realize that?"

"All the rest is irrelevant, you mean, like my children, my age, your age even more—"

He kissed her then because he didn't want to argue when he'd already made up his mind.

"There now," he whispered, lifting his mouth several moments later, "just so you don't forget me."

"Not likely," she breathed, her senses on fire.

He looked up at a sound in the corridor. "Stay away from Argyll," he abruptly said, reality returned.

"I'll try."

"Wrong answer."

"I'll really try," she lightly replied.

"Then I'll really try not to see you," he gently countered.

"I'll think of something to keep him away."

"Lord, how am I going to manage not seeing you?"

"Only until—what did you say—September?"

He swore. "That's a lifetime."

Footsteps approached the door.

"Go," Roxane nervously told him.

"Be careful," he murmured, releasing her.

Someone tried the knob and she pushed him away. The connecting door opened, and Amelia furiously motioned Robbie out.

He stood for an instant staring at Roxane, uneasy at leaving her within Argyll's ken, and then compelled, he turned and ran.

Chapter 8

"ᗞ ID YOU SEE WHERE HE WENT?"

Amelia, who had been standing by the windows facing the garden when Roxane entered the drawing room, turned at her inquiry. "No, and I don't want to know. *You* don't want to know. My majordomo was the one at the study door and I'm not so sure he wasn't eavesdropping. So just tell me Robbie Carre's going to be sensible and leave you alone, and I'll sleep much better at night."

"I think so."

Amelia rolled her eyes. "That's reassuring."

"We have an agreement of sorts."

"Humor me. Use less equivocal words."

Roxane smiled, in sublime favor with the world at the moment. "He's absolutely unbelievable."

"Unbelievably stupid? Unbelievably naive? Unbelievably sexy? Tell me when I'm getting warm. *Merde*," Amelia said in an explosive breath, regarding her friend's expression with unease. "You're in deep, aren't you?"

"There's no possible explanation. Don't ask me for one. If I were religious, I'd say it was God's will."

"But since you aren't, might it have something to do with his virile young body and flagrant carnality?"

"Definitely a factor," Roxane said with a grin.

"You're going to need a keeper if you don't get that lovesick look off your face. I mean it. Or Queensberry will put the thumbscrews on you and find your lover."

"I don't know where Robbie is, so I couldn't tell him anyway."

"He may not care whether you know or not. The man's not precisely normal, and who can tell what tales his army of spies may have fed him. Think of your children, too."

Her last words were like a drenching sluice of ice water, effectively obliterating any further lovesick fantasies. "You're right about Queensberry, of course," Roxane agreed. "Thanks for reminding me. I also have to discourage Argyll."

"That'll require a miracle of the first magnitude."

"If he's not cooperative, I myself might have to disappear for a time. Should you hear of such an event, don't take alarm."

"Don't tell me any more," Amelia quickly interposed. "I don't want to know."

Roxane nodded. "Understood. Now take the children, and go quickly in case Queensberry is already on Robbie's trail."

"You'll be careful."

"As cautious as possible considering I'm caught between the Carres and their enemies."

Amelia frowned. "Robbie shouldn't have done that to you."

"I could have made him leave two nights ago and I didn't. So some of the responsibility is mine. And they can't accuse me of anything more than sleeping with Robbie Carre, anyway," she dismissively added.

"Even that is considered treason by those who oppose him—and Queensberry is in the vanguard of his enemies. Remember that," her friend reminded her. "If you should need help," she went on, her tone worried, "old Lannie is trustworthy, even if some of the newer servants aren't. Send him to me with a message."

"I'll be fine," Roxane maintained. "Without the responsibility of the children, I'm relatively unconstrained in my options. Now go."

*W*HEN ROXANE ARRIVED AT KILMARNOCK HOUSE, she found Agnes Erskine standing beside her luggage, directing the porters and footmen with her cane. Her thin face was wreathed in smiles, her good cheer even extending to Roxane as she entered the entrance hall. "It seems young Angus will have his earldom," the old lady cheerfully remarked. "Argyll's ADC was here a short time ago. I hear you had the sense to take my advice and encourage Argyll," she said with a wicked crackle. "You're not completely witless, after all."

"Argyll promised me he'd have you gone by noon, Agnes," Roxane coolly returned, taking off her gloves. "Weren't his instructions clear? It's after two."

"I'll go home gladly, you nasty bitch, since it leaves you alone with Argyll. Now make sure you properly flatter the young commissioner."

"Advice on romance from you, Agnes? I thought you witches were heartless," she murmured, moving toward the stairway.

"Just do your duty to your son," her mother-in-law snapped, "or I'll see that you rue the day you entered the Erskine family."

"You're years too late on that score." She'd given in to her parents' pressure to remarry, and bitterly regretted her decision. Reaching the base of the staircase, suddenly tired of the years of viciousness, she turned back. "Henceforth, my doors will be closed to you and your family, Agnes. Don't ever return to this house."

"It's my son's house!" Agnes barked, banging her cane on the floor. "You can't keep me out!"

"I suggest you check the marriage settlement," Roxane calmly replied. "Your son was so eager to marry me, he was extremely accommodating to my lawyers' requests."

"I'll have Angus taken from you," the old woman screamed, the feather on her black bonnet quivering with her rage.

"He's gone. All the children are gone. Good-bye, Agnes, for the last time."

She swept up the stairs on a buoyant cloud of shameless exultation, undisturbed by the shrieks and threats following her ascent, the means to rid herself of Kilmarnock's hateful old mother a reality at last. Or perhaps she'd simply reached the end of her patience and would have sent her from the house with or without Argyll.

Being in love gave one an odd sense of invincibility, she reflected, imbued one with a new deep-felt sense of purpose.

She had her house to herself again.

She was legally in control of her life and finances.

She was no longer a young girl unsure of herself, but a woman with the means and ability to secure what she wanted.

And September wasn't so far away.

❧❧❧

𝒜T THE SAME TIME AGNES ERSKINE LEFT KIL-
marnock House, two of Queensberry's informers were
closeted with him in his apartments at Holyrood
Palace. They sat in a closely arranged circle of chairs,
their voices deliberately low, for no one trusted the
walls of Holyrood Palace, especially a man of Queensberry's ilk. His definition of loyalty was fluid and con-
ditional, aligned to any policy advantageous to his
fortunes.

Naturally he assumed no less from others.

"Argyll was closeted with lawyers all morning," one
of the men murmured. "A personal matter, the clerk in
his office said."

"Meaning?" Queensberry suspiciously inquired.

"There's talk he's accommodating the Countess of
Kilmarnock," a second man answered.

"In what way?"

"Rumor has it—" The man paused for effect. "The
Carre lands are the commodity of exchange for the
lady's favors."

Queensberry's face went pale, but he showed no
other reaction to these men who couldn't be trusted
any more than he. "Are you sure?" he calmly inquired.

"Argyll's intensely impassioned. The lady refuses
him without some guarantees."

"And those guarantees are my lands?"

Even English spies knew whose lands they were, but
they weren't disposed to argue. "So rumor maintains,
sir," the older of the men replied. "Argyll's counselors
might be able to enlighten you further."

"Their names, Defoe."[8] Once Queensberry was in

possession of the names, he dismissed the men and sat for a lengthy time in his high-backed chair, seething with the iniquity of Argyll's arrogance. "We'll just see who wins this game," he murmured, his hands steepled on his chest, his mind absorbed with the machinations necessary to thwart Argyll's plans.

Before long, he was en route to Kilmarnock House, walking the short distance down the Canongate, his methodology in place. His first step would be an interview with the countess. It always paid to be well informed. It was also useful to threaten one's enemies as soon as possible.

Often the initial warning was all that was necessary to accomplish one's mission. Although, after his conversation with the countess at dinner last night, he strongly expected her to use Argyll as a shield.

It never hurt to exert pressure, though.

Some people were fainthearted.

*N*OT ROXANE FORRESTOR, HOWEVER.

She abhorred Queensberry, and men like him, who felt they could manipulate people and events without any consequences to their own lives. And when Queensberry walked into her drawing room so close on the heels of Agnes's departure, she wondered if they were in partnership. She found herself considering again how lucky she was to love Robbie Carre, a not uncommon reflection since her meeting with him at Amelia's—actually, a joyous, blissful constant in her mind.

Queensberry, whose fortunes often depended on

reading people correctly, saw a woman in love the instant he stepped into the room. And she wasn't trying to conceal it, he noted. He gave her high points for self-assurance.

"I hear Argyll is giddy as a schoolboy over you," he said, waving the footman out of the room as though it were his house.

"You may stay, Ian," Roxane countermanded. "Is he really?" she mildly said. "I would hardly characterize Argyll as giddy, but suit yourself. I'm very busy, though, so please be brief."

Queensberry sat, making himself comfortable as though he intended to stay. "Agnes is gone, I see."

"How do you see that, James? Do you have your spies here as well?"

"Your caddy told me, if you must know."

"Did he really? I must see that he's fired."

"And your children are gone as well."

"Did he tell you that, too? He's much too loose-tongued."

"Do you want your servant to hear this?"

"Whatever you have to say, James, is best heard by others. You don't inspire trust, but then I expect you know that by now. How many years have you been working for the English?" she lightly queried as though she were asking him his latest golf scores. "So many lies," she went on with a flashing smile. "How do you sleep at night?"

"You seem particularly cheerful. Young lovers will do that to a person, though, won't they?"

"How would you possibly know? No offense intended," she sweetly said. "And yes, young lovers are lush, like fresh spring mornings or the delectable scent of lilac on the breeze. Would you like to hear more? I'm embarrassing Ian."

"What would you do to save him?"

"Why can't you say his name, James? You astonish me. Such fastidiousness from an evil man."

"Would you give me the land back to save him?" he blandly queried, relatively immune to barbed remarks in his profession.

She masked her surprise; his sources of information must be well placed. "Why don't you ask Argyll?"

"I prefer asking you."

"I'll discuss it with John. Why don't we leave it at that."

"I don't think you'll discuss it with him. The young boy must love you to risk his life. I doubt you can be false to such devoted passion."

"You're touching my heart with such sweet senti-ments, but consider—you're not the only person in Scotland with mercenary instincts. And after all, a widow who has to make her way alone in the world has to weigh all her options . . ."

"You should be on the stage, my dear," Queensberry silkily drawled.

"And you should be in prison, my lord."

"All this facetious banter aside," he crisply said, his gaze no longer affable, "let me give you a small warning. I have no intention of giving up the Carre lands, not for Argyll's lust, not for your lovesick heart, not for the honor of the Carres. And John Campbell is very young," he softly went on. "A disadvantage when dealing with me. So be careful in your bargains. I don't recommend you selling yourself to Argyll unless the stipulations of your agreement are altered to something less displeasing to me. Because you'll never collect your part of the contract. I hope I've been plainspoken enough. I wouldn't want you to misunderstand my intentions."

"You're quite lucid, James. However, let me leave you with some equally plain words. You didn't really think I was ingenuous enough to feel you would relinquish the Carre lands without a fight, did you? That's why I need Argyll. And it's a business arrangement we're considering, if you're thinking of relaying this conversation to him. He already knows why I'm interested in him. He's not looking for love, James. He's not ingenuous, either. I think that's why he's commissioner and you're not," she said, rising. "Ian will see you out."

But she was warned.

And she understood Queensberry would stop at nothing.

Her interview with Queensberry was simple, though, compared with her coming conversation with Argyll, she knew, and she made preparations in advance for that event.

She understood enough about predatory men to realize that John Campbell wasn't going to like what he heard. And rather than send for him, she waited for him to appear.

He came at dinnertime that night as though he'd been invited, and when he entered her dining room, he strolled across the large candlelit room, pulled up a chair beside her at the table where she was dining alone, and said, "I was expecting you to send for me this afternoon."

Putting down her knife and fork, she sent the servants away with a nod. Unlike Queensberry, who had no pride if he had advantage to gain, Argyll wouldn't allow himself to be publicly humiliated. Once the last servant had departed, she met his challenging gaze. "I've changed my mind."

"You saw him."

Her brows rose in query. Was he speaking of Queensberry?

"Robbie Carre. You must have seen him. And apparently he's not inclined to be reasonable."

"It's my own decision, John. I found the concept of selling myself unacceptable when actually faced with the prospect. But thank you for your kind interest."

"You don't really think I'm going to be well-bred and obliging about this, do you?" He pushed his chair away from the table and leaned back in a comfortable sprawl, his red uniform coat glittering with gold lace and braid. "Let's talk over our options," he suggested, leaning forward briefly to lift a bottle of wine from the table. "I presume your lover is opposed."

"Why not presume *I'm* opposed?"

"Because I've been negotiating people's lives and fortunes for many years now and I recognize interest when I see it, darling. You were quite willing to share my bed last night." He poured himself a glass of wine.

"Only with contractual stipulations."

"Those are still relevant." He drank deeply and then smiled his approval. "Excellent. Some of the Carre shipment?"

"Isn't all the good wine in Scotland?" she acknowledged. Wanting to change the conversation from the Carres, she said, "Queensberry came to see me this afternoon. You might wish to check the security in your office."

His expression immediately brightened. "Is it Queensberry? If that's your concern, leave *him* to me. I assure you, he'll be stripped of the Carre lands and you can forget any further problems with him. My word on it."

For the smallest moment she was tempted. How easy it would be—a sexual liaison of no consequence to her for so much in return.

He was watching her, his gaze insightful. "He'll get over it, even if he says he won't."

"Does your wife feel that way?"

He shrugged. "Hardly an apt comparison. Come now, Parliament should be dissolved by September, October at the very latest. A few months out of our lives—how can it seriously hurt Robbie Carre at eighteen? He'll hardly remember in a few years."

"You've never been in love?"

"This is the closest, darling," he said with a cloudless smile. "I'm looking forward to the experience."

"Unfortunately, it's not that simple."

"You're making it more difficult than necessary. My dear Roxane, surely you're sensible of the prize I offer. Even a woman of your renown is aware that this is not a bagatelle. And I'm not a callow young boy to be twined around your lovely finger."

"Is that a threat?" she murmured.

"Just a realistic appraisal of our circumstances."

"You'll make the decision—or you've made the decision? Is that what I'm hearing?"

"Darling, acquit me of such ruthlessness. You simply entice me—enormously. Tell me we have an agreement, and I'll treat you with the greatest deference."

"I'm truly sorry," she replied. "I can't tell you that."

His eyes lost their geniality. "That's your last word?"

"It's my choice."

"Actually, it's not. *I'm* sorry," he said with feigned courtesy.

"You mistake your power over me."

"Not in the least." He moved upright in his chair and placed his wine glass on the table. "My men are surrounding your house. They'll remain in place for the duration of our . . . liaison. Don't attempt to leave." He adjusted the lace at his cuffs and smiled faintly. "Although I'm not ungenerous. I'm more than willing to adhere to our agreement and free the Carre lands from Queensberry."

"That costs *you* nothing," she murmured, "so don't speak to me of generosity."

"It costs me Queensberry's enmity."

"Which you have already."

"Taking the Carre lands will cause him a major hemorrhage, my dear. I'm expecting retaliation above and beyond his normal animosity. So you'll be costing me, rest assured." He stood and sketched her a bow. "Enough of this useless debate," he declared, a touch of brusqueness in his voice. "Be ready within the hour with your lawyers. I'll return with mine."

"You astonish me. Is this normal for you, this coercion?"

He laughed. "Hardly. You're the rare exception, my lovely countess. You should be flattered."

"You're not the first man who's coveted me, Argyll. Pray mitigate your arrogance."

"Maybe not the first, darling, but the most fortunate of men, I assure you," he drawled. "I'll be back shortly. Do call your counselors. I don't wish any further delays."

She sat in stunned silence for a moment after he left and then, rising from the table, went to the windows and slipped back the draperies enough to look out onto the courtyard. He was serious. At least a troop stood at attention before her house. When she surveyed the other directions from a variety of windows she took note of the ring of soldiers surrounding her home.

He was indeed determined, she realized.

Which meant she didn't have much time.

Returning to her bedchamber, she dismissed her maid, telling her she had a headache and wished to lie down. She felt a small guilt lying to Geillis, who had been with her so long, but in these troubled times, excessive caution was required.

Quickly sliding her small pack from under the bed, she pulled out the clothes she'd taken earlier from her son's room. James was a big boy at twelve, and the riding pants and shirt would do nicely. Swiftly discarding her gown and petticoats, she dressed the way she had as a child in the country, when comfort was more important than decorum. In moments she was attired, her riding boots and a servant's jacket she'd plucked from the kitchen hall completing her ensemble.

Turning before the cheval glass, she decided her

disguise looked adequate provided the night was sufficiently dark, for although she'd bound her breasts, a side view still wouldn't pass muster at close range. Her hair of course would have to go, she realized with faint misgivings the heavy mane of curls was too difficult to hide.

She reached for her small gold scissors, and minutes later, her shorn tresses lay in silken heaps on the floor. Her remaining red curls were clubbed together at the nape of her neck, a tartan tam pulled low over her forehead. A stable lad gazed back at her from the mirror. With no moon, she thought, and a little luck . . .

Glancing at the clock on the mantel, she noted the time with dismay. A quarter of her hour of reprieve was already gone. But not wishing to leave evidence of her disguise, she took the time to clean up her hair from the carpet and stuff it into her rucksack.

Her jewelry had already been stowed inside, including Robbie's new necklace; she had money as well, and enough food to last her a day or so. Her main objective was simply to escape Edinburgh tonight. After that, she'd see if the route to Edgarhope Wood lay open to a stable lad taking his master's horse home.

With the pack on her shoulder, she surveyed herself one last time in the mirror, searching for any discrepancies that might give her away. Adding a scarf around her neck, she hid a bit more of her pale skin and a portion of her chin. At the last, she rubbed her fingertips in the ashes of the grate and smeared a light gray film over her face.

Better, she thought. Stable lads as a rule didn't have a freshly bathed appearance.

And now, she nervously reflected, glancing once more at the clock, to get past the circle of guards surrounding her house.

ARGYLL WAS MOVING AT AN EQUALLY SWIFT PACE, his subordinates assembled to perform the tasks necessary for his expeditious return to Kilmarnock House. Sitting at his desk, he delivered orders in a brisk staccato to functionaries standing at attention before him. "Have the lawyers brought round. I need my schedule rearranged for the morning—no appointments until noon. Where are those gifts I had Lawson buy? And have some champagne sent over to Kilmarnock House from my cellar. Agnes Erskine is gone from the city? Her departure monitored? Good," he pronounced with a nod to the young captain who answered in the affirmative. "Send a note to Queensberry—where's my clerk?" he queried, raising his voice, his impatience obvious. "Ah." He noted the man running through the doorway, papers in hand. "Tell Queensberry he is being formally apprised of the return of the Carre properties to their owners *and* of the revocation of the treason charges against them. I'll sign it before I go. Deliver it to him." Assured of his conquest of the beautiful Countess Kilmarnock with his troops in place around her house, he considered Queensberry's notification a courtesy to her. He would arrive at her home with that duty discharged.

A conciliatory gesture along with his gifts.

A peace offering.

⸻

HOLMES ENTERED ROBBIE'S ROOM OUT OF BREATH, his swift journey through the streets of Edinburgh and his racing ascent of the stairs leaving him gasping for air.

At the sound of running feet on the stairs, Robbie had risen from his chair, and he met his man with pistol drawn.

"Argyll's troops . . . have Kilmarnock House . . . barricaded," Holmes breathlessly announced.

"How many?" Robbie was already slipping his jack on.

"Three corps."

His scowl deepened. "Is he there with her?"

"He was . . . but he's back at headquarters now . . . with clerks and lieutenants scurrying as if a battle was about to begin."

"You're right there," Robbie curtly muttered, fastening the last buckle on his jack. "How many men do we have in town?"

"Sixty since morning."

"And there's a watch at Kilmarnock House?"

"Front and back . . . plus the garden wall. You knew he'd do it," Holmes asserted, the discussion of Argyll's motives and agenda much debated during the afternoon and evening.

"I didn't think he'd be so clumsy." Robbie's brows rose in derision as he slipped his sword baldric over his head. "He could have waited a day or so to woo her." The thought brought a grimace to his face. "Double our surveillance," he ordered, pulling his sword from its scabbard, lunging in a feint to test his pain levels and stability. "I have to know where she is, where Argyll is," he added, teeth clenched against the torment, a thin beading of sweat breaking out on his forehead.

"Send Mrs. Beattie inside." Geillis was a relative, the ranks of Edinburgh servants close-knit by blood ties. "Hurry. And tell the men I'll meet them at our appointed rendezvous in ten minutes."

ROXANE HAD TRAVERSED THE UPSTAIRS HALLWAY undetected and traveled down the servants' staircase without meeting anyone, but the kitchen was bustling with staff, some cleaning up the remains of dinner, others gathered round the fire with pints and pipes in hand, their normal duties lightened with the house empty of Agnes and the children.

She waited in the shadows of the pantry, but quickly realized that passing through the room without being seen was impossible. She decided to leave through the garden door, although the route required she cross a long open stretch of yard.

Moving back up the stairs, she carefully made her way through the reception rooms, on the lookout for servants, but she reached the library unseen. The glass-paned doors to the garden gleamed in the moonlight as she entered the room, as though beckoning her to freedom. Or luring her to disaster, she uneasily thought. The crushed rock of the garden paths shone pale under the moon. One of these paths led to the stable yard.

Her hands were shaking as she grasped the door latch and pulled it open, the metal hinges squeaking faintly in protest. Freezing at the sound, she waited, heart pounding. But the garden walls were high and thick, and after several tense moments, she realized the guards hadn't heard.

Taking a step outside, she held her breath while she closed the door again, not wanting to leave an open door behind her. And she endured once again that fearful interval while the sound of grating hinges died away in the night.

She could hear the horses in the stables, their soft nickers and movements reassuring. But in the quiet garden the voices of Argyll's guards were audible as well, their words drifting over the wall in bits and pieces, a word a phrase, a guffaw of laughter.

Campbell swordsmen—so close and waiting for her.

A church bell began tolling the hour. She silently counted to ten.

Which left her only thirty minutes before Argyll's return.

She wished for a moment, the way she might have in childhood, that she could fly over the garden wall and drift away like the wispy clouds above and find herself safe in Edgarhope Wood, where her mother's family had left her a small cottage.

But the fleeting whimsy passed. Steeling herself against daunting reality, she forced herself to move, because standing in fear at her library door would bring sure disaster. She didn't want to sleep with Argyll—not tonight, not ever.

She moved one terrified step at a time, and in a disjointed and shrinking way she progressed across the cultivated gardens over soft dirt under her boots, to the wooden gate that divided the garden from the stable yard.

Neither garden fragrances nor beauty struck her senses during her passage, her mind's eye focused only on reaching the gate. When she did, she pressed her face against the rough wood and waited for the fierce pounding of her heart to subside.

But she didn't allow herself much respite with time so urgent, and moments later, she eased the gate open a fraction so she could view the stable yard.

Her heart stopped.

Three Campbell swordsmen were lounging against the stable door, passing around a small earthenware decanter.

She had to walk through them to get to her horse.

It took a moment to gather her terrified wits into a modicum of calm, and a moment more to remind herself she had nothing to lose. If she stayed, she became Argyll's paramour for certain. If she could bluff her way past the guards, she had a chance at freedom.

Boldly pushing the door open, she stepped into the stable yard.

Three pairs of eyes immediately swung her way.

"D'ye ken how many o' these are in yon cellar?" Roxane called out in as deep a tone as she could muster, holding up a bottle of whiskey she'd brought along for possible bribery.

"And how did ye come by that?" one of the troopers gruffly queried.

"The mistress is alone, ye ken . . . an' who's to notice in a big manse if a bottle or two flies away."

"Na then, lad, ha'ye more wi'ye?" another man inquired, clearly interested in the extent of her cache.

"Mayhap I do." She pulled out a second from her pack. "But the cellar isna' so far ye couldna' fill your rucksack and no one the wiser."

Such temptation brought all three men from their lounging pose, and as she approached, their focus was not on her but on the two bottles she held.

The whiskey was swiftly grabbed away and lifted to their mouths while she stood hoping they'd move aside enough so she could enter the stable.

"Weel, that's mighty fine," one man murmured, taking a breath between gulps.

"What d'ye say ye show us yon cellar, lad, and ye can fill yer rucksack, too," a trooper declared, waving his bottle toward the garden gate.

"I couldna' leave my work right noo. But ye ken that door?" She pointed at the gate. "Through there and ye'll see the glass doors, wi' no one home but the countess upstairs waitin' for Argyll hisself."

"Och, ay, an' Big Red John will show the leddy a right fine time tonight," a trooper said, chuckling. "But show us yon cellar, lad, seein' ye ken the way."

The church bells tolled the quarter hour, and for a second she considered making a break for the street and running.

"Ay, lad, come wi' us." The soldier's tone had taken on a harsh rasp.

"The commissioner needs the lad," her stable-master brusquely said, coming out from the stables, leading a horse. "He says he wants this mount to be brought to him at half past the hour, and ye best hurry, laddie, or hisself will ha' your skin."

"Ay," Roxane croaked, her nerves stretched so taut her stablemaster had to wrap the reins around her hands and give her a push. "Now don't ye dawdle, laddie, or I'll see ye get the whip when ye come back. Hisself said half past, and half past he means."

Forcing her feet to move faster, she passed through the gate into the street, offering up a thousand prayers for Alec's nervy inspiration. She needed her horse tonight, she'd told him earlier, but no more; he'd improvised with panache.

Obliged to walk past the entire line of troops guarding the front of her house, she stayed in the shadow of the huge roan, running the gauntlet with a wildly beating heart. But Holyrood Palace was up the hill, and up the hill she must go.

Until, finally out of sight, she leaped into the saddle and galloped away.

Chapter 9

$\mathcal{M}$RS. BEATTIE ENTERED THE KITCHEN AT KIL-marnock House without difficulty; a servant, parti-cularly an old woman, was above suspicion. And after taking Geillis aside, she quietly said, "I need to talk to the countess. Don't look at me like that. We both know she doesn't care for Argyll's company, and he's on his way back here. I have a message for her from my young master."

Geillis nodded; last night's activities were common knowledge to everyone in the house. Motioning Mrs. Beattie to follow, she took her upstairs to Roxane's bedroom. "She's resting, she is, with a headache from all the pressures, ye ken, and she dinna' want to be disturbed."

"I'll speak to her for a second only. My master wants to know she's still in good health."

A minute later, Mrs. Beattie scurried down the stairs in as near to a run as a plump, sixty-year-old woman could manage. Five minutes later she met Holmes out of sight of the guards and hissed, "She's gone."

"Where?" Holmes gripped her shoulders as though she'd stolen her herself.

"Just gone. No one knows."

"Does Argyll have her?"

She threw her hands up and shook her head. "She told no one her plans, not even her maid, who's crying rivers for being left behind after serving the countess since childhood."

"It could be Argyll, then. Go home. I'll tell the master."

*Q*UEENSBERRY WENT TO ARGYLL'S OFFICE AT HOLYrood Palace with guards of his own this time, a dozen Douglas men to give credence to his anger. But Argyll had fought foreign armies for a decade; he wasn't easily intimidated by marching feet.

Queensberry barged into the anteroom of Argyll's headquarters, and stormed through to the office, his face red with fury. "I'll take this to the queen, to the House of Lords, damn you!" he shouted, waving the paper delivered to his apartments by Argyll's man. "If you think you can take these lands away from me for some cunt you crave, you're mistaken!"

Argyll's subordinates registered various stages of shock and consternation at Queensberry's intrusion and outburst, but Argyll didn't move from his lounging pose. "But I already have taken them from you," he casually noted. "You see the seal of England is displayed at the bottom of the document. My authority is supreme here in Scotland, while yours . . . is not," he succinctly pointed out. "And kindly remember, too, why you're in Scotland, James, in the event you've forgotten. You're here on my sufferance." His voice was low, temperate, like a parent indulging a tantrumish child. "So go to the queen if you wish, kiss her fat ass for all I care. But she prefers my ass-kissing at the moment, which is why I am in charge here in Scotland, and you are merely a necessary political tool."

"I'll see that you pay dearly for this," Queensberry blustered, Argyll's words too chillingly accurate for comfort. "I have friends in London, too."

"But not many."

"Enough," James Douglas ground out. "Enough that you need me to get this treaty through Parliament. Have you thought of that in your hot rut for the countess?"

"You need me more than I need you, James. In fact, your nephew, Mar, would be more than happy to usurp your role in serving me," he said, lifting a letter opener from the desk and jabbing it at Queensberry. "As I see it, you're not in a strong position right now. So kindly see that the Carre properties are immediately emptied of your staff. I've already sent clerks and troops to them to protect their inventories, so don't think of cleaning them out. The countess is particularly interested in Goldiehouse, I hear. You will not be allowed on that property at all. Good night, James. I'm rather in a hurry," he said, standing up, his height dwarfing Queensberry.

"You might have won this engagement, Argyll, but not the campaign, believe me," Queensberry said through clenched teeth, having to look up at Argyll. "You'll be hearing from me, so don't let the countess get her hopes up."

The young general sighed. "Please, at least don't bother me before tomorrow afternoon. I have plans, and I've left orders not to be disturbed. You understand."

"How do you find time for work, Argyll, with your unbridled taste for cunt?" Queensberry snapped.

John Campbell stared at Queensberry for a moment, as if questioning his sanity. "I find it intensely invigorating, if you must know—as you find the Machiavellian jobbery that rules your life. But then you're getting a little old for cunt, aren't you, James? A shame. The rewards are so much more gratifying than fucking someone out of their money." He turned away and spoke quietly to his ADC, as though Queensberry no longer existed, and then walked from the room.

An awkward silence ensued.

Queensberry's face was so mottled he looked ready to burst, and Argyll's staff wondered if he was going to have an apoplexy right before their eyes. But the duke, despite this current loss to his political and personal fortunes, was still a man of considerable power. So they cautiously refrained from further aggravating him and waited for him to leave.

Which he did after another uncomfortable moment, turning on his heal and stamping out of the room like an angry child.

"Argyll *does* like cunt overmuch," the commissioner's ADC murmured into the silence.

"Which may have its advantages on occasion. He charmed the queen." The clerk who spoke had been with Argyll in London during his negotiations for Commissioner.

"Which is more than Queensberry can do," an adjunct noted. "She hates his very guts."

"Although Argyll's charm hasn't worked with the countess, I hear," a young captain said.

"With her house surrounded, I don't expect she can long defend herself against Big Red John."

"The Carre laddie's going to be furious," a lieutenant cheekily declared with a grin.

"He had his turn. Argyll's in line tonight," the ADC quipped.

"I'd like my turn with her, damned if I wouldn't," the captain said with a low whistle.

"And what would your wife say to that?" one of the men inquired with a wicked smirk.

"What wife?"

WATCH ARGYLL, WATCH THE HOUSE, WATCH THE countess's servants—where they go, who they talk with," Robbie quietly said, giving instructions to the men he was adding to those on surveillance. "I want to know where the countess is as soon as possible." He paced as he talked, his long strides crossing and recrossing the great hall of the house on the outskirts of the city where the Carre troops were assembling. The men had been coming in all day in response to their summons, the number rising near eighty now, the full complement expected within two days.

"As soon as Argyll leaves headquarters I want a report."

"Mrs. Beattie's gone back into Kilmarnock House," Holmes said, coming in from outside.

"Then we sit here and wait," Robbie gruffly said, his sword hand lightly tapping the hilt of his weapon.

"We should know something soon. Argyll's scheduled to come back within the hour, the footman at Kilmarnock House said."

Roxane's conversation with Argyll in the dining room hadn't been private. Servants listened; it was a fact of life.

$\mathscr{A}$T THAT MOMENT, ARGYLL WAS STRIDING DOWN the Canongate, two footmen in his wake, one bearing his gifts, the second his portmanteau, three lawyers behind them, followed by two clerks. He was inattentive to his entourage, his thoughts consumed with anticipation of the coming night. He intended to take up residence in Roxane's home—actually, in the comfort of her boudoir—as often as his schedule permitted. He was looking forward to the months in Edinburgh with the most pleasant expectations.

He felt overcome with an odd enchantment or bewitchment, as though he were in the grip of some rapturous spell. And now he understood why men wrote sonnets—it was for women like Roxane Forrestor, he thought. She had the luxurious sensuality of a royal courtesan—pampered, indulged, more beautiful than God should allow, intriguing, as if lying in her arms would offer one the most ravishing glimpse of paradise.

The Royalist poets understood that; cunt had a special, captivating appeal when a woman enticed one's senses. And seduction took on a titillating allure, in contrast to just fucking, the young general reflected.

Strange, different.

Fascinating.

Like entering a foreign land.

He was smiling when he took the entrance steps in a bound and knocked a quick rap on the door.

The footman greeted him blankly; the majordomo behind him wore a look equally void of expression.

"The countess, if you please, " Argyll crisply said. "Tell her I've returned."

"She's not here, Your Grace," the majordomo pronounced.

"What?" the general exclaimed, his voice sharp as a knife blade. Infuriated, he moved forward as though he were about to attack the two servants. "Where the hell is she?"

"She's disappeared, my lord." The majordomo held his ground, his dignity intact, unlike that of the footman, who had slipped behind the door.

"Disappeared with my *men* surrounding the house? Impossible!" he barked. "Have the house searched," he rapped out. "Immediately." Turning back, he pushed through the cluster of men behind him, leaped down the stairs, and shouted for his troops.

Within minutes, the Campbell swordsmen were swarming over Kilmarnock House, from basement to attic, looking through armoires and under beds, searching linen closets and water closets, flipping draperies aside and tipping over sofas. And so they continued scrutinizing every cubic inch of the large house for nearly an hour before their commander, seated in the drawing room, white-faced with rage, ordered a halt to the search.

Argyll had interviewed the servants while his men had torn the house apart, but without success. A turncoat Scot who thought he ruled Scotland for the queen wasn't likely to get any information from the countess's loyal staff. Not even on threat of imprisonment.

The general's questions secured only blank looks or denial; no one had seen the countess since she'd dined with him.

Even Geilis remained silent; she had no intention of telling the traitor Campbell a word about her mistress, threats or no threats. As if he could force the poor wee babe—Roxane would always be that to her former nursemaid—to sleep with the English queen's flunky. Not likely while she had breath in her body, she silently vowed, her mouth set in stubborn defiance.

𝓑UT IT WASN'T LONG BEFORE ARGYLL'S SPIES HAD extracted the information he needed. Skilled at their craft, they'd talked to the soldiers guarding the house, questioning them on details, ostensibly one soldier to another, gossiping about the events of the night. And they discovered a young lad had walked away with a horse from the stables. In fact, that the boy had strolled by every soldier on guard on the Canongate side of the house.

"When?" Argyll asked, not lounging behind his desk at headquarters this time, but sitting bolt upright, tapping his fingers in a rapid tatoo on the desktop.

"Two hours ago, probably . . . or close to that."

"And where did she go from there? I want answers," John Campbell growled, taking exception to being hoodwinked by a mere woman, stung at having to curtail his lust, his particularly eager lust. Damn her, he'd fuck her senseless when he found her. And find her he would, if he had to turn every house and crofter's hut in Scotland inside out.

"Our feeling is that she headed south."

"Feeling?" he roared. "You'd better have something better than that, or I'll send you back to London and your dull duty watching Godolphin's fat mistress," he spat out. "Now give me specifics. Why the route south?"

"We had two reports of a young lad riding a horse too fine for the likes of him. South of Gilmerton and again at Dalkeith."

"That's more like it," Argyll said with a sharp rap of his fingers and the beginning of a smile. "When did this lad pass through Gilmerton?"

"No more than an hour ago."

"Find me someone who knows the countess and is willing to tell me why she might be riding south. Her properties are north. Does she have friends in the south? And if so, where?"

"Only her enemies are likely to tell you anything. And they'll ask for payment."

"Give it to them, then, dammit. You know how this works." The concept of enemies had given him an idea. "I'll meet you back here in a half an hour. Have the troops ready to ride."

Forgive me for calling so late," Argyll said short minutes later, bowing to Catherine Haddock, who was having tea with several ladies in her drawing room. The men from her dinner party were still in the dining room with their port.

"It's never too late, my dear Commissioner, for a call from you. Do come in," she replied, beaming smugly at her friends. Had she not lured Argyll here after all, her smile seemed to say.

"If I could have a word with you in private," he murmured.

Her soft titter brought a knowing smile from her friends, and reminded him why he found it so tedious courting ladies. Well-born females played at flirtation, pretending they didn't want what you wanted. The posturing always annoyed him. Better the middling-class or servant girls who didn't hide behind such vanities.

But he cautioned himself to politesse as he followed the flaunting sway of her hips into a small parlor. Turning to him in a swish of aquamarine silk and swinging whalebone petticoats, she purred, "I knew you'd come."

He gritted his teeth against his first response and said instead, "I'm afraid it's a matter of business."

Her pouty look, immediate and artful, wasn't attractive. Someone should tell her. Nor did pale blondes appeal to him; they always looked breakable and cold. Unlike Roxane, he thought, whose titian hair and warm skin tones glowed with sensuality, while her voluptuous body would welcome a man softly. "I was hoping you might help me," he went on with a well-bred smile.

"Of course, John," she dulcetly replied, the sound of his invitation more pleasing. "*Whatever* I can do . . . I'll do."

"I came to ask you something of the Countess of Kilmarnock, who's in trouble with the law," he quickly added to deter the scowl forming on her porcelain white forehead. "She was under house arrest for harboring the young Carre—"

"Good for you," Catherine tartly said. "Throw her in prison."

Her need to inflict punishment was so blatant, he knew he'd come to the right person. "As a matter of fact, while she deserves exactly that, unfortunately she's escaped."

"The bitch! It was Robbie Carre who liberated her, you can be sure."

"Do you think so?" he politely noted, not sharing her opinion. None of his spies had reported parties of significant numbers riding out of the city tonight. And Robbie Carre wasn't in Edinburgh without a substantial bodyguard. "What I hoped you might be able to help me with," he tactfully went on, "was the possible location of any friend or acquaintance of the countess's on the Jedburgh road."

"Her mother was from Lauderdale."

He could feel the hairs rising on the back of his neck. "Where, exactly?"

"I'm not sure . . . but if I find out," she murmured with a coquettish giggle, "would that entitle me to some of your undivided attention?"

"Definitely." He forced himself to smile. He'd sleep with old Haddock himself if it got him the information he needed.

Having won the prize she'd so long sought, Lady Haddock turned ingratiatingly helpful. "I'm sure Janet knows. She grew up in the same dismal little place. I'll ask her and be *right* back," she added in a velvety murmur.

Who would have ever thought of some small parish so far off the beaten track? he reflected. No wonder Roxane ran there. It sounded as though the village was incredibly remote. Itching to get on her trail, he forced himself to an appearance of calmness when Catherine returned.

She blew him a kiss from the doorway. "I'll expect you to devote a great deal of time to me now. I *have* your information."

"You'll have my utmost devotion, my dear, I assure you." He'd spoken to the queen, once his demands had been met, in like fashion, and had meant it as little.

"Roxane's mother grew up in Edgarhope Wood, and Janet says while the country house is in ruins because of a fire several years ago, the dowager cottage is still in good repair. Aren't you pleased with little old me?" she inquired with an affectation of demureness. And holding her arms open, she lifted her mouth for a kiss.

There was nothing for it but that he must kiss her in her pose of mannered innocence, and so he did. But he felt nothing, his mind already contemplating the road south. Gently uncoiling her arms from around his neck a moment later, he set her away with as much courtesy as he could muster in his impetuous need to be gone. "I thank you most kindly."

"Thank me when you return, John, in a decidedly more intimate way," she replied, simpering.

One would have to be very drunk, he thought, to climb into bed with her. But smiling politely, he replied, "I certainly will," and quickly bowing, escaped.

∞∞∞

MRS. BEATTIE HAD ASKED GEILLIS SIMILAR QUES-
tions for Robbie, his queries having to do not only with
possible sanctuaries, but whether Argyll might have
spirited her away.

"My cousin Geillis doesn't think so, my lord," Mrs.
Beattie reported to Robbie, back from Kilmarnock
House with additional information. "Argyll was right
angry, Geillis maintains. His men fair tore the house
apart, she said, and there wasn't need for that if he had
her. She said they were all threatened with the Tolbooth, too, unless they gave him her direction."

Robbie silently thanked all the benevolent gods. At
least Roxane wasn't with Argyll, which partially explained why the Campbell troops were being readied
for a night ride. His scouts had just come in with the
information. "Thank you, Mrs. Beattie, for all your
help," Robbie said. "And thank your cousin as well."

"I hope you find her first," his housekeeper asserted,
having taken note of all the preparations for departure.

"I intend to. We can't have her falling into Argyll's
hands when she's managed to elude him thus far."

"The men are all saddled up, sir," Holmes declared,
walking in, the light metallic jingle of his spurs and
sword resonating in the quiet. He'd fought in the
Dutch wars and carried himself with the vigor of a
trained soldier. "They're awaiting your orders."

"We'll move out quietly and stay well back of Argyll's rear guard," Robbie declared, pulling on his
gloves. "And if Argyll knows where the countess went,
we'll find out soon enough. If not, at least she's safe
from him."

"And we're no worse off for a night ride," Holmes
said with a smile.

"I only hope she's far away."

"For now, perhaps," Holmes noted. "But Argyll's army of spies told him something."

"So we presume. Make sure everyone's well armed," Robbie briskly charged, flexing his fingers in his soft leather gloves. "How many men do we have?"

"Just over a hundred since morning."

"And Argyll?"

"A few more in his troop."

"How many?"

"Three hundred."

Robbie smiled faintly. "We should manage. The Borderers could always outfight the Campbells."

"Aye, sir," Holmes replied with a grin.

*I*N A SUITABLE, TIMELY FASHION, THE CARRES FOL-lowed the Campbells out of Edinburgh on that moonlit night, the two large cavalry units passing by in such close proximity, the inhabitants on the road to Jedburgh were wakened from their sleep.

Argyll was up to no good, muttered those who recognized the standards of the commissioner's troops, peering out their windows. But their spirits rose when the Carre reivers thundered by in the Campbell's wake. Some Scots loyal to their country were going to teach the hated Campbells a lesson or two, it seemed.

Driven by anger and lust, Argyll led his men at a wicked pace, intent on overtaking Roxane. Robbie Carre and his men maintained his whip-and-spur speed, but at a prudent distance. Hours later, Argyll's troop took the southeasterly fork at Oxton. Turning to Holmes as they sat on the crest of a hill some miles distant, Argyll's troops strung out before them on the road below, Robbie said, "Now why didn't I think of that? Roxane's mother was from Edgarhope Wood."

"It's a mighty small village for four hundred men, Holmes laconically said.

"Or even a hundred." Robbie leaned forward, stretching after hours in the saddle. "I'd say we'll have to take him on earlier."

"It would save the lady from danger."

"That's what I'm thinking. Tell the men we're cutting cross country at Cleekhimin Bridge. We'll set up an ambush for the Campbells at Scour Glen."

𝒪N THE EAST COAST OF SCOTLAND, IN A SECLUDED cove north of Dunbar, a ship that had been lying at anchor most of the night let down a longboat carrying a crew and six passengers. The sea was choppy with three-foot waves, and the seamen had to pull hard on their oars to bring the boat slowly to shore.

When the small craft scraped onto the rocky shoals of Margret's Cove, a tall dark man, his cape whipping in the strong breeze, jumped into the water first and strode through the breaking foam to shore. The other passengers followed, each man moving briskly from the exposed shore to the shadows of the rocky cliffs.

The men climbed quickly and silently, their weapons muffled, only the crunch of their boots against the rough gravel occasionally heard above the soft wailing sound of the wind. A copse of beech and chestnuts stood at the top of the rough path from the sea, and in a few swift strides, the men reached the security of the trees.

"Welcome back." A tall, tawny-haired man put out his hand.

"It feels good to be in Scotland again." An errant wisp of breeze found its way into the trees and blew a lock of long black hair across the man's face. He brushed it away before reaching out and gripping the other man's hand in a firm handshake.

"Your brother shocked all the spies by showing up at the countess's house. They hadn't expected such audacity."

Johnnie Carre smiled. "He's still safe, I presume, or you wouldn't be here."

"He was when we left Edinburgh."

"Good, because Elizabeth would have my throat if I let anything happen to him."

"She sent you, then."

"I'm here on orders," the Laird of Ravensby said with a grin.

"I got that impression from the note she sent me, even couched as it was in the bland language necessary to outwit all the spies in this country. She always did know what she wanted," said the man who had served as her bodyguard for a decade.

"So it seems. I've been told it's up to us, Redmond," he said, his eyes amused, "to save my brother from his indiscretions."

"Not so easy a task," Redmond said, smiling back, "with Argyll and his Campbells in town. And the queen's commissioner intent on having the fair Roxane for himself."

"Really?" Johnnie Carre murmured. "An added intricacy."

"How intricate you can see for yourself in a few

hours. And perhaps talk some sense into your brother."

Johnnie chuckled. "You *do* have a sense of humor. Had I been able to do that, he'd still be in Holland. You know everyone, don't you?" the Laird of Ravensby noted, gesturing at his entourage.

"How many men did you bring with you from Three Kings?" inquired Johnnie's cousin, Munro, reaching for the reins of one of the horses held by Redmond's cohorts.

"Three hundred, some already in the city."

"And we can bring together—"

"Five hundred," Munro finished.

"That should give Argyll pause," Johnnie said with a smile. "And then we'll see whether we have to muster more, or if he's willing to negotiate."

"Argyll can be bought, or else he wouldn't be pimping for the English," Redmond brusquely said.

"My thought exactly," Johnnie softly murmured. "Are we all ready?"

Chapter 10

HE CARRE TROOPS FLANKED THE FORD, WAIT-
ing for Argyll's scouts to appear, the country road no
more than a rough track—a decided advantage. Argyll's men would be strung out thin, the path allowing
no more than two horsemen to ride abreast.

"Load pistols." The order went down the ranks in a
murmur, a formality to men who had been trained to
battle from childhood. But with the sound of riders
carrying into the quiet vale, they checked their
weapons one last time. Screened by underbrush and a
dense growth of beechwood, Robbie's forces were
drawn up in tight ranks on both stream banks and the
border of the road, their vantage ground raised above
the rutted path and streambed.

Only a brief, laconic discussion had been necessary
to agree on strategy. Familiar with night raids, every
man a reiver to the bone, they understood the hit-and-
run tactics that allowed for minimum casualties and
maximum rewards. And tonight, Argyll was their
prize.

No one spoke, their eyes trained on the slight rise
over which their enemies would come, night shadows
making visibility difficult, the heavily forested glen
adding to the gloom. The moon had gone behind

scudding clouds halfway into their ride, and more than one man had muttered about the bad road and smothering darkness.

A glint of metal suddenly gleamed through the murky veil, and hands automatically went to weapons. The Campbell scouts in their breastplates and helmets had crested the rise and were slowly riding down toward the ford, cautiously navigating their way through the treacherous footing. Just as the scouts reached the streambed, the distant glitter of Argyll's gold-trimmed uniform caught everyone's attention.

The men in ambush glanced at their neighboring kinsmen, smiled, and nodded. A showy fop like Argyll would make easy picking, even if he were in the center of his ranks. But a degree of patience was required to effectively ambush the large force. Robbie's troopers quietly waited until half the column had passed over the ford, everyone understanding the necessity of splitting the company in two. Motionless, mute, they bided their time.

Surrounded by his cousins, Robbie maintained the position at the ford, counting the Campbells as they passed, Argyll with the center slowly moving toward the crossing. Impatient for the skirmish to engage, ready to strike, Robbie could barely contain his urgency. Dammit, hurry, he silently ordered.

After what seemed like an eternity, Argyll finally reached the ford. Robbie's gloved hand went up in signal, the gesture passing down the ranks in the darkness, each man watching the man beside him.

When Argyll reached the midpoint of the shallows, Robbie's hand slashed downward, he spurred his horse, and the Carre battle cry exploded into the night. A hundred reivers, screaming for blood, their guns blazing, swept down on the Campbells, galloping out of the blackness like fiends from hell.

Argyll's men barely had time to wheel and meet their attackers. Some pushed their horses to a gallop and bolted; those caught in the ford fought to keep their mounts in hand in the soft streambed. The forward ranks were cut off, most of the rear guard in flight, isolating Argyll and his guard, the clash of swords replacing the initial barrage of gunfire, the melee a scene of slaughter and confusion. Argyll's guard put up a stout resistance, but the Carres recklessly slashed their way through, intent on taking their prize. The first line of defenders fell, fatally wounded, and then the second line was scythed away, the contest not only a personal vendetta between Carre and Campbell, but an age-old rivalry between Lowlander and Highlander.

Argyll and his bodyguard were soon overwhelmed. Robbie was at the center of the bloody combat, and when at last his sword was poised at John Campbell's throat, a sudden silence fell. "Call your men off or I'll kill you," Robbie brusquely ordered.

Argyll understood when a battle was lost, and understood as well that no woman was worth dying for. He quickly had his trumpeter call retreat.

"Now tell your troops they'd best be back to Edinburgh," Robbie commanded.

Argyll complied.

"There's a sensible man," Robbie noted, restoring his sword to its scabbard.

Still mounted, the two men looked at each other at close range, the queen's commissioner furious beneath his feigned calm. "While you're not sensible at all," Argyll coldly replied. "You could have had your lands back without this unnecessary exertion and that musket wound. The queen is always ready to forgive a supporter."

"I don't want the queen's forgiveness," Robbie said.

"You're a principled fool."

"We can't all be politicians." Taking a bandage from one of his men, Robbie began wrapping it around his reinjured right arm, his jacket sleeve torn open by a grazing musket ball, the damaged flesh beneath ragged and bloody.

"I can see that your lawsuit is tied up indefinitely in the courts," Argyll threatened. "You should have considered that before you attacked me."

"And you might consider the thought of your pompous ass incarcerated in a well-concealed prison until such a time as I have what I want," Robbie countered, tying a tight knot on his makeshift dressing, gritting his teeth against the sharp pain.

Argyll was an intelligent man; he knew there were dungeons in Scotland where a man could be lost forever. "What do you want?"

Robbie looked up, his gaze bland. "Just what's mine. I'm not greedy."

"And if you have it, what then?"

"Then you won't have to sit in a dank, dark hole where no one can appreciate all that fine gold lace," Robbie murmured.

"And you want?"

"Two things. The Countess Kilmarnock is mine. Stay away from her. And should you make our court case unnecessarily difficult, we'll see that you don't enjoy your stay in Scotland."

"I can agree now and change my mind later."

"So can I."

"So I would be witless to argue."

"And having arrived at such lofty eminence at your age, I rather doubt you are."

The obscuring clouds cleared the moon for a moment, and Argyll's crafty gaze was transiently exposed.

"Agreed."

Robbie nodded, not gullible enough to actually believe him, but interested in buying some time to take Roxane away. "You'll be escorted back to Edinburgh."

"And the fair Roxane is yours."

"Remember, I don't allow poachers. A caveat I suggest you heed."

"As you wish," Argyll smoothly said.

Too smoothly for anything but dissimulation. But he had a few hours at least to see that Roxane was escorted to safety, Robbie thought. That much Argyll's capture would allow.

Soon ARGYLL, UNDER HEAVY GUARD, WAS ON HIS way back to Edinburgh—by a circuitous route well out of the way of his troops, who were taking their dead and wounded home. The Carre wounded were escorted to the nearby estate of a loyal friend, while Robbie with a minimum guard continued his journey to Edgarhope Wood.

The cottage looked deserted when they arrived, and for an anxious moment, Robbie wondered if he and Argyll had both miscalculated. But on closer inspection, he saw that a single window in the back was dimly lit. As his men waited, Robbie dismounted and approached the kitchen entrance.

The door was bolted, so he knocked.

The light immediately went out.

He called out to Roxane, and a second later candlelight flickered again and the bolt was drawn back. Opening the door, Roxane surveyed him with surprise. "What are you doing here?"

"Were you expecting someone else?" He was instantly suspicious, and his voice had turned gruff. Had she been waiting for Argyll?

"In this remote village—hardly. I'm surprised, that's all. I thought you weren't supposed to see me until September."

"Argyll was after you, so I changed my mind."

"Was?"

"He reconsidered. But we should leave immediately. He can't be trusted."

"Just a minute," she said. "Do I have anything to say about this?"

"Would you rather spend the next few months with Argyll?"

"Would I have run if I did? I can be rude, too."

He exhaled. "I'll start over. We rode south to stop the Campbells from bringing you back as Argyll's paramour. Now, would you please accompany me to a more secure location? Despite his word, Argyll may return for you."

A slow smile greeted his explanation. "That's better."

"I'm learning," he replied with a grin. "Although you're damned touchy."

"I don't respond well to orders."

"I'll keep it in mind. Now if we're friends again," he murmured, his smile widening, "dare I ask, what the hell did you do with your hair?"

"I had to pass as a stable boy to escape the house. Don't you like it?" She brushed a hand over the short curls.

"I adore it." His voice was amused. "Was that sufficiently diplomatic? Although I think mine is longer than yours now."

"Perhaps I should take the male role then," she teased.

His gaze narrowed and he shook his head. "Not likely, darling." Moving forward, he was already reaching for her hand. "We really do have to go."

"You're wounded!" she exclaimed as he stepped into the light.

"Damned thing reopened. It's nothing. How much baggage do you have?"

"Robbie, you're bleeding through." Even in the dim candle glow, the amount of blood visible was alarming.

He glanced down. The wetness extended down past his elbow. "I'll have a new dressing put on once we reach the Cheviots."

"But that's hours from now."

"If the bleeding begins to leave a trail, I'll have the dressing changed. How would that be?"

"You should change it now. So it doesn't become infected."

"Mine never do," he dismissively replied. "Darling,"

he admonished, "we really have to leave. Get your things."

They were on the trail minutes later and rode until just before dawn when, concerned their well-armed escort would call attention to them, they separated south of Galashiels.

"We're for Leithope Glen," Robbie said to his men, "where we should be safe. Once you return to Edinburgh, send a note to my brother in Holland and tell him my plans. And don't travel in daylight. Argyll will have his spies on full alert."

"Mossburnford Forest should give you cover, at least for today," Holmes said.

Robbie nodded.

"And have that arm looked at." Holmes handed Robbie a pack of dressings and medicines Mrs. Beattie had sent along. The snuff-colored wool of Robbie's coat sleeve was completely blood-soaked. "You couldn't have gone much farther anyway without leaving a trail."

"I'm warned, Holmes," Robbie said with a small smile, the pain in his arm a torment the last few hours. "The countess will see that your orders are fulfilled, I'm sure."

"As soon as we stop, Holmes," she firmly declared. "I've been holding my tongue with difficulty."

"There you see," Robbie said, grinning.

"Be on guard. Even in the hills a herder or woodsman might see you. Loyalties are no longer secure with Argyll's bribes and threats common currency."

"We'll be caution itself."

"I told my children I'd see them in a fortnight,"

Roxane said. "Could you have someone bring Amelia a message?"

"Tell her we'll come north in a fortnight," Robbie added.

Roxane shook her head. "It's not necessary, Holmes. The children will understand if Amelia talks to them."

"Tell her we *may* come to see them in a fortnight," Robbie instructed, a finality in his tone Holmes recognized.

Holmes tipped his head in understanding. "We'll see that she's informed."

As pale gray lighted the horizon, Robbie and Roxane set off on their own. The landscape of rolling hills and streams, dotted with small groves of beech and oak, offered a degree of security, but Mossburnford Forest was still miles away and they had less than an hour to find concealment.

ARGYLL WAS PLOTTING HIS VENGEANCE AS HE rode between his Carre guards, mentally recalling the southern counties, contemplating the best areas of concealment. A nation as small as Scotland couldn't long hide a fugitive from the queen. He'd have posters drawn up, he thought, and criers sent out with the offered reward for Robbie Carre, dead or alive. The young earl had already been put to fire and sword—outlawed—without Argyll's help. As for the fair Roxane, she'd pay in her own way for the inconvenience she'd caused him. And for his humiliation.

He'd whip her first—not enough to do damage to that beautiful flesh, just enough to teach her compliance. And a silver collar around her neck might be useful, something he could shackle with a chain. Then he'd see that she offered herself whenever he wished, wherever he wished. Maybe he'd even have Robbie Carre watch, if he was brought in alive. He had to shift in the saddle to accommodate his erection, the salacious fantasy vivid in his mind.

$\mathscr{R}$OBBIE CARRE AT THE MOMENT WAS FAINT FROM pain, undergoing the torture of having his bandage removed. He and Roxane had found shelter in a woodcutter's hut, a rough shed made from logs and wattle, the roof thatched with brush.

His arm was dangerously swollen, the mutilated flesh crimsoned and hot. Roxane resisted the impulse to gasp at the gory sight.

Robbie silently swore, recognizing a wound beginning to go bad. And he clenched his teeth against the agony as Roxane wiped the pus away with a piece of bandage wetted with brandy from his saddlebags.

"You need a doctor."

"No doctor." He took a sustaining breath. "Mrs. Beattie sent a salve. Put that on."

"This wound might need to be lanced."

"You can do it later. I'll lie in the loch at Leithope Glen. Water does wonders for suppurating wounds."

"How much farther do we have to ride?"

"Another night."

"Dare we travel today?" She left unsaid the possibility he might be unable to ride by nightfall.

He gazed at his wound and then at the dense

growth of trees around them. "Tie this up, and we'll go as far as the limits of the forest."

Turning pale as his coat was pulled on, he suppressed the groan rising in his throat. And moments later, almost faint after mounting his horse, he whispered, "Give me another drink." Only his hands, clenched hard on his saddle pommel, held him upright.

What have I done? Roxane fearfully thought, rushing to pull the silver flask from his pack. He might die from his putrid wound, all because she hadn't been resolute enough to send him away. She should have considered more than her own pleasure; she should have insisted he leave that first night in Edinburgh.

"I wouldn't have gone," he whispered, as though reading her mind.

She stared at him, nonplussed.

"It's not your fault, none of this is. I'll be fine." His smile took effort, she could see. "Once I have a drink."

Quickly thrusting the opened flask into his hand, she watched him drain half the contents in one swallow. "There, now," he said with a sigh, putting the chained stopper back in with his teeth. "Come, darling, it's not so bad. I've been wounded before. Let me show you the way out of here."

He drank the first flask dry and emptied a second one before they reached the end of the forest. With his pain dulled by the liquor, his color improved; he could even stand to move his arm marginally.

"Could we try the country lanes?" she asked, aware of the necessity to reach safe haven quickly. "Even if someone were to see us, we could offer them a bribe to forget our passing."

"Argyll travels with an intimidating number of men," Robbie cautioned. "I'm not sure a local can withstand that pressure, bribe or not."

"But the Borderers don't like the militia. Nor the Highlanders either. I think we should travel in daylight and take our chances."

"I won't argue." He understood the limits of his endurance. Brandy or not, he knew he wouldn't survive another day in the saddle.

"How *are* you?" she murmured, alarmed by his ready acquiescence.

"If I black out before we reach Brundenlaws, tie me to my saddle, stay on the path to the right at Upper Hind, and keep moving toward the outcropping on the crest of the hill. Wake me up somehow at that point and I'll take us the last few miles."

"You need a doctor," she whispered.

"I can't put someone at risk. And there's not much a doctor can do for this, anyway. Get me to the loch at Leithope Glen"—he smiled faintly—"and roll me into the water."

She took the reins of his horse and he didn't dispute her actions, which frightened her even more. For the next few hours they rode in silence except when he'd quietly say "left" or "right" at a crossroad, or point out a landmark—"in case you need it later," he'd say. An ominous foreboding would overtake her as she'd glance at the distinctive feature, but with their journey taking them through uninhabited country, she paid heed to his words.

Twice they saw shepherds, but from a distance, and the only village they came to they bypassed without incident. "The alarm hasn't reached this far yet," Robbie murmured, his voice tight with pain. "The government troops aren't out."

"How much farther?"

"A quarter mile closer than when you asked me last time." His low chuckle ended in a suffocated groan and he didn't talk again until her exclamation, "There's the outcropping!" brought his head up.

"Brandy." His voice was no more than a whisper.

Unbuckling her saddlebag, she pulled out the last flask, drew their horses to a halt, and helped him put the flask to his mouth. He slowly swallowed the last two inches in the container.

"Let me get you some help," she pleaded. He was burning with fever, his shirt and coat drenched with sweat, his face ashen.

"Almost there. . . ." And with gritted teeth, he kicked his mount forward.

Quickly following, she rode closely behind. The path narrowed as they climbed the hill, low-hanging branches and brambles tearing at them. It was another half hour more through dense undergrowth, and she wondered at the brave spirit that kept him conscious and moving.

His fingers were white-knuckled on his pommel, sheer will keeping him upright in the saddle. The small fishing lodge in the valley of the Cheviots would offer not only sanctuary, but a plentiful supply of liquor, he knew, the thought sustaining him through the excruciating agony racking his body.

When they finally reached the small hidden valley, the lodge barely visible through the dense plantation of silver fir that had been planted by an "improving" laird decades ago, she realized she'd just been witness to a miraculous act of courage.

He rode directly to the small mountain lake framed by alpine flowers, and fell from the saddle before she could help him dismount. He was unconscious before he hit the ground, landing on the soft, green, flower-strewn verge without a sound.

Taking advantage of his insensibility, she gripped his booted feet and literally dragged his body an inch at a time toward the water. Cutting his coat and shirt away with her dirk, she undressed him to his breeches, a lengthy ordeal made more difficult by his inertness. Once he was partially unclothed, she pulled his feverish body into the shallows. Her boots sank into the soft sand as she struggled to bring him to a depth that would cover his wounded arm. Making a rough pillow of their jackets to keep his face above the water, she crouched beside him. He stirred at last, moaning as the cold water seeped into the fetid, mutilated flesh of his damaged arm, but his eyes only flickered briefly before he sank back into unconsciousness.

She didn't know how long she sat beside him, watching him breathe, regularly surveying the purulent wound as if she could will the damage to heal with keen enough surveillance. But as the sun set and the temperature dropped, she began shivering uncontrollably. She didn't dare leave Robbie, and it was out of the question to build a fire in the open with possible pursuers behind them. Rising to her feet, she ran in place on shore to warm herself. Uncertain, confused, she began to question whether chilling Robbie's body was appropriate treatment.

Was it worse for him to be feverish, or was she killing him by doing his bidding? Helpless to move his large frame save by inches at a time, she wondered: How was she going to get him to the distant lodge if need be?

As the first stars began to appear, she decided she had to bring him inside, or they would both freeze in the chill temperatures of the high altitude. She couldn't drag him now that he was half-nude, nor would their few remaining garments withstand the pressure of hauling his weight.

Utterly frustrated, she swore into the twilight.

"Need some help?"

At the blessed sound of his voice, however faint, she broke into tears.

He tried to move when he heard her sobs, half rising on his uninjured arm, but the movement brought such excruciating pain he fell back into the water.

Splashing toward him, she dropped to her knees and repeatedly kissed his face in exultation. "Thank God, thank God," she murmured, her mouth warm on his cool skin.

"I'm cold," he whispered, not daring to move, raw agony still vibrating through his senses from his impulsive movement.

"That's wonderful," she breathed, placing her hand on his forehead. "That means your fever is down. Now we have to get you inside."

"I'm going to need liquor to walk. It's in the lodge."

"Dare I leave you?"

"Why don't I wait here?" he murmured, his mouth lifting in a whimsical smile.

Leaping to her feet, she ran across the small

meadow, raced up the gentle rise, and took the stairs to the entrance porch in two bounds. Wrenching the door wide, she left it open, allowing the moonlight in.

For a moment she stood in the center of the entrance hall, wondering where the liquor was kept. Candles and flint lay in a row on a porter's table convenient to the door, and after lighting a candle, she began her search. Reaching the dining room, she smiled as her gaze fell on the sideboard, well stocked with aqua vitae.

In moments, she was back at the lake, holding a bottle to Robbie's mouth. And fifteen minutes later, anesthetized by a goodly portion of brandy, Robbie slowly came to his knees in the water. Leaning against Roxane, he rested until his breathing slowed to a more normal rhythm, until he was able to separate the general agony from the more specific areas of pain.

"When I count to three, help me to my feet," he whispered, "and don't stop lifting even if I scream."

It took another few moments to brace his sensibilities to the impending torture, and as he began counting, he drew on his last reserves of strength. At the count of three, with heroic effort, he shakily rose to his feet and, swaying, clutched hard at Roxane.

Leaning into her, teeth gritted, panting, shaken by a cold sweat, he doggedly braced his legs to remain upright. Taking a moment to gather his strength again, he rested his weight heavily on Roxane and forced himself to take a step, then another and another, moving in a halting, slow progress through the crushing pain that threatened to smother him, keeping the lodge in sight as his salvation. Light-headed, nauseated by the time he reached the stairs, he sank to his knees, crawled up what seemed an endless mountain of steps, at last crossed over the threshold, and, having reached his goal, collapsed into unconsciousness.

Unable to wake him, Roxane made him a bed on the floor of the entrance hall, dragging down a feather mattress from the floor above, piling it high with quilts. Then, with the technique she'd perfected in bringing him into the lake, she tugged and pulled him by the feet into his bed. He was shivering in his sleep, so she covered him and, knowing the smoke wouldn't be visible at night, she made a fire in the huge fireplace that dominated the entrance hall.

While Robbie slept, she brought the temperature of the room up, and once he'd stopped shivering, she quickly saw to their horses. Leading the animals into the stable, she readied them for the night. She was reminded of her childhood in the country when she'd cared for her ponies, the sweet-smelling scent of hay pleasant, the buckets of water she carried for them like those she'd carried as a child. Before long, their mounts were settled in for the night, munching oats in their stalls.

A brief time later, after carrying their gear into the lodge, she was able to contemplate their situation with a small degree of satisfaction. They were safe—temporarily. Stripping off her damp clothes, she changed into the gown she'd brought along. The brushed twill of the serviceable garment felt smooth on her skin, familiar. Padding barefoot over the floorboards warmed from the fire, she knelt beside Robbie and touched his forehead with her fingers. Better, she thought. Not hot, not cold, and for the moment he seemed to be sleeping peacefully.

While he rested, she searched the kitchen for food. To her delight, she discovered a treasure trove— shelves of preserved and dried fruits, pickled fish and eggs, several containers of dried oatcakes scented with cardamom and cinnamon. Putting together a tray of edibles, she brought up a bottle of wine for herself, and some more brandy for Robbie. Carrying their supper *à deux* back to the entrance hall, she decided their circumstances had considerably improved from an hour ago.

Familiar with country living, she settled comfortably on the floor beside Robbie and, nibbling on her supper, waited for him to wake. The pungent aroma of spiced vinegar struck his nostrils, and he half opened his eyes. "I need a drink," he murmured, his voice stronger.

"You should eat something, too." Putting the bottle to his lips, she raised his head on her arm.

"Later." He winced as she lowered his head back onto the pillows.

"I have dates, preserved apricots, and orange marmalade on oatcakes."

"And pickled eggs," he added, the acrid scent stinging his nostrils.

"Would you prefer herring?"

"Not now," he said. "I'm not quite sure I'm alive yet."

"The lake brought your fever down."

"I'll take another soaking later. Holmes taught me the merits of water therapy. He has more wounds than an Italian duelist."

"I do want you to eat."

"Yes, Mama." His smile flashed in the firelight.

"I mean it. And don't remind me how young you are," she murmured with a raised brow.

He grinned. "Old enough to love you. Old enough to love you well and good."

"Don't remind me. If you hadn't, none of this would have happened."

"How could I be in Scotland and not make love to you? And if not for Agnes, no one would have known."

"Unfortunately, most of the population is now informed."

"We'll have to invite them to our wedding, then."

"You *are* feverish."

"Probably. But I'm marrying you, so you might as well get used to the idea."

"Maybe I don't wish to marry again," she lightly retorted. "Have you considered that?"

"Not for a second. I have a Covenanter's aversion to living in sin."[9]

"Obviously a recent conversion," she sardonically observed.

"Very." His smile dazzled for a moment. "And I have every intention of changing your mind."

"That might not be possible."

"Give me a half hour for this liquor to take hold, and once I dare move again"—he grinned—"I'll convince you."

She cast him a warning glance. "Don't even consider it."

"Give me another drink," he ordered. "I like a challenge."

But even with liquor, his pain was too intense to do

more than lift his head so she could feed him. Later that night, when his fever rose again, they struggled down to the lake and sank into the cold, healing water. Twice more they made the round trip before morning, when at last they fell into an exhausted sleep, their hands entwined.

Chapter 11

$\mathcal{O}$NCE ARGYLL HAD BEEN DELIVERED TO THE OUT-
skirts of Edinburgh, his Carre guards abandoned him,
wheeling and galloping away without a word. Immediately making for Holyrood Palace, he was in a foul
temper when he strode into his office. He shouted for
every member of his staff, his voice roaring down the
halls and corridors like a daunting wave of terror. And
once his subordinates were assembled, he set about
seeing that the Countess of Kilmarnock came under
his control with all due speed. His instructions were
rapid, brusque, systematic, sending aides and clerks
scurrying in all directions to see that his wishes were
carried out. Roxane's brother, Colter, was to be fetched
from London. Once he arrived, he was to bring his
niece and nephews back to Edinburgh. In the meantime, the countess's servants were to be placed under
house arrest. "And bring me Queensberry's best spies. I
want to compare reports on the number of men the
Carres can bring into the field."

Later that day, he met with the agents who were the
eyes and ears of the English ministry in Scotland.
Queensberry's men were cautious at first, not knowing
why they'd been summoned by their employer's rival.
But the commissioner's bluntness quickly reassured

them; he wished only information unrelated to
Queensberry. At which point, they willingly added
their knowledge to that of Argyll's spies.

"The Carres hold the loyalty of most of the Border
counties," the Queensberry man assigned to the south
noted.

"While the counties near Edinburgh are sympa-
thetic to the young Earl of Greenlaw," another said.

"How many men can they muster?" Argyll bluntly
queried.

And the discussion began.

"Four thousand," one man asserted. "Maybe five.
Considerably more than the regular troops in Scotland."

"Not counting those from the Laird of Ravensby's
wife," pointed out the man who oversaw information
from the southwest.

"Give me a number," Argyll growled.

"Another thousand."

"A thousand? Why the hell does she need an army
like that?"

"To guard her Redesdale inheritance. A right fair
sum."

"A king's ransom, they say," the spy from Redesdale
interposed.

"The Carre kinsmen and *soutenirs* from their lands
near Leith could amount to another five hundred," a
small man declared, his amused gaze on Argyll's
stormy expression.

"And the local militia, including that of Edinburgh,
might not be dependable if it came to choosing sides
between the queen and the Carres. The earl is a favorite with the city mobs." Defoe knew of what he

spoke, since part of his duty while in Scotland was to report on the political agendas in and out of Parliament. "The Carre influence will see their titles returned shortly. Bets are a month on the outside."

Argyll swore. The size of the Carre troop outnumbered his own. He gave them credit for good judgment. They could have used armed threat to regain their estates. "That will be all," he brusquely said, waving the spies out. He sat at his desk after they left, pondering how best to meet his aims without incurring a full-scale engagement.

*N*O ONE IN JOHNNIE CARRE'S PARTY HAD SLEPT, their arrival in Edinburgh following close on the heels of Robbie's returning troop. They were quickly apprised of the skirmish with the Campbells, as well as of Robbie's journey south. And when Holmes appeared the next day, he was able to add further details concerning Robbie's destination, easing the worry lines from Johnnie's brow.

"Although he's badly wounded," Holmes added, "and should be under a doctor's care."

"You and Munro take a force south, along with a doctor," Johnnie ordered, "and see that he has the necessary care. We're assembling our men in five days. Orders have already gone out. The Duke of Argyll needs to be apprised of the limits of his powers in Scotland."

"Which don't include imprisoning the Countess of Kilmarnock," Munro noted.

"She's a friend," Johnnie murmured. "Perhaps he doesn't understand."

"We'll tell him, along with his Campbells," asserted

his kinsman Adam Carre with a grin. "It's good to be back." The forced inactivity in Holland the months past had sorely tried the patience of the younger members of Johnnie's retinue. They were used to the exhilaration of raiding as sport.

"We'll wait for news of Robbie first." Johnnie glanced over at Munro. "You stay with him, though, along with a guard. He's too impulsive."

"Don't want him riding back to challenge Argyll to a duel?" Munro lightly queried.

"Definitely not."

"I don't expect he'll be riding anywhere for a time," Holmes observed. "Between his wound and the bonny countess, the lodge will serve as a right fine refuge."

"Try to keep him there if you can, Munro," Johnnie charged.

His cousin cast him an amused glance. "I can't, but perhaps the countess might."

"Granted. Talk to Roxane, then. We don't need any duels, we don't need him wounded again. Once I see Argyll, perhaps he'll set his amorous sights on someone else."

"If you pay him enough. The Argylls are for sale. Not just him, but his father before him," Kinmont said with a derisive snort.[10]

"Which makes negotiation so much easier," Johnnie observed, lounging in his chair. "Men of principle are discouragingly slow to settle on a price."

Munro's eyebrows rose. "So cynical."

"These are cynical times, with the Darien adventure gone bad, the years of bad harvests, the Alien Act almost closing Scotland to trade. All the lairds and magnates are desperate for cash. The only men of principles are the rare ones of wealth or those without families."[11]

"So we see Argyll first, and if that doesn't work—"

"We'll see if Red John of the Battles can fight as well on home ground," Johnnie softly said.

*I*T TOOK THREE DAYS OF HARD RIDING FOR ARgyll's message to reach Roxane's brother in London. As ordered, Colter immediately took the road north. The agents on watch at Longmuir were augmented by several of Argyll's troops, with instructions to bring the Countess of Kilmarnock's children back to Edinburgh as soon as the soldiers were notified.

*T*HE FIRST DAYS AT THE HUNTING LODGE PASSED IN blissful isolation, as though the fugitives had been offered respite from the world. After two days of soaking his wound in the lake, Robbie's arm had begun to mend. His drinking had diminished to social rather than medicinal portions, and he was able to walk down to the water unaided. Late in the afternoon, he and Roxane lay in the green meadow, warming their chilled bodies in the sun. She'd joined him during his last water cure, taking the opportunity to wash her hair and her gown.

"I haven't lain in the sun like this since I was a child. Look at that cloud," she murmured, gesturing with her hand.

"A bear."

"A bouquet of flowers."

He turned his head and smiled at her. "Definitely a bouquet of flowers."

"You don't have to charm me. It's quite enough being here like this, alone with you, in the warm sun and quiet."

"I just want you to be happy—always."

She rolled over on the scented grass and, lying on her stomach, leaned forward and kissed him lightly on the cheek. "I'm more happy than I've been in years. You're healing, we're safe, I adore you."

"We could stay here." He gently touched her face, slid his fingers through her damp curls.

"Wouldn't that be nice." She rolled away and arms stretched over her head, she softly added, "If the world was without greed."

"Argyll?"

"All of them—Queensberry, Seafield, Tweeddale, Argyll, his brother Archie . . . The list is endless."

"They can't touch us here, not until we decide to leave."

Her eyes were tinged with sadness when she turned her head to look at him. "But then it all starts again."

"He frightened you."

She took a small breath, remembering the fear when she escaped. "He's ruthless."

"You're not alone now. You won't ever be alone with him again."

"He's in Scotland until fall at least."

"I've enough men to protect you."

"And my children?"

"Yes, more than enough." He slowly sat up, his injured arm still painful. "If you're worried about the children, we can go to Amelia's tomorrow."

"No," she quickly said, sitting up too, brushing his fingers with hers. "I'm just being overanxious. We'll leave once your arm is better. Amelia's not expecting me for at least ten more days."

"Are you going to be able to relax? If you can't, I'd rather go to Longmuir now. My arm is healing well."

"I'm perfectly fine, really." She smiled.

"I know a sure way to help you relax," he playfully murmured.

"If you wouldn't faint from the effort."

"I don't think I'd faint."

Her gaze was stern. "No, Robbie. Be sensible. You're just barely mobile, and if your wound opens—"

"Then maybe you should put some clothes on. The sight of you lying in the grass like some dew-fresh nymph is damned distracting."

She glanced at her gown and chemise spread over a bush to dry, gauging their dampness.

"Or you could give me one little kiss," he murmured.

"Do I look that gullible?" She took cautious note of his erection, quickening, surging upward. "I'll put on a gown from the lodge," she declared, pushing herself up into a sitting position.

"Oh, hell, don't bother. I'll behave."

"You're sure, now? It's for *your* own good," she added, with a modicum of lecture in her tone.

"Yes, ma'am," he replied with mocking obedience.

"Don't get moody, now."

"I'm not moody." But he turned away, his gaze fixed on a point across the lake.

"I've seen a sulky child once or twice before, darling," she noted, lying back on the grass, shutting her eyes. "And the best way to deal with the situation is to ignore it."

"A shame," he murmured, "when I wanted to suck on your nipples... until you came."

His words drifted through the balmy summer air, instantly dispelling her smug equanimity.

Her breasts began to tingle as her nipples firmed into taut crests, the lust in his voice triggering a thousand sensual receptors. "Damn you," she whispered, shutting her eyes tighter as if to protect herself from him, from the promise in his words.

"All I need is your approval." He recognized her sexual response with a connoisseur's eye. Slowly rolling on his side, careful not to jar his wound, he sprawled beside her. She was gloriously nude, utterly delectable, he thought, watching the subtle transformation his words had incited. Her skin was taking on the rosy glow of arousal, her nipples stood upright, taut and waiting, her breathing had changed, and shifting restlessly, her legs half opened, as though inviting him in.

"Maybe I should just put this hard cock inside you instead," he quietly declared, "and see how far I could go in, how long it would take to reach that tantalizing limit where you gasp."

"Stop it, Robbie!"

Her voice was strained, her hands clenched at her sides, her eyes shut tightly against temptation, but she didn't get up and leave. So he took care not to antagonize when he mildly said, "I wouldn't even have to move. You could sit on me. My arm will go unscathed, and you could come as many times as you like." His voice deepened, turned velvety. "Think of how good it feels when I'm filling you, when your little clit is quivering and engorged, when the throbbing ache between your legs melts through your body like liquid ecstasy. How you always scream at the end," he finished in a whisper.

Her hips stirred at his lascivious description, wanton need flooding her senses.

"You'd be doing me a favor. After—"

"No," she sharply said, but she still didn't dare look at him, nor did she flee. Both facts duly noted.

"I feel as though I'm going to explode if I don't climax," he said. When she drew in a great restraining breath he softly added, "After these days of celibacy, I could fill you with rivers of come."

"Robbie, please," she whispered, "I shouldn't."

Her equivocation instantly added dimension to his erection. "My cock is so hard I'm in pain. Darling . . . look."

No longer able to resist, she turned her head, and when she saw his splendid length, she flushed hot pink. His flagrant erection lay flat against his belly, the pulsing veins feeding his arousal, stretching it, the head gleaming a deep crimson in the sunshine, the magnificent size intoxicating.

She hadn't climaxed either . . . for days.

"If I agree, you have to lie still."

He barely heard her hushed words, her voice the merest wisp of sound. "I promise," he quickly agreed, his own feverish excitement mitigating the pain in his arm as though his sensory nerves had better things to do than remind him of his wound. "Come closer to me," he whispered, "so I can touch you."

She hesitated a moment more before giving in to her covetous longings. As she moved nearer, a soft moan caught in her throat, her sleek, pulsing labia rubbing together, the friction luxuriously carnal.

Gratified by her feverish utterance, his own anticipation acute, he rolled onto his back, waiting.

"I'll make you pay for this someday," she threatened, rising to her knees, her body reacting traitorously to his ostentatious size with a rush of liquid heat.

"Why not pay me back now?" he seductively murmured, holding out his hand to help steady her as she moved over him. "Any way you want."

"And if you faint?" She balanced on his thighs.

"Not likely with my heart beating in triple time."

He hardly looked the invalid. His lean muscled body gleamed in the sunshine, the flagrant virility of youth, potent, intense. Even with his bandaged arm, his brute strength was palpable. "We really shouldn't be doing this," she equivocated, a fragment of reason still operating in the hotbed of her arousal. "Are you *sure*?"

"You aren't?" He traced the curve of her waist, his touch gentle

She took a deep, sustaining breath. "I'm not completely mindless yet."

"Really." He slid his hand downward, slipping two fingers into her vagina with ease. His grin was impudent, shamelessly cheeky. "Ready and waiting from the feel of this," he murmured, sliding a third finger upward into her moist, heated recess, softly stroking.

Trembling at his expert ministrations, her mind in tumult, she simultaneously wanted and didn't want him to stop, chided herself for her susceptibility, resentfully reminded herself that he was too practiced, skillful, too accomplished in seduction, yet too fragile in health as well. But his delicate massage was bringing her senses to fever pitch, his long, slender fingers magical in their expertise, and her transient reservations faded before the exquisite ecstasy flooding her brain.

When he quietly said, "You should be able to take me now," she felt as though she'd been favored by the gods.

Sliding his fingers out, he urged her up on her knees, guiding her into place, his thumb holding his erection upright, his index and middle finger spreading her labia to accommodate him. Gently forcing the engorged crest of his erection into her pulsing cleft, he whispered, "Careful now as you go down."

Her eyes were half-closed, consummation beating at her brain. "Yes, yes," she whispered, heedless of all but her insatiable need.

"Slowly," he cautioned, arresting her swift downward progress, sliding his hand between her legs to curtail her descent.

She tried to push his hand away.

"Not yet." Firmly restraining her, he eased her down another small distance. "You'll be hurt."

She squirmed against his coercing hand and they both felt it—slick, liquid pleasure, skittish, taut nerves, tumultuous desire.

"You won't hurt me. Robbie, please, I can't wait, you're going too slowly, I'm going to die if you—"

"I'll keep you from dying," he promised. "Look at me, darling, look." He allowed her to slide down a marginal distance. And when she reluctantly opened her eyes and gazed down at him, he said, "Just for the first time. After that"—he allowed her the next small descent—"you'll be fine."

"I'm fine *now*." She struggled against his hold.

But he could feel the reluctant yielding of her pulsing flesh. "A minute more, darling, please," he soothed her, not sure himself that celibacy was the sole cause of his extreme arousal.

Less than a minute passed, every sensation goaded almost beyond bearing, overwrought, seething, time seemingly suspended, stalled, Robbie's deliberate penetration the rapt focus of every fevered nerve, cell, body, and brain.

Perhaps they were both mindless when he rested at last where he most wanted to be, when she beheld the finite limits of ecstasy, when the warmth of the sun no longer touched them and the scents of the flowering meadow disappeared. Neither remembered Robbie's wounded arm nor their disparate views on his convalescence. Only flagrant pleasure held sway.

Half-breathless, he paused. "Are you—"

"Greedy," she whispered, her eyes ablaze.

"How unusual." His smile was audacious.

"So take me where I want to go."

And he did, in a driving rhythm that urged, incited, heated, tantalized, bringing them swiftly to a wild, fierce, scorching orgasm that left them reeling.

Her hands braced against his chest, panting, she barely held herself upright, while he was grateful for the stability of his grassy bed as his heartbeat thundered in his ears, his breath rasped in his throat. Once his pulse rate returned to normal, he brushed his hair back from his sweat-sheened temples, and opened his eyes to the perfection of the world—a world that required his darling Roxie in close proximity.

"You saved me," he murmured, satisfaction and contentment in his voice.

"You saved us both, my bonny lad," she whispered, her orgasm still a lingering bliss in her mind.

"You're a damned fine rider." His smile was benevolent.

"With the best of studs under me." Her mischievous gaze shone through the tangle of her curls.

"The only stud you're allowed," he growled.

Pushing herself upright, she swept her unruly hair away from her face. "You mean the only one I want."

"That, too," he acknowledged. "We can define the boundaries of ownership in the next few hours of riding."

"Hours?" A wanton heat flared in her eyes.

"Hours," he softly affirmed.

"Notice I'm on top," she playfully murmured.

"Only temporarily."

In the course of the summer afternoon, their various differences were disarmed, mollified and appeased in the most enchanting of ways. And later, in the unfolding of amorous events when Robbie supplanted her in the superior position, she only gazed up at him from the languorous depths of dissolute sensation and murmured, "How strong you are."

"The better to fuck you, my lady," he said.

THEY WERE SITTING BEFORE THE FIRE IN THE parlor when they first heard the sound of horses; a second later, the battle cry of the Carres rang through the night. Robbie dropped back into his chair with a smile. "Holmes must be back."

"With food, I hope. I'll never make a cook."

"You were more resourceful than I, but Holmes actually cooks very well."

Moments later, Robbie and Roxane stood on the small porch, watching a wave of mounted men ride into the meadow. "They do give one a sense of security," Robbie noted with a satisfied smile.

"Yes." Roxane felt more relieved than she'd expected. She'd never been hunted before, nor in personal danger. The large number of Carre troopers was reassuring.

Very shortly the table in the dining hall was crowded with Carre clansmen, and everyone was exchanging greetings while the liquor decanters were passed around. Roxane sat beside Robbie, her hand in his, his frequent smiles in her direction obvious to all. Every one of his kinsmen understood the extent of his involvement with the beautiful countess.

"So tell me," Robbie said, once all the explanations of their arrival from Holland were discussed, "what are Johnnie's plans?"

"To save your ass, at the moment," Adam answered with a grin.

"He worries too much. I don't need saving."

"Protection then," Munro said. "Argyll will be

pushing hard for vengeance. Your brother's called out the whole force."

"Seriously?" Robbie glanced over the rim of his glass, his dark gaze mildly surprised.

"A precaution," Holmes explained.

"Against?" Robbie sat up straighter.

"His discussion with Argyll."

"Good." He leaned back in his chair. "Argyll needs a better understanding of his position in Scotland. He wasn't sent up here as God."

"I think Johnnie intends to point that out to him," Munro noted.

"Along with a proposition he might find lucrative," Adam added.

Robbie glanced at Roxane and smiled. "I sense a lessening of his interest in us."

"I'm sure he'll be willing to compromise for a suitable sum," Munro murmured. "So rest here until your arm is healed, and Edinburgh should be a friendlier town on your return."

"Are the court hearings *en train?*"

"Johnnie came prepared to release the merchant and burgess funds from your bank in Rotterdam, in return for a favorable decision."

"He wants to participate in the Parliament, doesn't he?" Robbie intuitively queried.

"He's been deluged with pleas from those in the Country Party."

"Now that Hamilton is out for bids with France and England."

Munro grimaced. "Exactly."

"So I'm on holiday?"

"We're all on holiday," Munro replied.

Robbie's eyes narrowed slightly and he grinned. "I have this many warders?"

"Johnnie thinks you might be impulsive."

"And he never has been?" His tone was light with mockery.

"He's hopeful his experience might save you from a difficulty or two."

"Listen to him, Robbie," Roxane murmured.

"We do have to go back for Roxane's children soon, though."

"Why don't we escort them?" Munro proposed.

"Or I could just go," Roxane suggested.

"Not while Argyll is still in the country." Robbie's voice was brusque.

"When do you have to leave?" Munro recognized the determination in Robbie's voice.

"In eight days."

"Then we'll have a short holiday," he genially replied. "Are the fish biting?"

In the following days, regardless of the large guard in place, Robbie and Roxane were left alone. Robbie would spend an hour or so with his kinsmen, very early before Roxane woke, keeping abreast of the latest developments in Edinburgh, with Johnnie's daily messenger apprising them of the current news. But he made it clear he wished privacy, and when Roxane's breakfast was prepared, he'd bring it upstairs himself and wake her with a kiss.

They often rode in the morning when the dew was fresh on the ground and, taking a picnic basket with them, would lie on the grassy hillside high above the lodge and pretend they were alone in the world. They found another small lake, clear and cold, where they swam and treated Robbie's arm and made love, sleek flesh against flesh, the heat of their bodies making them indifferent to the chill of the water. They treasured their time together, for both understood that, no matter how wishful their dreams, the uncertainties and dangers of the outside world would soon intrude.

They slept near the mountain lake the night before they were to leave for Longmuir, wanting to be alone, aware their brief idyll was coming to an end. With the morning light, they knew they must return to the city.

"Argyll should be brokered out of our lives soon," Robbie noted, trying to assuage Roxane's apprehension. "Once he returns from his tour of the west, Johnnie intends to meet with him. Our lives should be more pleasant then."

"Wouldn't that be nice," Roxane murmured, her head cradled on Robbie's shoulder. Lying in a bed of fur rugs, they were toasty warm despite the cool upland air, the stars brilliant in the velvety blackness of the sky.

"It's not a dream, darling."

"I hope you're right." She'd never forget Argyll's blunt menace that night. Nor Queensberry's sinister threats. And when powerful men were pitted against each other, the outcome was never certain.

"I'm right," he firmly said. "So we should set a wedding date."

The days at the lodge had been so filled with contentment, she no longer found her reservations against marriage so compelling. "You're sure you want to take on my wild brood?"

"I've been sure much longer than you, darling."

She'd vowed after Kilmarnock not to have her children suffer another stepfather, but Robbie was so unlike Kilmarnock, they could have come from different worlds. "I'm very tempted," she whispered, understanding her love for him was certain even if little else was.

There was no ambiguity in his love for her. He'd risked his life in coming back. "Tempted is good enough for me. Let's say next week."

"Next week?"

"Say yes, or I'll keep you prisoner in this upland meadow."

"That in itself is tempting," she playfully murmured.

"I'm waiting. . . ."

"Yes," she whispered, knowing he wasn't a man to be denied, knowing as well the secrets of her heart.

His exultant cry rose into the starry night, echoed over the hills and vales, set the dogs baying at the lodge below.

Made her laugh.

"I'll make you happy, my darling Roxie," he promised with joy and tenderness. "For a million years . . ."

Chapter 12

$\mathscr{A}$NGUS IS SICK. HE SHOULDN'T BE TAKEN ON a long journey," Amelia pleaded. "At least leave him with me, if you must take the other children."

"He'll be fine," Colter Forrestor replied, flicking a speck of dust from his coat sleeve. "Send along all the servants you wish. Where the hell is that coach? I don't have all day to play nursemaid to Roxane's brats." Scowling, he gazed down the lane to the stables.

Roxane's children were clustered together on the gravel drive at Longmuir, dressed in their travel cloaks, their eyes large with fear, tightly holding each other's hands. Jeanne held little Angus close beside her, trying to comfort him when he coughed, his pudgy face pinked with fever.

"At least let me go along," Amelia cried. "I promise to explain to Argyll that I insisted. He won't blame you." She desperately wished David was home to deal with Roxane's arrogant brother. But he'd gone hunting, and wasn't expected back until tomorrow.

"Look, Amelia, my answer was no the first time you asked, and the second and twentieth time, too. Now get the hell out of my way or I'll have you carried into the house."

A small, thin man, he hadn't the physical strength to carry her himself, she unkindly thought, but recognizing the futility of her efforts, she went to offer what comfort she could to the children. Talking to them in low tones, she promised she'd follow them into the city and see that their mother was immediately informed of their abduction.

"Why is Uncle doing this?" Jeannie asked for the tenth time, as if hoping the latest answer would offer more solace.

"He's with the English, like Argyll. So they follow orders from the ministers in London. But I'll find a way to get you back with me as soon as I reach Edinburgh. Try not to worry, and see that Angus is kept warm and has plenty to drink." Grief-stricken, terrified herself, she tried not to alarm the children, and went on in what she hoped was a calm voice. "Colter is just following orders. We'll have this all straightened out as soon as can be."

"Mama doesn't like Colter," Jeannie murmured.

"He's a gutless cur," Jamie muttered. "I should challenge him to a duel."

"No, no, don't do anything to anger him, darling," Amelia soothed him. "He's short-tempered after riding for days from London."

"He's a priggish popinjay, too," Jamie sneered, and all the children tittered. Their uncle's attire was so flamboyant it was difficult to tell if he was truly a soldier. His velvet coat dripped with lace, his breeches were lined with rows of gilded braid, his white kid gloves were more suited to a ball than to horseback, and his elaborate curled wig looked out of place in the country.

But their eyes were all bright with tears as they

climbed into the coach a few moments later, and Amelia was sobbing as she waved good-bye.

She watched only until the coach disappeared around the curve in the drive, and then called her steward forward from the huddle of servants crowded around the door. "See that horses are ready for us in ten minutes. You must come with me, Crauford, in David's absence. Bring what money you can find, and send a message to David so he understands he's to follow us immediately." She called her lady's maid over and instructed her to gather the bare necessities for a swift journey into the city.

Only twenty minutes later, she and Crauford, mounted on their best thoroughbreds, galloped after the children, and within an hour had caught up to the slow-moving carriage. Careful to remain out of sight of Colter and his troopers, they followed the children into Edinburgh. As they entered the city, Amelia instructed her steward to stay with the vehicle until it reached its destination, and then report back to her. She was headed for Steil's Tavern; the owner was known as loyal to the Carres.

Despite the late hour, Johnnie received Amelia's message and ten minutes later, a servant came to fetch her.

They took a circuitous route through darkened streets and wynds, stopping occasionally to see if they were being followed, and before long she was being greeted by Johnnie.

"I hope I misunderstood your message," he said, his anxiety plain.

"Unfortunately, it's true. Argyll had Roxane's children taken."

"Jesus," he muttered, his mind racing with possible methods of retaliation. He escorted her to a chair. "Tell me what happened."

"Colter appeared with a troop of Argyll's men and simply took them. And Angus is sick." She wrung her hands in despair.

"I'll send a message to Argyll immediately," Johnnie replied. "We'll have them back posthaste. Don't worry."

She seemed to collapse where she sat. "Thank you, oh, thank you." Her eyes were suddenly bright with tears. "Thank God you're here." She didn't ask how or why, content a savior was on hand.

"I'll have a servant see you home, and you needn't worry anymore. I'll see that the children are freed."

"Crauford followed the carriage. He'll return to Steil's with information on their destination."

"Good. You've done marvelously. Now let me take over." The Laird of Ravensby was already debating the exact wording of his message to Argyll. "I don't dare mount a raid tonight—the children might be hurt in the attack. I think its best to talk to Argyll first."

The moment Amelia was shown out, Johnnie called for Kinmont to deliver his note to Argyll.

But Kinmont reported back with unsatisfactory news. "Argyll's out tonight. His subaltern doesn't know where. Some lady, no doubt." He grimaced. "I gave his batman twenty pounds to see that Argyll has the letter the minute he returns."

"We can't wait with Angus sick. Notify the caddies. I want Argyll found."

⸻ ❈ ⸻

ARGYLL WAS LOCATED WITHIN THE HOUR, AND once he'd read Johnnie's message, he left the lady whose bed he was occupying without so much as a glance at his partner.

Near morning, the two powerful men met alone, on neutral ground, without an entourage. Arriving at the altar rail of the Tolbooth church, weaponless as agreed, the Laird of Ravensby and the Duke of Argyll viewed each other like circling gladiators.

"I could have you arrested," Argyll threatened.

"But that wouldn't be very profitable for you." Johnnie knew what had brought Argyll here alone. His offer had been discreetly put, but the lure of money was unmistakable.

Argyll had dressed in full uniform—red military coat, medals from his Continental wars, decorated sword scabbard—all emblems of his subservience to the English, and Johnnie wondered for a moment what kind of man would betray his country.

"How profitable?" Argyll bluntly asked.

That kind of man, Johnnie cynically reflected. Luckily, the kind of man most useful to him at the moment. "Tell me what you think of fifty thousand pounds. English of course."[12]

"If I married Roxane, I'd get half that amount and the countess as well."

"Unfortunately, you're already married."

"She's sickly."[13]

"So you have plans already."

"Any sensible man would."

Johnnie thought himself very fortunate not to be sensible, to be deeply in love instead, and when he spoke, his voice was smooth with sarcasm.

"Would a sensible man consider seventy-five thousand pounds?"

"A hundred, and your troops disbanded within the week. Plus, keep your brother leashed. No woman is worth a duel."

"The countess's children will be released immediately?"

"When I receive the money."

"I'll meet you at their lodgings with the funds." With Angus sick, they couldn't afford delay.

"I envy your liquid assets," Argyll silkily murmured.

"That liquidity is yours as soon as you wish." Johnnie deliberately owned banks for that reason.

"One of the brats is sick, I'm told."

A flash of alarm raced through Johnnie's brain. If Argyll had been informed, Angus's condition must be serious. "I suggest we waste no time, then."

"No troops."

"Only a man to help carry the coin."

Both men knew the other would have reserves in the wings but each had something the other wanted, too. So for the moment they were in agreement.

JOHNNIE HIMSELF DROVE THE COACH TO THE children's lodgings, and he and Kinmont carried the sterling into the house in three trips. Only when the last bag was deposited on the table did Argyll hand Johnnie a key.

"Upstairs," he curtly said.

"Just a precaution." Johnnie indicated Kinmont, his two handguns pointed at Argyll. While his cousin guarded the Campbell chief, Johnnie ran up the stairs and unlocked the door at the top of the landing.

The children were in a tight group around Jeannie, who held Angus in her lap, the fear on their faces pitiful to behold. When Johnnie stepped into the room, the twins ran to him, their faces streaked with tears. "Uncle Johnnie, please help," they cried in unison. "Angus is terrible sick."

He and Roxane had been friends for years, and he'd spent a great deal of time with her children. He loved them and they him, and it broke his heart to see little Angus so still and white.

"They took our servants away," Jeannie sobbed, "and Angus hasn't moved for ever so long."

"He'll have a doctor in ten minutes," Johnnie promised, picking up the small child from her arms. "Follow me now. Kinmont is downstairs to help." Carrying Angus gently down the stairs, he saw the children into the coach, placing Angus in Jeannie's arms. "As soon I get Kinmont, we'll leave. A minute more, that's all." He shut the carriage door.

Striding back into the room where Argyll waited under guard, Johnnie surveyed him, his gaze cold as the grave. "If that young boy dies, Argyll, I'll see that you die, too. It's not an idle threat, so you might want to pray for his recovery." Followed by Kinmont, he turned and left the contemptible man who ruled Scotland for the English queen.

Short moments later, Angus was being put to bed, Mrs. Beattie already brewing a posset for him. A servant was racing for a doctor, and Johnnie was soothing the children as best he could. "The doctor will be here in a few minutes. Mrs. Beattie knows how to make anyone well, and I've already sent word to your mother."

"Thank you, Johnnie," Jeannie gravely said, seated on the bed beside Angus, holding his hand. She looked so much like her mother had when she was young that Johnnie was reminded of his adolescence, when he and Roxane had fished and ridden together with all his Drummond cousins and Jamie. "Angus should have lots to drink, Aunt Amelia said."

"Should we see if he'll take a sip of water before Mrs. Beattie comes back?" Johnnie poured a small portion of water into a glass, understanding that doing something helped to ease the anxiety. "Here, let me hold him up a little, and you see if he'll drink some."

When Johnnie gently eased Angus's head up, the young boy's eyes fluttered open, his gaze terror-stricken—until he saw Johnnie. He tried to smile, but his eyes filled with tears. "I want Mama," he croaked.

"She's on her way," Johnnie murmured. "Jeannie wants you to have a drink now."

Obediently, Angus opened his mouth for his sister, but he swallowed with difficulty. "I want Mama," he rasped, the congestion in his throat and lungs audible, his tears spilling over, running down his flushed cheeks.

"She'll be here very soon," Johnnie assured him, but the fluid in the young boy's lungs alarmed him, his labored breathing a fearful sound in the quiet of the room.

Mrs. Beattie bustled in at that moment, carrying a tray with steaming jugs and cups and bowls. "Now we're going to see that this little laddie gets weel, right quick," she cheerfully declared, moving toward the bed. "And your brothers and sister can drink a wee bit of this broth and lemonade, too." She set the tray down beside the bed. "D'ye want the lemon sweet first, or a bit o' beef broth and oatmeal bread?"

Her good cheer and optimism altered the mood in the room, and before long, all the children were busy eating, little Angus fed his broth and lemonade a spoonful at a time by Mrs. Beattie, who regaled them with stories of ghosts and wee people.

The doctor came with an array of medicines and before long, Angus was sleeping peacefully, helped by a small amount of laudanum. Beds were arranged for the children, with Jeannie set up in a cot in Angus's room along with Mrs. Beattie. Johnnie sat up in a chair near the bed, feeling responsible for the children in the absence of their mother.

By morning, Angus's breathing had improved—not dramatically, but enough to allay everyone's anxieties. When he asked for oatmeal with raisin faces for breakfast, his sister beamed.

"He's ever so much better," Jeannie whispered to Johnnie as they watched Mrs. Beattie tuck Angus into a freshly made bed. "He didn't want to eat anything at all yesterday, not even a sweet Amelia had sent along."

"Mrs. Beattie's beef broth cures anything," Johnnie said with a smile. "Your mother will be pleased."

"Not with Uncle Colter." The young girl made a face. "He's hateful."

"He won't bother you again."

"Did you scare him off?"

"Not exactly but I think his orders have changed. I wouldn't be surprised if he's on his way back to London."

*B*UT HE WASN'T. IN FACT, COLTER WAS QUEStioning Argyll's sudden volte-face.

With an arrogance Argyll found annoying.

"Why in the world was I hied from London to pick up Roxane's brats if they're sent away again?"

"If you needed to know that, I'd tell you," Argyll coolly replied wondering what Marlborough saw in the man.

But then, Marlborough and Argyll disliked each other intensely, a point not wasted on the young Earl of Garrin. "Am I free to return to London, then?" he haughtily inquired, raising his chin above the expensive Flanders lace of his neckcloth. "Marlborough's office is exceedingly busy with the campaign."

"Not just yet," Argyll said, flexing his power at such haughty insolence. "I may still need you."

"For what pray tell? I'm not usually employed as a nursemaid."

"I'll employ you in whatever capacity I wish, Forrestor. Or have you forgotten your rank?"

"No, sir," Colter murmured, the sneer in his voice blatant. "I'm at your disposal, my lord."

"Kindly remember that."

With a wave of his hand, he dismissed the young officer.

Sulky and restive, Colter spent the afternoon drinking in the officers' mess. With evening, he strolled down the Royal Mile to Kilmarnock House, where he'd taken up residence. He had to change into his finery for the night's entertainments.

THE JOURNEY NORTH FROM THE FISHING LODGE was leisurely, the pace dictated only by the need to reach Longmuir on the fourteenth. And the company had left in plenty of time.

Robbie and Roxane, surrounded by mounted clansmen, rode at a slow canter. The spring days were splendid, the sun warm, the political turmoil in Edinburgh and London seemingly distant in the balmy beauty of the green landscape. Roxane rode in her boyish garb, her short curls gleaming in the sun. And she and Robbie smiled at each other with lover's smiles, intimate, exclusive, contented.

But just as they were leaving the Cheviot Hills, they were intercepted by Johnnie's messenger, and before his gasping report had fully ended, Roxane had whipped her horse into a full gallop.

Quickly following her, Robbie drew alongside and tried to offer comfort but, tearful and angry, she vehemently brushed him away. Leaning over, he tried to grab her reins to draw her to a halt so he could talk to her.

"Stay out of my way!" she screamed, slashing at his hand with her quirt. "I don't want to talk to you!" She forced her mount to more speed. Riding one horse almost to death, Robbie finally convinced her to stop long enough to get a fresh mount, and in the remaining miles to Edinburgh, she maintained a stony silence.

What could Robbie possibly say to relieve her fear

and guilt? How could any words mitigate the terror overwhelming her, the terror of not knowing where her children were, or how frightened, or who had them? She blamed herself for not being with her children, and as the hours passed, she blamed Robbie as well for involving her in Argyll's vengeance.[14]

A bitter sense of déjà vu obsessed her, the relationship between love and male possessiveness too prominent in her life. It was never worth it for a woman, she thought, this giving in completely to love, because men always compromised the purity of the emotion with their need for power or mastery over a rival, their compulsion to covet, to win at all costs.

She should have know better than to give in to desire. She actually did, in her rational moments when Robbie Carre wasn't holding her close. But if anything happened to her children because of him, she'd never forgive him—or herself. Never.

Please, God, she prayed, spurring her horse to more speed, her heart pounding as fast and hard as the hoofbeats on the road, please let my children be safe.

While Johnnie's message had been written directly after his conversation with Amelia, he'd assured Roxane of her children's safety. But the long ride did little to alleviate her worry, nor mollify her resentments. Only the blissful sound of her children's voices when she arrived at Johnnie's lodging offered her relief. Racing up the stairs, she followed the familiar noise, and dashing into the bedroom, she saw them all assembled around Angus. Cries of delight greeted her arrival, and laughing, crying, she ran toward them.

Angus was sitting up in bed eating a pudding.

"Your favorite, Mama!" he cried, holding it out to her. "Apple pudding!"

Smiling through her tears, she hugged her small brood as they crowded round her, trying to listen to the tumble of conversation with all of them talking at once, breathlessly conveying the story of their abduction and Angus's illness. With her arms around them, she approached the bed and hugged her youngest son, too.

"You're dressed like a boy, Mama," Angus said, his voice still husky.

"I could ride faster, darling." Sitting beside him, she stroked his tousled hair.

"Johnnie saved us from bad, bad Uncle Colter," Angus exclaimed. "And I was sick, but I'm better now. See, feel my forehead. Mrs. Beattie says it's cool as a cucumber."

Roxane placed her hand on her young son's forehead and, smiling, agreed. "Are you ready to go home?" Her voice was composed, her gratitude profound, but beneath her joyful happiness she wanted to take her children home away from everyone, away from any further danger.

"Can Mrs. Beattie come? Her pudding is really, really good."

"Of course, she can," Johnnie interposed, standing off to one side.

"Then I think we're ready to go," Roxane declared.

"Everything's taken care of," Johnnie quietly reported, a cryptic message in the brief phrase.

Color flared in Roxane's face. "Children, why don't you gather your things." A modicum of restraint cooled her voice. "I have to talk to Uncle Johnnie for a moment."

The Laird of Ravensby had enough experience with women to recognize her tone, and with great courtesy he ushered her out of the room. "Why don't we discuss this downstairs?" he suggested.

"So the children don't hear me scream."

He knew her temper. "That's what I was thinking."

She surveyed him for a taut moment and then turned, descending the stairs so swiftly he was hard-pressed to keep up with her. But he took that last four stairs in a bound and, touching her arm, guided her into a small room filled with armor and weapons.

"How convenient," Roxane snapped, seeing Robbie discarding his weapons. "You can both hear what I have to say."

Johnnie shut the door and leaned against it. "I understand your anger."

She turned on him with fire in her eyes. "You couldn't possibly understand my anger. You couldn't come within ten leagues of understanding my anger. You men think you can do anything you want and then all you have to say is, 'It's taken care of,' and we're supposed to thank you and consider ourselves fortunate. Well, for your information, both of you," she heatedly rebuked, rounding on Robbie, "I don't want anyone taking care of me. Not either of you, and not Argyll or Queensberry, not my damned brother, nor the Erskines. From this moment on, I stop being a pawn to be fought over and possessed. Kindly leave my children and me out of your damned male contests for supremacy. I want all of you"—she swung her arm to include both men—"to leave me alone!"

Spinning around, she stalked toward the door.

Johnnie quickly moved aside, and seconds later the slam of the door echoed through the house.

The brothers looked at each other.

"She's always had a temper," Robbie murmured.

Johnnie exhaled softly. "I think she means it."

"Is Argyll stopped?" Robbie asked, his concern for Roxane's safety foremost in his mind.

"Paid off."

"Stopped?" The emphasis was delicately put.

"One's never completely certain with him, but I think so. He knows how many troops we can muster. It's a concern for him. And he likes the money, of course."

"How much?"

"A hundred thousand."

"English?"

Johnnie nodded.

Robbie's nostrils flared briefly. "That should purchase a degree of courtesy."

"Even from a Campbell."

"Who's seeing her home?"

"Kinmont and Munro. They'll know enough to stay, if she wants company."

Robbie looked at his brother with a sidelong glance. "Not likely, in her present mood."

"I don't blame her. Angus was very sick last night."

"Argyll's a fucking animal," Robbie muttered, beginning to unbuckle his jack.

"He's not familiar with a woman like Roxane."

"You mean a woman who doesn't faint at the sight of his uniform?"

"Or grow weak in the presence of a queen's commissioner," Johnnie wryly noted.

"And now I'm going to have to suffer for his stupidity."

"For your stupidity, too. You shouldn't have endangered her by so blatant an entrance into town."

Robbie dropped into a chair and slid into a disgruntled sprawl. "I'd missed her—which isn't a good excuse, I suppose."

"Some might think not," Johnnie observed.

"I don't imagine I could abduct her the way you did Elizabeth?"

"It might be a shade harder with five children," Johnnie answered. "Let her temper cool for a few days."

"And if I don't want to wait?"

"You'll be wasting your time. She's damned angry. Besides, I need you for a week or so while we deal with the justices in the Privy Council. Coutts tells me we're very near a settlement on our properties."

Robbie shrugged out of his jack and reached for a bottle of brandy on the table. "If I decide to be prudent and polite and leave Roxie alone for a week, tell me what you want me to do. Who do we have to win over? And don't say it's Macfie, for he's the most boring man on the face of the earth."

"He's an ardent opponent of Queensberry, however," Johnnie said, sitting across from his brother.

"In that case, he's suddenly acquired a riveting personality. And talk of torts and petitions has my undivided attention."

"It's not as though you haven't had training in the law."

"Like any Scottish gentleman," Robbie drolly remarked.[15] "But acquit me of an inspired enthusiasm such as Macfie's. Rumor has it he's aroused by the mere mention of a tort."

"As long as he's willing to vote against Queensberry, I don't care if he's aroused by a donkey's behind."

Robbie poured himself a glassful and lifted the goblet to his brother in toast. "If I'm obliged to bide my time with my lady love for a few days, I might as well contribute to the Carre cause."

"Which is partially why we're both in Scotland. Parliament opens soon."

"And you're determined to be there to fight the union treaty."

"We're both going to be there. Scotland needs our votes."

"I'm more cynical than you, dear brother. I think we're fortunate to have our wealth well away from English interests."

"Don't think me naive. But in the process of hammering out whatever agreement is finally reached, Scotland must be defended as fiercely, as ardently as possible. And those who don't resist the grasping English are simply allowing our country and heritage to be taken away without a fight."

"I'm with you, of course," Robbie quietly said. "How can one not be, when people like Argyll and Queensberry are planning on ruling Scotland? But, realistically, will our case be settled before Parliament sits?"

"Coutts assures me it will."

"I'll drink to that," Robbie said with a grin, "and to beautiful red-haired countesses."

"To the Carre interests and to the women we love," Johnnie said, lifting his glass.

Chapter 13

$\mathcal{R}$OXANE WAS INCENSED TO DISCOVER HER brother in residence when she returned to Kilmarnock House. Shepherding her children and Mrs. Beattie up to the nursery, she stayed with them until everyone was comfortably settled once again, until all the servants had been informed of the last fortnight's events and assured of everyone's safety. Until she'd been apprised as well of her brother's high-handed treatment of her staff. Excusing herself from her children with the stipulation that she would return shortly, she proceeded downstairs to find her villainous brother.

But not before instructing her majordomo to see that Colter's belongings were all packed and set outside on the steps, nor before making a short detour to the stables.

She found him in her drawing room, lounging in his boots on her primrose silk sofa. Shutting the door behind her, she said, vicious and low, "You have five minutes to vacate my house. And if you ever dare to return, I'll have my footmen whip you."

"Don't take that imperious air with me, sister dear. I'm here on Argyll's orders."

"Angus could have died because of Argyll's orders and the treatment you accorded him, while the other children were terrified out of their wits. Get out of my house now, or I'll whip you myself."

"You look like some damned urchin," he drawled, his gaze insulting. "Does young Carre like the boyish look?"

She gently flicked the horsewhip she held in her hand, and the long braided leather uncoiled at her feet. "That fine silk shirt is going to be damaged, if you don't move."

"You wouldn't dare." His brows rose negligibly.

Her arm flashed up and down in a blur, and a thin red line appeared down the front of his shirt.

Screaming he leaped from the sofa as her second blow struck him, the shoulder of his shirt ripped away, another slice of his flesh oozing blood. "Damn you!" he roared, racing toward her, but her next snap of the whip coiled around his ankle and, with a powerful jerk, she yanked his foot out from under him. He fell hard, his shriek bringing the front hall servants running to the drawing room door to listen.

Swiftly unloosening the whip from around his ankle with an expert flick of her wrist, she struck again, laying another lash mark across his shoulders. And then another and another, each whip stroke retaliation for her children's suffering, for her own violent rage, until finally, breathless and panting, her arm dropped to her side, the whip trailing on the floor.

Uncurling from his protective huddle, Colter sat up and snarled, "You should be whipping Argyll, you bitch."

"And you shouldn't grovel to masters like him," she retorted, her voice like ice. "Get out of my house now. And if you have any sense you'll get out of Edinburgh, too."

He slowly came to his feet, his shirt in tatters, blood-spattered, his eyes bitter with hatred. "You chose the wrong side this time, darling sister. The English are going to take this country over. And when they do, don't come to me for help."

"Don't worry, Colter. I'll never be that desperate."

"The beautiful Roxane always has options from the circling tomcats," he sneered. "I hope the wealthy Carres protect you, because Argyll believes in vengeance."

"I'll protect myself."

"As you always have in the past," he jibed, pulling the shreds of his shirt together. "With one man or another."

"Just get out, Colter. I don't need your venom and treachery. There's more than enough of that in this town, with all the Scots turncoats scrambling for English gold and favors."

"If I ever have the opportunity to return this favor," he said, indicating his bleeding flesh, "I intend to take advantage of it."

"Am I supposed to be frightened? Of you, Colter? All you know how to do is lick English boots. Although I suppose you might be brave enough to take on a woman."

"We'll see, won't we, who wins in the end."

"I don't want to win anything, Colter. I just want you out of my house." She turned and opened the door. "You know the way."

She washed her face and hands and changed into

fresh clothing before she returned to her children, calmer now that she'd exorcised not only her brother from her house, but some of the inchoate fury from her mind. She spent the day with her family, grateful to be home, pleased her children were safe and secure once again. She hoped the violence and personal challenges were over—Argyll pacified, Colter gone, the Carres aware of her feelings. It helped to be in the bosom of her family, in the familiar setting of her own home. It helped to focus her attention on what was truly important in her life—her children.

When Amelia came to visit later that day and saw how well the children were doing despite their ordeal, she was relieved. "Angus looks remarkably well," she said as the ladies moved off to an area of privacy in the nursery.

"Mrs. Beattie's regimen is wondrous. Thank you so much for your help as well." Roxane smiled at her friend.

"I was just the messenger. Johnnie saw that the children were freed. Argyll is no longer a danger?"

"So I'm told."

Amelia searched Roxane's face at the small testiness in her voice. "That's good news," she carefully remarked. "Is Colter going to be a problem? I know how vicious he can be."

"I think revenge is low on his list of priorities at the moment. With luck, I won't see him again."

"Johnnie was a miracle worker. He had the children back within hours of my contacting him."

"I appreciate everything he did. I really do."

"Why do I sense a but somewhere?" Amelia queried.

"Because I'm feeling misanthropic at the moment. I no longer care to be manipulated for some man's purpose, nor to have my children exploited for male whims and ambitions. And while I know it was Argyll who ordered my children's abduction, if I hadn't been involved with Robbie and, by extension, with Carre politics, he wouldn't have taken such drastic measures. Also, Johnnie made the mistake of patronizing me when I wasn't in the mood to hear a dispassionate, 'It's all taken care of.' After terrifying hours of not knowing my children's status, I was supposed to ignore everything that had happened and go back home to my embroidery."

"When you've never embroidered in your life," Amelia said with a small smile.

"More to the point, when I've finally made an independent life for myself and can decide whether I even *want* to embroider."

"Johnnie did get your children back, though. He deserves your gratitude at least."

"I know. As well as repayment for Argyll's sizeable bribe. I know John Campbell didn't free my children out of kindness or charity. I'll send Johnnie a thank-you note," she acknowledged, "and a bank draft tomorrow. Right now, I'm still furious at men using me for their own selfish reasons. No one's considered whether I may have selfish motives of my own. Perhaps I have my own vision of a contented life."

"Without Robbie Carre?" Amelia softly queried.

Roxane sighed. "I don't know . . . but I do know I'm still too angry not only at myself but at him for my children's ordeal. And Robbie Carre and rational thought are still too tenuous a supposition to be sure of my feelings. Even before the children went to Longmuir, I told him I needed time before deciding on life-altering judgments. And I do, even more so now. I want respite for myself, for my children, without any man coaxing or cajoling or threatening me."

"Will you be allowed your privacy?"

"I intend to find out. I'm staying home for a fortnight at least and *won't* be home to anyone. If any of our friends inquire, tell them with Angus recuperating, I'm currently devoting myself to my family."

"And after a fortnight?"

A fierce gleam shone in Roxane's eyes. "Then I'll get on with my life."

QUEENSBERRY TRIED TO CALL FIRST, BECAUSE HE was intrigued by Colter Forrestor's fabrication about being waylaid by rogues. Every caddy in Edinburgh knew Colter had been tossed out of Roxane's house with all his luggage, looking very much the worse for wear; the duke didn't need his spies to tell him that.

Additionally, Queensberry wished to know why Argyll had suddenly withdrawn from his pursuit of the lovely countess, and set her children free. He suspected the Carre brothers were instrumental. But it never hurt to hear the same story from several different sources.

Unfortunately, he was refused admittance to the countess, and when he attempted to push his way into the house, two young, strong footmen lifted him under the arms and placed him back outside. Undeterred, he moved to his second visit, Lady Carberry's home, only a short stroll away. It was a pleasant sunshiny morning and the walk gave him time to compose his thoughts. He'd been so long in the political game that at times like this, when the vast wealth of information was yet to be uncovered, he felt truly exhilarated, as though these initial moves in a mysterious drama required his skill and expertise to be fully revealed.

But Lord Carberry met him instead when he was ushered into the drawing room. And he understood that mining this particular field of information was going to be more difficult than he'd expected.

"My wife's indisposed," David gruffly declared. "Although she wouldn't wish to see you anyway. We're not interested in your company."

"You're in town early," Queensberry pleasantly observed, as though David hadn't insulted him.

"Leave your smooth-talking, James. I have no intention of telling you anything."

"What makes you think I want you to tell me something?"

"Because you and I haven't had a conversation for ten years. I'm sorry your army of spies is derelict in their duties, but I can't help you."

"Not even if what I wish to know might help your friend, Countess Kilmarnock?"

David snorted. "Help? You? I don't think anyone in Scotland can remember the last time you helped anyone. Except maybe helping yourself to their fortunes or estates."

"The Carres are both back, I hear."

"Are they now? Good for them. Disturbs your sleep, does it?"

"You haven't seen them?"

"Now, would I tell you if I had? Look, James, I don't

know if you don't have anything better to do, but I certainly have. I'll show you out." David took the much smaller man by the elbow. Like so many of his countrymen, Lord Carberry was tall and fair, his hair and beard red-yellow, his countenance and manner affable. His taste was for country life and country sports, and men like Queensberry with their penchant for evil offended him, when he bothered to notice. Forcing the queen's Lord of the Privy Seal toward the door, he hurried the slighter man's exit with a purposeful gait. "Lord Queensberry is leaving," he said to his footman when he opened the door and shoved Queensberry out into the hall. "Show him the door."

ROXANE MAINTAINED HER HERMITAGE FOR THE following fortnight, content with her children, pleased to be removed from the machinations and treachery of the world. Angus recovered completely, and the round of schoolwork and lessons for the children filled her days. Amelia came to call, but no one else was admitted, and from her Roxane heard what she wished of the round of social activities surrounding the upcoming session of Parliament.

Robbie had sent flowers, gifts, notes of apology, and love. But she'd not answered and she'd returned the flowers and gifts, not yet ready to forget all that had happened because of him, still not sure of her feelings. No revelation, prophetic or otherwise, had appeared to resolve her compromised emotions. But when she'd heard from Amelia that the Carres had successfully concluded their court case and that their titles and properties had been reinstated, she'd sincerely wished them good fortune. Several days later, however, over tea, when Amelia mentioned the Carre brothers' appearance at Janet Lindsay's dinner party, Roxane found herself far from pleased with the news. "Robbie didn't waste much time, did he?" she pettishly declared.

"Her husband wanted to be the first to offer congratulations once the brothers returned from surveying their properties," Amelia replied. "He and Johnnie are old friends."

"I don't doubt Janet has set her sights on Robbie, now that Johnnie is no longer available."

"You know Janet," Amelia evasively murmured.

"I see. So how did Robbie respond?"

"He was gracious, I suppose."

"How gracious?" A touch of aspersion colored her tone.

"You've returned every note and gift he sent you, including those fabulous diamonds. Are you expecting him to pine? Is that what you want?"

Roxane crumbled the cake on her plate with her fork. "I don't know. I suppose I do want him to pine."

"Forever? He's eighteen, darling. Not precisely the age when women like Janet Lindsay are refused."

She looked up. "Are you telling me he slept with her?"

"How should I know? Culross was there, though. Perhaps Janet is on her good behavior with her husband in town."

"How fortunate," Roxane sardonically retorted.

"You could have him back."

"Until the next Janet Lindsay looks his way, or God knows who. How long did he wait after his heartfelt declarations of love to me—two or three weeks?" She pushed her cake plate aside. "Certainly an indication of true love if I ever saw it."

"You *could* talk to him, respond to his notes."

"Why? Because he's making eyes at Janet Lindsay now? I don't think so. My God, if he's going to succumb to Janet Lindsay's overtures so readily, I really have been right in my hesitation. Blandishments of love that persist mere weeks," she crisply noted, "don't exactly fall into the category of undying affection. Janet Lindsay *would* be the first to offer herself, wouldn't she?"

"She's a predator of the first rank, no doubt of that. And she particularly likes young men. Remember, Lady Binns threatened to disinherit her son if he persisted in his amorous intrigue with Janet, and she finally had to show up one night and drag him out of Janet's bed."

"Good Lord, how old was Dalyell?"

"Old enough. He was just back from the Grand Tour. But Lady Binns wanted him for her sister's daughter, and Janet's allure was detrimental to her plans."[16]

"On second thought," Roxane said, "perhaps I'll attend your dinner tomorrow night after all. As an observer."

"A little jealous?" Amelia remarked with a faint smile.

"Curious."

"Are we going to be entertained by a lover's quarrel?" she teased.

"I'm sure I can be as civilized as Janet Lindsay."

"She's a vicious little bitch, and you know it."

Roxane's eyes narrowed. "Do tell."

ROBBIE HEARD THE SOUND OF HER LAUGHTER AS he reached the top of the stairs.

"Roxane's here," Johnnie casually said, keeping pace with his brother.

"I heard." Shock vibrated through Robbie's senses, and his pulse quickened. The light, joyous sound trilled again above the muted sound of violins, and all he could think of was wanting her. The feeling was so instinctive and compelling, he wondered how he'd survived without her. Rationalization and logic, his frenzied activities in their legal fight, cool pragmatism—everything he'd brought to bear to suppress emotion the last fortnight—instantly vanished.

"She seems in good spirits."

"Doesn't she," Robbie grimly said, catching sight of her, coming to a sudden halt on the threshold of the drawing room. There she was, manifest in all her beauty, conspicuously female in a room of females, the only woman surrounded by a throng of eager, panting men.

Outrage flared through his senses at so many hopeful men smiling at her, laughing with her, wanting her attention—wanting more. But she was his, he moodily thought. She would always be his.

Radiant in cobalt green silk embellished with Brussels lace, she fairly glowed, the elegant gown a perfect foil for her sun-kissed skin and glorious red hair, the twinkling diamonds in her ears and at her throat drawing attention to her beautiful face and lush breasts. Not his diamonds. Some other man's.

Damn her. How dare she flaunt herself before all those covetous gazes? How dare they think she was available? The need to possess her twisted through his gut.

"Roxane must be feeling better." His brother's voice sounded distant through the roaring tumult of his thoughts. "She's looking well."

Robbie's furious gaze swiveled around.

"Don't make a scene," Johnnie warned.

"I'll just say a few words to her." The explicit anger in his taut words brought stares from the footmen posted on either side of the portal.

"Keep your temper." Johnnie's brows had drawn into a scowl.

"Too late," Robbie hotly retorted, and taking leave of his brother, he plunged forward, a man on the attack. The small groups of conversing guests in his path fell back before his determined advance, a sudden hush descending in his wake.

Everyone knew of his provocative arrival into Edinburgh, and his and Roxane's sojourn in the south was equally the stuff of speculation and gossip in the small circle of Edinburgh society. As was her refusal to continue their relationship.

So titillation ran high as all eyes followed the Earl of Greenlaw's purposeful passage across the drawing room. Breath-held expectation held sway.

Glancing up at the deepening silence, Roxane saw him, splendid in black velvet, fine lace at his throat and wrists, his hair ablaze under the crystal chandeliers, his temper equally aflame—on his face, in his eyes, in the marching tread and the sharp tattoo of his embroidered black kid shoes on the polished floor. A flush of color rose on her cheeks, her chin came up in defiance, and she snapped her fan shut as though readying herself to use it as a poniard.

When her circle of admirers turned to follow her gaze, they had brief seconds to step aside or be bowled over—or worse, from the glowering look on Robbie Carre's face. A space immediately opened up before Roxane as they scrambled to withdraw.

"Are you done pouting?" Curt and hard, his words struck her like a blow.

Fuck you, she mouthed, which elicited a small gasp from her audience, and then she added in a sweet voice, "You must be mistaken, my lord. I never pout."

"Then we can talk." An emperor's fiat would have been more gentle in tone.

Bristling at his arrogance, she crisply said, "I'm afraid I'm busy."

"Really." His dark gaze swept the ranks of her suitors and, aware of Robbie's reputation as a duelist, they quickly retired, his look a caveat to all but those most reckless with their lives. "There now," he softly declared. "You're no longer busy. Come, we'll find some privacy." He stood before her elegant as a courtier, yet unmistakably threatening, the width of his shoulders blocking the room from her view, his height shadowing her.

She surveyed him with flashing anger in her eyes. "I find it inconvenient right now. Though you may intimidate others, I'm not afraid of you."

"Perhaps you should be," he silkily murmured, reaching out to take her arm.

"How nice to see you back in society, Roxane," Johnnie interposed, smoothly insinuating himself between Robbie and Roxane, brushing his brother's hand aside.

Flicking open her fan, she smiled at the Laird of Ravensby and spoke in a temperate voice. "Thank you. My congratulations on your success in court."

"It was just a matter of time," Johnnie replied with a deprecating shrug.

"And . . . money," Amelia added, arriving slightly out of breath after having rushed across the entire length of the room in an effort to defuse what looked to be a nasty encounter.

"Always money," Johnnie agreed. "A necessity for the proper functioning of the wheels of justice, is it not?"

Glancing at Robbie's surly expression, Amelia quickly suggested, "Why don't we adjourn to the dining room. I see Carter giving me the signal," she mendaciously added, her majordomo nowhere in sight. She took Robbie's arm and turned her gaze to Johnnie. "If you'll escort Roxane, Robbie will see me in. How handsome you look tonight," she said, her attention back on her escort, her smile bright with cheer, as though she were immune to the crackling tension in the air, blind to the rapt curiosity of their audience.

As they moved toward the dining room, the silence was so profound their footsteps rang out. Even the musicians had stopped playing, until Amelia gestured sharply to them with a whisk of her fan. The remainder of their gauntlet through the fascinated guests proceeded to the accompaniment of a brisk country air.

After Roxane and Amelia were seated and the

dining room began filling with guests, Johnnie took his brother to one side. "I expect you to behave," he said. "Roxane's not your personal property."

"So I surmised from all her ogling suitors."

"She's allowed admirers."

Robbie's mouth twisted into a bitter grimace. "We'll see." He shook his brother's hand off. "You've done your duty. I'm warned."

"I won't have you embarrass her." But he understood jealousy, too. "Look," Johnnie kindly said, "if you want to talk to her, just do it with a degree more courtesy."

"Like the courtesy you extended to Elizabeth when you took her from the church on her wedding day?" Robbie insolently noted.

Johnnie sighed. "It's not exactly the same."

"Pretty damned near. Although we have less of an audience tonight—far from the five hundred soldiers and wedding guests watching you."

"I can't justify what I did," his brother gently said. "But do me the favor, anyway."

"Why?"

"Out of courtesy to Amelia and David, if nothing else."

A slow grin lifted the corners of Robbie's mouth, shameless in its effrontery. "Why didn't you say so. And here I've been rude."

"Keep it up, baby brother, and David and I will haul your ass out of here."

"That would be *really* interesting."

"How much have you drunk?" The Laird of Ravensby scrutinized his brother.

"Not enough, if I have to watch Roxane flirt with a

roomful of men." Robbie lifted his dark brows in warning.

"I should have found you an accommodating wench tonight and left you home."

"I can find my own accommodating wenches, thank you."

"You have to consider, though, Roxane might have really changed her mind," Johnnie quietly declared. "You know her children mean the world to her."

"This has nothing to do with her children. They like me."

"Whatever it is, she seems convinced."

Robbie's eyes narrowed. "We'll see."

"Promise me," Johnnie cautioned.

Robbie shook his head. "Not a chance."

Johnnie sighed. It was going to be a long evening.

AMELIA HAD SENSIBLY PLACED A TABLE LENGTH between Robbie and Roxane, and while she'd also arranged that Janet Lindsay be well away from Robbie, she'd not taken into account Janet's boldness. The predatory countess had quickly exchanged places with Lady Paton, and Amelia inwardly groaned, watching Janet slip into the chair next to Robbie.

Roxane, thin-skinned and moody, took a more acrimonious view of the Countess of Lothian's advances. She shouldn't, she told herself. She should be indifferent to Robbie's dinner partner. But a sharp-set jealousy remained, despite her attempts to quell it.

And to make matters worse, true to form, Janet was whispering in Robbie's ear before the first course had been served, her invitation eliciting a sidelong look. "That's damned plain, Janet."

"I prefer being direct," she purred, leaning forward to more fully display the plump ripeness of her breasts.

"I'll have to let you know," Robbie evasively replied, his gaze drifting away from her bounteous bosom to the only woman who held his interest.

Unfortunately, Roxane happened to be laughing with Lord Jeffrey at the time and, warnings or not, social courtesy be damned, he felt an overwhelming urge to thrash her dinner companion and wipe the smile from her face. His knuckles went white on the silverware he was holding, and he gently placed the knife and fork down before he did something unforgivable.

"Not hungry?" Janet murmured. "I can think of something you might like to eat."

His gaze flickered sideways at such blatant invitation. "You're persistent."

"But then you have something I want." Her gaze drifted downward to his crotch and she delicately licked her lips.

"Your husband continues to be understanding. I'd not allow my wife such indiscretions."

"I doubt *your* wife would wish them. Although," Janet went on, aware of his wandering attention, "I'm not sure Roxane is the type of woman to settle down."

"Perhaps the choice won't be hers."

Her brows arched. "Are you going to be outrageous like your brother and imprison her?"

Robbie's smile was bland. "I've been warned to behave."

"But will you?"

His long lashes lowered marginally, shuttering his dark eyes. "That depends."

"You could imprison me anytime you want," she whispered with a little frisson of pleasure.

He laughed. "That stirs your lust, does it?"

"Everything about you stirs my lust, you darling boy. How old *are* you, by the way?"

"Old enough to fuck you, Janet, should I fancy the notion."

"Please do, you sweet, *sweet* boy."

Their murmured conversation engaged the interest of many of the guests, for Janet's breasts were nearly falling out of her gown as she leaned toward Robbie. And knowing her reputation for amorous adventure, the guests had no doubt of her intentions. Understanding better than most how determined she could be in pursuit, Johnnie found himself feeling uncomfortably like a chaperon, trying to constrain personalities too unruly and volatile to control.

Roxane included. She was responding to Janet's open coquetry with a brittle flirtatious air, her temper high. And her wine glass had been refilled too many times for his peace of mind.

He found himself monitoring the liquor his brother and Roxane consumed like a butler with the keys to the wine cellar. And becoming more uneasy with each glass.

He met Amelia's amused gaze as his own glass was being refilled. Seated to his left, she sportively murmured, 'Need a drink, do you?"

"Or a dozen," he responded with a grin.

And so the evening progressed through numerous courses, an undercurrent of debacle shimmering beneath the banter and repartee, the level of noise rising as the wine bottles emptied.[17] Janet became more shameless in her actions, Robbie drank two bottles himself, and Roxane felt unsure if she should laugh or cry in her unsettled mood. One moment she wanted to slap Janet's face, the next moment Robbie's. And more than once she wished to flee all the curious, avid attention of the other dinner guests and retire to her country estate, away from indecision and tangled emotions and the frenzy of society.

But once the last sweet was served and the final toast was drunk, the seemingly interminable dinner concluded, putting an end to the painful proximity of Robbie and his flirtatious dinner partner.[18]

With dinner over, dancing was about to commence, and the overwhelming question on everyone's mind was whether Roxane would take Robbie Carre's hand in a dance or offer him a set-down. No one questioned whether he would ask her; his smoldering attention had been fixated on the Countess Kilmarnock despite Janet Lindsay's concerted efforts to the contrary. When Amelia said, "Are we all ready to dance now?" the guests rose en masse as though anticipating a command performance.

Johnnie made a point of reaching Roxane before his brother.

"I'm hoping Robbie's not going to be difficult tonight," he said, offering her his arm.

"He seems to have been well occupied during dinner."

"Everyone knows Janet," Johnnie said with a dismissive shrug.

"And everyone's waiting for her to seduce him before our eyes."

"I doubt he's interested. You should tell him it bothers you if it does."

"*She* bothers me."

"He's *tried* to see you, as have I."

"I know," she said with a sigh.

"I practically had to tie him down to keep him away."

"I'm not sure what I want. I'm not sure of anything."

"Tell him that. Tell him something."

"I have. Angus's illness was utterly terrifying. I told him that. Guilt still eats away at me—at my selfishness, at my willingness to yield all to passion. What if my son had died?"

"Argyll was to blame."

"And myself—for not being with my children."

"I'm not trying to change your mind."

"Thank you. And I'm not willing to become dependent on anyone again."

"I'm not sure Robbie will give up until he understands. Until you make him understand."

"It looks as though Janet is doing her best to distract him at the moment," Roxane sarcastically said, nodding toward the dining room. Draped across his chest, Janet was feeding Robbie a morsel of cake.

"Should I go and get him?"

"Not for me. He's old enough to know what he wants to do."

"Or drunk enough not to know what he wants to do."

"Dance with me once, and then I'm leaving," Roxane murmured, dragging her eyes away from the dissolute spectacle. "I shouldn't have come."

Chapter 14

THE FIRST DANCE, A FRENCH CONTREDANSE with improvisations of the Scottish reel, was well under way before Robbie appeared in the ballroom, Janet clinging to his arm. Ill-tempered and moody, he stood near the doorway, a scowl drawing his dark brows together, the sight of Roxane in his brother's arms galling.

"Why don't we leave," Janet murmured, twining her fingers through his. Leaning into his arm so her breasts swelled above her décolletage, she swayed closer.

Glancing down, he took in the deliberate display, his gaze neutral. "You're wasting your time, sweet." He eased his fingers from hers and unclasped her arm. "Now be a good girl and find someone else to seduce."

"If you're waiting for Roxane, she doesn't seem to be grieving," Janet snidely noted. "Maybe you're wasting *your* time."

His eyes flared wide for a moment, both in astonishment and pique, and then he smiled faintly. "I make it a point never to waste my time."

"You might with Roxane, my pet. She eats up little boys like you every day."

His glance flickered to the dance floor briefly before returning to her. "We'll have to see who eats whom."

"Who's eating what?" Giselle Duncan flirtatiously queried, coming to within inches of Robbie and tapping her closed fan on his chin. "And I do hope some salacious topic is under discussion."

Her sister, arriving a step behind, leaned against Robbie's free arm and gazed up at him. "Do come home with us, sweetheart. We have a *very* large bed."

"He's resisting amorous intrigue tonight," Janet lightly countered, although her frustration at being interrupted was apparent in her gaze.

"Maybe he's only resisting you, darling," Mary Duncan observed. Her voice dropped to a seductive whisper. "No one's at home for a week, Robbie, dear. We'd have great leisure to entertain you."

Roxane could see the fawning ladies around Robbie, the Duncan sisters and Janet so adulatory they looked like purring cats rubbing against him. Which of them would he choose? she fretfully wondered, and when he disentangled himself from them instead, she chastised herself for feeling such satisfaction.

She understood she couldn't expect him to remain celibate. But maintaining that practical logic was infinitely easier when remote from the blatant infidelities of the fashionable world.

When the dance came to an end she wished above anything to quickly escape the crowded ballroom and the parade of females intent on capturing Robbie. Unprepared for the extent of her resentment, she couldn't bear another minute of the ostentatious display. As the introductory chords to the next set began, Johnnie po-

litely inquired, "Would you like to dance again?"
Roxane shook her head.

Nettled to see two more ladies join Robbie's admiring throng, she crisply said, "I'm ready to go."

"Good, I'm more than willing to leave this crush."
Placing his hand on her waist, Johnnie began guiding them through the milling dancers.

They'd managed to wend their way through the press of guests, responding to conversational gambits with only minimal answers or polite smiles and brief nods. The door was within sight when Robbie stepped into their path.

"Give me five minutes," he murmured, slightly breathless after having swiftly shouldered his way across the crowded room.

"Are you sure you have time?"

He didn't pretend ignorance of the number of sexual overtures offered him tonight, but he had no intention of arguing. "I've all the time in the world. Please talk to me."

"I'm more in the mood to box your ears."

"Be my guest," he proposed, leaning forward, brushing his long hair aside, turning his cheek to offer her a better target. "I'm completely at your disposal."

"Save your suave charm for all the others."

He gave her a sidelong glance. "There aren't any others."

"It appeared as though there were a bevy of hopefuls at least."

He wasn't about to discuss that highly charged topic. Turning to her, he softly said, "I sent you dozens of letters and tried to call countless times. I've really missed you."

The husky undertone in his voice brought sudden tears to her eyes, instantly obliterating a fortnight of practicality, and she wondered whether it was possible to ignore wisdom and judgment for this inexplicable craving.

"Don't say that." Her voice was no more than a whisper.

"Do you know how many times I tried to see you?"

Someone coughed, the sound loud, and glancing up, Robbie took note of their attentive audience. "Could we go somewhere? They're all waiting for a fight, and I don't want to fight."

She hesitated, trying to stem the rush of emotion he provoked.

"They're betting on the outcome."

"Don't they have something better to do?" she muttered, offended by the hopeful malice in everyone's eyes.

"Not at the moment. We're center stage, darling."

Her violet eyes sparked. "I'm not your darling."

She'd always be his darling, he thought, but conciliatory and obliging, he diplomatically said, "Forgive me. Come and talk to me." He nodded toward a nearby anteroom. "In there."

"For only a minute," she agreed, nervous, aggrieved, taut with conflicted feelings.

"Whatever you say."

She cast him a searching glance. "Such unreserved appeasement."

"I offer you any and all appeasements, now and always." Putting his hand out, he waited, his heart in his eyes.

She'd seen him last like that at the lodge and she

could no more resist than she could resist the inexplicable joy that began filling her heart. Her fingers grazed his heated palm, the merest tactile contact, and she felt a miraculous wonder, as though happiness had been restored to her soul.

Cautioning himself not to frighten her with the intensity of his need, he closed his hand tenderly over hers and, with a deferential nod to his watching brother, Robbie drew Roxane away. He navigated a path through the buzzing crowd, his shuttered look discouraging conversation, his size and power intimidating to any who considered interfering.

After escorting Roxane into the small chamber, he shut the door on the fascinated and curious, on all the raised brows and titillated glances, and a sudden quiet settled over them. Aware of her strained patience, the undercurrent of disagreement palpable, he spoke immediately. "Whatever you want, I'll do. Whatever you need, I'll give you. These last weeks have been desolate without you."

"You didn't look desolate with all the flirtatious ladies around you."

"I'm not interested in them."

"And I should believe you?"

"It's the truth. Look, I don't want to fight about other women. Tell me what you want and I'll do it."

"I'm not sure you can give me what I want." But her voice was hushed, his nearness disturbing to all her carefully wrought arguments.

"Make me understand, then. Tell me how you could walk away from what we had." He didn't touch her; he knew better, although it took every ounce of will he possessed to restrain himself.

"For a host of reasons, some of which wouldn't make sense to you, maybe not even to me. Lord, Robbie, this isn't the time or the place, with everyone waiting with bated breath for that door to open."

"When, then?"

She sighed, the tumult in her mind immune to logical assessment.

"Tomorrow morning." His voice was insistent, tight with restraint. "Your place or mine?"

"Mine." She opted for the safety of her home, as if her feelings would be less volatile and chaotic in her drawing room.

"Early. You rise early as I recall." His long lashes drifted downward for a moment, insinuation in his gaze.

"Don't. It's not right that you have only to stand before me and all my resolve is gone. That you have but to remind me of our time in the Cheviots and my resentments fade."

He smiled. "I wish I had known that sooner."

She made a small moue. "Don't be urbane when I'm still struggling with my anger."

"I'm being honest, not urbane. Making up was always . . . the sweetest pleasure."

"We *haven't* made up. I'm not so easy as Janet Lindsay and all those other fawning females tonight. I hate them all, by the way."

"I understand. Lord Jeffrey was very close to being skewered with my butter knife at dinner. You were smiling at him much too often."

"I find it unnerving—this adolescent, temperamental yearning. I dislike intensely how you've disrupted the tranquility of my life."

"What I feel for you has nothing to do with tranquility. Not since that first night on Johnnie's yacht."

"Don't remind me. I should have had better sense."

"I'm glad you didn't."

"It was slightly difficult, with your insatiable libido." She could feel the blush warming her cheeks; that night of unbridled passion would be emblazoned forever on her memory.

"I wanted you to remember me," he said with a faint smile.

She blew out a great exhalation, frustration, skepticism, a host of disconcerting perplexities running riot in her brain. "I wish I could deal with our relationship more casually."

"So it would be safer."

"More impersonal," she added with an ironic glance.

"I *could* call you Lady Kilmarnock."

She suddenly grinned. "Damn you. I hate these wretched complications."

"Or I *could* call you the love of my life," he said. "And I'd take care of all the complications."

Her gaze instantly narrowed. "I don't *want* to be taken care of."

He groaned. "Strike those last words. Please. I temporarily lost my mind."

"Tell me, why is this so difficult? I should just walk away from you and save myself a lot of aggravation."

"I could kiss you for that uncertainty"—his mouth quirked in teasing—"but I won't, because I'm on my very best behavior."

"Meaning you haven't tried to bed me yet?"

"Meaning I've become innocent as a choirboy for you."

Her eyes widened. "Really."

"Word of God," he quietly said. "I'll tell you all the sordid details in the morning. Come, let's escape all the curiosity seekers now and enjoy what's left of the evening."

"How tempting, but there's a veritable gauntlet to run," she noted with a grimace.

"I'll brazen it out with the gossipmongers. You slip out the back way and meet me downstairs in a few minutes."

"You wouldn't mind?"

"The men will be careful what they say to me," he said, knowing his reputation for dueling would serve as a deterrent. As for the ladies, he'd perfected the art of evasion years ago.

"I wonder if I drank too much tonight. I'm actually agreeing to everything you say, after I swore I'd—"

"Hush," he murmured, daring to brush her mouth with his fingertips. "You can bring out your list of demands tomorrow morning."

"The list is long."

"Then, we'd both deal with it better when we're sober," he said with a grin. "I'll see you in five minutes."

*B*UT IT TOOK LONGER THAN THAT FOR ROXANE TO make her way down the back corridors, since she had to wait for an amorous couple stealing a kiss in the hallway to return to the ballroom. Once they were gone, she rushed down the back stairs, feeling

strangely liberated, not only from the evening's entertainment, but from the melancholy of the days past.
She briefly chided herself for not demonstrating more
restraint, but decided a moment later she much preferred this joyful elation to the dreary pragmatism of
the last fortnight.

Running through the enfilade of parlors, she arrived
at the entrance hall. Searching for Robbie, she twirled
around, her arms flung out in lighthearted abandon,
her ball gown flaring wide, a jubilant cheer warming
her senses. Until she froze in midturn.

Half-concealed in the shadow of a column, Robbie
and Janet Lindsay were locked in a heated embrace.

Her arms dropped to her sides, and it seemed for a
moment as though she were suffocating. But a second
later, she drew in a ragged breath and rage flooded her
mind. "Forgive me for intruding," she said with bitter
sarcasm, "but I'd like my cloak." She gestured toward
her silk wrap, which was folded over Robbie's arm,
trailing down the countess's back.

Robbie's head came up at the sound of her voice,
and she saw the shock of his face.

He swore—not an apology, she thought, only annoyance for being caught. Furious, she castigated herself for her gullibility.

Janet turned around slowly, her body brushing
against Robbie's tall frame. Her lips were wet from his
kiss, her eyes taunting. "Let her have her cloak," she
drawled.

A small, wretched cry escaped Roxane's lips. Humiliation flared crimson on her cheeks and, spinning
around, she fled.

"Jesus, Janet, look what you did now," Robbie

growled, pushing her away in disgust. "You and your fucking games." Brushing past her, he sprinted after Roxane.

Could there have been more perfect timing? the Countess of Lothian mused, a satisfied smile on her face as she watched Robbie dash through the door held open by a footman. Poor Roxane had looked *rather* displeased, she cheerfully reflected, which meant Robbie Carre would require a great deal of consolation tonight. A pleasant thought, with Culross away from home for a few days. Times like these actually made one consider the possibility of a God. Beckoning for a footman, she ordered her carriage. Now would Robbie prefer wine or whiskey? Should she be fully dressed or in dishabille? What of food? Should she wake her chef? So much to do . . .

$\mathcal{R}$OXANE'S HOUSE WAS NEAR, HER PORTICO IN sight, when she heard Robbie's shout. His cry only impelled her to more speed, reinforced her desperation to reach the sanctuary of her home. Humiliated, outraged at being so easily deluded, she never wanted to see him, never wished to be the recipient of his seductive charm, hoped never, *never* to be so mortified again.

Dashing into her house, she gasped, "Lock all the doors! The windows, too. Hurry!" She ignored her servants' shock, not caring if they thought her mad or drunk or both, so long as they kept Robbie out of her house.

Just in time her porter slid the bolt home on the

front door, for a second later Robbie's fists slammed into the stout oak.

Turning to her footmen and porter, she grimly said, "Don't let him in. Not now, not ever." Turning away, she walked across the white marble floor to the staircase. Immune to the stares of her staff, she ascended the carpeted steps to the floor above, wanting to remove herself as far as possible from the man who manipulated her feelings with shameless ease, destroyed the hard-won equilibrium of her life. Reaching her apartments, she dismissed her maid with a polite excuse and, shutting the door, leaned against it, feeling hurt, exasperated, utterly weary—of the Janet Lindsays of the world, of the men who welcomed them, of the whole gamut of fashionable amusements that passed for pleasure.

But perhaps more, she felt a self-loathing for her rank credulity about a man whose libertine reputation was legendary. She'd not soon forget her shame at Janet Lindsay's impudent smirk. How could she have been so ingenuous, accepting Robbie's sweet smile and facile gallantry like a damnable, grass-green maid. Renewed anger surged through her at the brazen insult. Damn him and damn his careless charm and damn most of all his shameless taste for vice. At least he'd found a suitable companion in Janet Lindsay—along with the Duncan sisters, who spent more time in bed than the whores at Madame Meline's brothel.

The thought brought a modicum of relief. Thank God she'd witnessed that embrace before she'd naively welcomed him back and added her name to the list of his female houris.

She smoothed the skirt of her gown with her palms, a mindless gesture, and then inhaling deeply, she reminded herself of all she could be grateful for. She was safely home, far from the vicious gossip and self-indulgent diversions of society. And more than many women, she was capable of taking charge of her life.

So Robbie Carre could indulge in his libertine amusements, and she'd concentrate on living her life without men of his ilk. She should have known better, anyway. The Carres had never been monkish.

Pushing away from the door, she walked toward her dressing room, feeling more composed. Perhaps she should thank Janet for exposing the true nature of Robbie's sense of commitment; she should send a polite note of gratitude. A smile flitted across her mouth at the droll anomaly. On second thought, she decided she'd much prefer slapping the little slut's face. Reaching out, she began to open her dressing room door, but her fingers slipped from the handle, the door swung open, and the man she least wished to see stood on her threshold.

"You didn't really think you could keep me out, did you?" he drawled.

"Leave this instant or I'll see that you're thrown out." Her voice was cold and flat.

"I wouldn't recommend that." There was anger in his voice as well.

"Fortunately, I don't take orders from you." Sweeping away from him, she moved toward the bell pull.

She'd taken no more than two steps before his hand closed hard over her mouth and he pulled her to a stop. "I'm afraid you *will* take orders from me. Now we can try to come to some understanding like adults, or—" He caught her swinging fist with effortless ease. "Don't even start," he growled. "I'm not in the mood."

Eyes flashing, she struggled against his hold, wildly kicking and squirming, refusing to submit, and when her heel solidly connected with his shin in a powerful blow, he grunted in pain. Swearing, he bound her arms in a vicelike grip and shoved her forward, his stride so rapid she was hard-pressed to keep from falling. Reaching the hall door, he leaned into the door enough to grasp the key with his fingers and turn it in the lock. "How convenient you dismissed your maid," he murmured, releasing her arms for a split second to drop the key into his coat pocket before redirecting their course toward her dressing room.

Her wrathful answer was muffled against his hand.

"Now we'll have some privacy," he softly breathed, tightening his grip on her, his sense of affront no less righteous than hers. He'd never groveled for forgiveness before, never in his life, and after weeks of trying to appease and act the gentleman, he'd reached the limits of his patience.

Marching her before him into the dressing room, he locked that door as well, and holding her hard against his tall frame, he said, "If you scream, I'll gag you." Lifting his hand a fraction, he waited, ready to muzzle her again if necessary.

"Will I have something to scream about?" she coldly inquired, brushing his hands aside and turning to face him.

"That depends."

"On?"

"Your maturity."

"Don't talk to me of maturity," she snapped. "You can't distinguish between love and lust."

"And you can?"

"Damn right I can. Although I'm sure Janet Lindsay's heaving bosom can be distracting to rational thought," she tartly observed.

"Fuck Janet."

"Don't let me keep you." Mocking, contemptuous, she glared at him.

"I suppose you'd take offense if I slapped you," he murmured, his jaw set.

"Not if you don't mind a kick to your balls."

"Sit down," he ordered, his voice tight with restraint. "Over there." He indicated a chair in the corner, needing distance in addition to self-control at the moment, with his temper barely curbed. "You're really trying my patience."

She didn't move.

"Jesus God, you're obstinate." He moved away himself before he did something ungentlemanly. Sitting down, he gazed across the room at her. "Explain to me why we're not lovers anymore," he brusquely said, unbuttoning his jacket. There were degrees and then more subtle degrees of gentlemanly behavior, and his conduct tonight would press the limits of both.

"You don't need me, with your harem. Don't take that off." The smallest touch of panic infused her swift warning.

"You didn't answer my question." Ignoring her command, he slipped his jacket from his broad shoulders.

"I prefer my independence." But her pulse quickened as he kicked his shoes off.

"I'm not interested in curtailing your independence."

"And yet somehow, as in recent moments," she went on, tartly sarcastic, "you take on a dictatorial male role that offends me."

He looked up, his silk hose slipped partway down his calves. "Then I'm sorry."

Words, she thought, only words, without a hint of apology in his tone. "As you'll be sorry a thousand times in the future, each time you choose to have your way." Her violet gaze burned into his. "Maybe I'm not interested in a thousand more apologies. Maybe I'm not interested in a love affair that doesn't take into account my protective feelings toward my children. I'll never forget what happened to them, not if I live a thousand years. I should have been there when they needed me. So forgive me if I take a strong dislike to men who think they can order my life. Like now," she ascerbically added. "And seeing you tonight with all your dear, *dear* lady friends reminds me afresh of your libertine ways. I'm sure you understand that I prefer to avoid such distasteful scenes in the future. So I'd suggest you go to see Janet. I'm sure she's waiting."

A muscle twitched along his jaw. "Are you finished?"

"For the moment," she churlishly said, as sullen as he.

"Believe me, I deplore what happened to your children, and if I could apologize enough to placate you, I would. But I doubt I can ever sufficiently atone for that disaster. As to your independence, it's bloody stupid to even argue about that. Everything's different now. Argyll's taken care of." He put his palms up to allay her heated remark. "Let me reword that. Argyll is paid off, and no one wants to order your life, least of all me. And regardless of what you think, other women don't appeal to me. Janet literally threw herself at me in the hall, and I was trying to shove her away."

"Spare me," she retorted, her lips curled in cynical disbelief.

"Maybe I don't want to."

"You don't have a choice."

"There are always choices," he said, menace in his tone.

"Am I supposed to be intimidated?"

"I was thinking more of . . . accommodating. It was a long climb up here."

"Why didn't you say so," she derisively jibed. "Certainly I should be willing to oblige an unwelcome intruder if he's put himself to such effort."

"You seemed willing earlier."

"Before Janet, you mean." Each word was clipped.

"Do I need a note from her exonerating me?"

"Would she give you one—without a *special* favor?" Roxane insolently murmured.

"You *are* a bitch."

"And you're interested in fucking any female within range."

"How convenient for me, then. I scarcely have to move. Think of this as a farewell fuck," he mockingly noted, "if you really mean what you say."

"You question my sincerity?"

"I question the extent your temper might govern your feelings." He came to his feet, moving toward her, tired of talking, tired of apologizing and explaining, weary of arguing nuances of perception. Wanting to take care of their differences in his own way.

Quickly backing away, she put out a hand to protest his advance. "Stay away from me."

"I don't want to."

"I'll scream."

"Not if I'm kissing you."

"Damn you, Robbie." But her lips began to tingle as though he were kissing her already and her voice had turned hushed.

"Damn us both, then," he whispered, following her retreat, "because you've made my life a living hell the last weeks. Do you know how much liquor I've drunk to sleep at night without you? Do you know how many times I've walked by your house like a lovesick boy? Too much and too many, and I'm going to make love to you now. And if you're not sure, I'm sure enough for both of us."

She'd come up against the locked door. "What if I hate you for this?"

The equivocation warmed his heart. "What if you love me instead? It's been two weeks, three days, fifteen hours, give or take twenty minutes, and I'm dying without you."

"Fourteen hours," she whispered.

"It seemed longer," he said with a faint smile. "But whatever you say, darling. Whatever you *want*. *Whatever* makes you happy in all this world. And I suppose I could get a note if I had to," he finished with a grin.

She looked at him, the smallest twinkle of amusement in her eyes. "You're not allowed within a mile of her."

"Done."

"I'll keep you leashed."

"Sounds intriguing," he impudently returned.

"Oh, Robbie." She sighed. "What are we going to do?"

"First I'm going to kiss you." He bent to brush her lips with his, the pressure delicate. After a moment, his mouth lifted and he said, so low the words were scarcely a vibration on her lips, "Tell me I'm forgiven."

She shook her head.

"Maybe I could earn my way into your good graces," he murmured, a teasing heat in his words.

"Take the easy way out, when I want a decade of penance."

"Why didn't you say you wanted me on my knees?" He began to kneel.

She pulled him up by his hair, grabbing thick handfuls of his long silken tresses. "I want you to be serious."

His expression immediately turned grave as he stood upright again. "If you want penance, I'll do penance," he said, covering her hands with his, drawing them to his mouth, brushing them with his lips. "But love me as I love you."

She did; she had for ever so long. "Tell me I won't regret this," she whispered, frightened at how much he meant to her.

"I won't let you."

"I'm crazy enough to believe you."

"And I'm crazy in love. Could I interest you, Lady Kilmarnock, in some very casual lovemaking? I understand you prefer that."

"I prefer anything, so long as a bonny young man with red hair and the devil's own charm is beside me."

"That's what I was hoping as I scaled those damnably slippery granite walls tonight."

"Next time I'll open the door."

"That won't be necessary. I'm not letting you out of my sight again."

"Nor I you. There were too many women purring around you."

"We won't speak of the men," he gruffly said, curbing his displeasure in the interests of their new détente.

"You frightened them away. I should take lessons from the Janet Lindsays and the Duncans."

"Don't waste your time. I felt like a monk with them, totally uninterested—and you felt the same with *your* admirers?"

"Yes, yes," she laughingly replied. "Like a nun."

"Sensible answer," he murmured.

She drew back a step, her gaze disconcerted. "I don't like your tone of voice. Nor do I have to be sensible for you."

A small silence fell. The emotion-fraught evening, their jealousies, the reasons for their separation, were all deterrents to a facile reconciliation.

"My apologies," he finally said.

"You're sure."

Silence again.

"You want me to beg, don't you? When—" He took a deep restraining breath. Supplication was disastrously new to him.

"When what?" Perhaps she'd drunk too much wine

tonight in the debacle of Amelia's dinner party, she thought, her temper high. Or maybe she *did* want him to beg.

His dark eyes narrowed and he looked for a moment at his fingers, scraped raw by his climb. "All right, then. When all the men around you at Amelia's seemed to be enjoying your seductive charms without groveling."

"I'm singling you out, you're saying?"

"Do you want the truth?"

"By all means."

"I don't think I can grovel."

"But you're not sure."

"Fuck you."

"Go home. I didn't *ask* you to come."

"Would you prefer Lord Jeffrey?"

"Hardly."

"Or Winton?"

"No."

"The Marquis of Rosslyn, perhaps?" They'd all been around her tonight, eager and waiting.

"No, no, no to all of them. Does that soothe your ego?"

"My ego isn't involved."

"And what is?"

"My heart."

"And?"

He sighed. "Don't bait me, Roxie. I didn't come here to fight."

"And yet you do."

"I care too much. It's easier to charm when you don't give a damn."

"Casual amours are less unnerving."

He grimaced slightly. "Lord, you're in a mood."

"Perhaps watching you with a dozen other women put me out of sorts. And then, of course, that scene in the entrance hall rather nicely sealed my evening."

"Mine wasn't much better," he muttered, thinking of the banal company he'd had to endure. "But I can improve the remainder of the night if you'd let me. Look." He held out his hands. "This is the third time I've bled for you."

"I'm supposed to be placated by your blood?"

"No, you're supposed to love me as much as I love you," he gently said. "Please, Roxie, haven't we fought enough?"

His words, soft as velvet, seemed to insinuate themselves into her outrage and smooth away the worst of her ire. But uncertain still, her feelings disastrously in flux, she wasn't sure she could deal with all the complexities of loving Robbie Carre. "I need an apology at least. Or maybe a shipful."

"I'd gladly lay ten thousand apologies at your feet. Or a million, if you'll smile for me again."

His pride and arrogance tightly curbed, he stood before her, barefoot, half-undressed, tall, and powerful, his hands bloodied for her, his apology laid at her feet.

"I don't know," she said on the faintest breaths, overcome by his earnestness and her own desires, by an enticing happiness that always overcame her in his presence. "I don't know if I love you as you love me— or more."

"No, not more," he quietly answered. "It's impossible."

To be loved so much was like putting flame to the tinder of her impressionable, flaring passions, and she smiled, an open, warm smile.

His face lit up.

"I've missed you," she murmured.

Swiftly closing the distance between them, he took her in his arms and held her tight, and for several moments they savored the bliss. "I was miserable without you," Robbie murmured, lifting her chin to brush her mouth with a kiss.

"I missed you every second." The corners of her mouth curved into a teasing smile. "Especially at night."

"I know. I drank every night. In fact," he whispered, a half smile playing over his lips, "I've been celibate so long, I'm not sure I remember what to do."

His celibacy pleased her, more than she thought possible after having lived so long in the fashionable world where fidelity was only for the naive. "Such self-discipline builds character, I'm told."

His brows flickered in roguish dissent. "A delusion. I'm only extremely horny."

"Which accounts for your climbing three stories."

"With ease and no memory of so doing," he replied with a grin. "It must be love."

"It had better be, if I'm going to throw my life away for you."

"I'm worth it."

"So it seems," she murmured, the feel of him like going home after a lifetime in the wilderness.

"You're my everything," he whispered, stroking her back.

"A fortnight is a very long time." He'd always represented the most intoxicating kind of physical temptation to her; desire shimmered through her senses.

"Thirteen and a half days too long. But you set the pace," he offered, intent on pleasing her.

The gracious yielding in his tone encouraged an impertinent impulse, predicated perhaps by the minutest need for vengeance against the Janet Lindsays in his life. "I can order you about?"

His audacious gaze held hers for a moment, and then he murmured, "Be my guest."

"How intriguing."

His smile was wicked. "We try."

"Would you undress at my bidding?" She moved back a step to better appraise his reaction, but after the smallest hesitation he dipped his head in acknowledgment and began untying his neckcloth.

Further encouraged in her sport, she pulled up a chair and motioned him back a few paces. "So I can see *everything*," she dulcetly murmured, sitting down in a rustle of cobalt green silk.

"You're enjoying this, aren't you?" But beneath his careless flippancy echoed an inherent restraint.

"It's not every night I have the opportunity to order you about," she playfully observed. "Do turn around, darling, so I can peruse all your considerable charms."

She didn't notice his minute hesitation before he complied, so involved in the game was she. When he faced her once again, his erection straining the black silk of his breeches, she murmured, "Mmmm. The *full* extent of your enthusiasm is very enticing."

"I live to entice you," he drawled.

"Soon, perhaps," she casually noted, as though she were considering the advantages of his offer. "Do take off your shirt."

He obeyed, the smallest tension evident in the set of his shoulders.

"Now your breeches."

He'd not taken orders since early childhood, and even then only sporadically. He was uncomfortable in his submissive role. But he acquiesced nevertheless, unbuttoning his breeches, sliding the dark garment down his slim hips, kicking it aside. "Have you had enough sport?"

"Indulge me, darling. You look magnificent— everywhere," she murmured, her gaze on his splendid erection.

"And you look like a woman ready to be fucked."

She tipped her head slightly and gazed at him with a discriminating fastidiousness. "Not yet."

He smiled tightly.

"You find it difficult to be docile?"

He shrugged. "Not my choice of words."

She offered him a speculative glance.

"I was thinking impossible," he quietly said.

"And if I were to insist?"

"I'd have to change your mind." He advanced toward her.

She stiffened slightly. "You weren't tractable very long."

"Sorry." Restless under his sexual urges, impatient, he spoke with the greatest constraint. "Perhaps I could indulge you some other way."

"Such as?" He was very close. She had to look up.

"Three guesses," he whispered.

"Is there a prize if I guess right?"

"There's a prize even if you don't guess right."

"Ummm. Are you in a rush?"

"Take your time." He picked her up from the chair with an effortless strength and carried her through the dressing room into her bedroom. "You can deliberate at length while I'm making love to you."

"What if I took issue with your presumption."

He smiled down at her. "If you didn't want to be fucked so badly, you might."

"If I didn't want *you* so badly, you mean. Or don't you differentiate?"

"You're asking me?" His gaze narrowed as he placed her on the bed. "When I could have had any of a dozen women tonight?"

She wrinkled her nose at him.

"But then, I'm a one-woman man," he whispered, moving over her, lifting her skirts away with a deft touch, settling between her warm thighs.

"You'd better be."

"Or?" He guided his arousal to her heated warmth.

"Or I'd have to refuse you."

The most frivolous of words, for her thighs were opening wide beneath him. Slowly sliding into her, he murmured, "Why don't we talk about it later?"

How could one forget the flamboyant, dissolving pleasure, she wondered, as he slipped deeper, the exquisite rapture trembling down her spine, thrilling her senses, heating her blood so she felt as though sunshine were streaming over her. How strange that those finite degrees of sensation weren't etched indelibly in one's memory. How strange that she could think for even a second of never feeling this again.

"I promise to be tractable tomorrow," he whispered,

wanting to please her, wanting to give her everything in the world when she could make him feel like this.

"Love me instead," she breathed, overwhelmed by his strength and power, selfishly wanting all of his deft, lascivious skills, wanting his love always. But she knew better than to verbalize that wish in these troubled times. These moments were enough, this glorious bewitchment and luxuriant rapture plenty.

"I'll always love you," Robbie replied, younger, less buffeted by adversity.

"Perfect." She wanted to believe in transcendent perfection, and thought she was presently experiencing the ultimate, unparalleled masterstroke of that conceit.

"On both counts," Robbie whispered, as though he could see into her mind and feel what she was feeling.

They joined completely, their every nerve and impulse quivering susceptible to his extreme invasion—she engorged, he engulfed. Pulsing tissue and silken flesh touched and melded, with his large, rigid length buried deep inside her. They were both momentarily breathless and still. Then he moved first. Or did she? With sensation peaking by swift, excitable degrees, neither was completely capable of clear thinking.

"I'm never letting you go," he growled, gliding deeper, feeling, remembering, vetting the blissful familiar, insensible to all but his overwhelming need to possess her completely.

"I'm keeping you in my bed."

He lifted his head marginally and looked into her eyes.

"I can be possessive, too," she murmured.

Balancing on his elbows, the scar on his biceps

conspicuous, he exuded potent virility and power. "Lucky me."

Wanting to savor the moment, he took her slowly to climax, but she was more insistent, impatient as always, and twice he had to calm her, partially withdrawing while she whimpered and pleaded.

"Wait, wait, it's better," he whispered.

"No, no, no, no, no . . ." An ardent hedonist, she rebelled at his delay.

But he knew exactly how to keep her just short of orgasm, and when at last she was at fever pitch, when the world had disappeared and desire alone infused her mind and body, he slid so deeply inside her, she screamed in ecstasy.

"Now," he whispered, as if she could stop.

She came and came, endless spasms of rapture coiling through her hot, rapacious core as she melted around him. And in the grip of two weeks' celibacy, he forgot himself that night and met her whimpering orgasm with a violent, fierce, raging release, as if he didn't know better, as if he owned her body and soul.

Chapter 15

$\mathcal{W}$AKING EARLY, HAVING HARDLY SLEPT THAT night, they smiled at each other in the dawn's light. "Stay for breakfast," Roxane murmured, his body warm against hers.

"I'll send for my valet."

"If you don't mind the children. We always breakfast together."

"Do they still throw their food at one another?"

"Does it matter?"

He grinned. "Hell, no. I just thought I'd warn Gordie. He thinks my clothes are his personal treasure."

"Wear something washable."

"Are you trying to scare me off?" He knew her family, had known them for years. And they weren't any more wild than he'd been as a child.

"I just want you to be aware—"

"Of what I'm taking on?"

"Don't jump to conclusions. You haven't heard my list of demands yet."

He lifted her onto his chest in a ripple of honed muscle and took her face between his large palms. "I don't care what your demands are, you're marrying me just as soon as I can get a license and minister."

"I so dislike domineering men."

"We'll have plenty of time to discuss that in the next fifty years. But you decide how to tell your children."

"That their new stepfather is only five years older than Jeannie?"

"Don't even bring up that tired old argument. I can show you any number of marriages like ours. You're too damned vain. Now let me distract you from idiocy like that. Hmmm, you feel—"

"In love?" she whispered, smiling.

"Sexy and in love. My favorite kind of wife."

"We don't have much time."

"This won't take long. You're so easy," he said with a grin.

And as first light framed the rooftops of Edinburgh, the lovers greeted the new day in their own style of heated welcome. Until Roxane, breathless and newly sated, said, "The children will be up soon."

Robbie's valet arrived fifteen minutes later, and their baths and toilettes were completed in a rushed half hour. When the children trooped into the breakfast room shortly after, their mother and Robbie were drinking their coffee and reading the latest news in *The Edinburgh Courant*.

"Uncle Robbie!" they cried, throwing themselves at him as if he were a long-lost playmate. "You've been gone ever so long!"

"I've been busy with the parliamentary debate," he replied, hugging them en masse. "But your mother has graciously invited me to spend more time here now, and I will."

"Can we ride your racers?" Jamie exclaimed.

"I'll bring them over."

"And bring your rapiers, too," Alex said. "Everyone says you're the best in Scotland. I want to learn."

"Me, too." Angus exclaimed, dancing from foot to foot.

"And what can I bring for you?" Robbie said, addressing Jeanne, who stood slightly apart. "A new gown or some pearls? You're old enough for your own pearls, aren't you?"

"Let me ride Titan."

Robbie glanced at Roxane. "It's up to your mother." Titan was a brute of a horse that had taken most of the purses last year on the downs.

"Under supervision," Roxane quietly agreed.

"I can hold him, Mama. Uncle David says I can ride anything."

"Why don't we all go to Bransley Hill next week and do some riding at my practice track?"

The children's screams were deafening.

Roxane smiled across the table at the man who brought such pleasure into her life.

Robbie smiled back and, putting his paper aside, said, "As soon as we're done with breakfast, let's go and see if Wilson's has any new toy shipments."

"I'm thirteen," Jeanne said.

"Some fashion dolls, then, from Madame Tonnere's shop."

Jeanne cast a questioning glance at her mother. "If you like, darling," her mother replied.

"And why not a grown-up gown," Robbie added.

"Mama," she breathlessly declared, beaming with delight.

"Don't spoil them completely," she warned Robbie, but she was smiling.

"No more than their mama," he pleasantly replied.

𝒜FTER BREAKFAST, THE CHILDREN LEFT TO GATHER their coats for their shopping excursion, and Robbie and Roxane shared a quiet moment before the bustle began once again. "Don't be too extravagant with them," Roxane admonished.

"Just a few things," Robbie declared. "I'll have the most fun."

"They could be overwhelmed."

"Your children? Please. The only thing that might overwhelm them would be the hand of God himself. And I'm inclined to think even He might be run over in the charge to first shake His hand. I'm not disparaging them, darling," he quickly interposed. "I like children with spirit. You've raised them beautifully."

"How charming you are."

"Am I not," he teased, winking at her. "Later tonight, I'll show you the full extent of my charm."

She laughed. "And modest, too. How can I refuse?"

"How indeed, when I know everything you like."

She put her hands to her cheeks. "Behave. You're making me blush."

"But then, I so enjoy it."

And into this charming scene Roxane's majordomo entered with a message.

"A Mrs. Barrett is here to see you, my lady. She wished to see the earl as well. I'm afraid we had to lock her in the drawing room. She's quite unruly."

"Thank you," Roxane blandly said. "We'll be there

directly." Once the servant left the room, she turned on Robbie and coolly said, "Are they going to be joining us for breakfast now?"

"I have no idea why she's here. I haven't seen her since before I left for Holland. And there's no need for you to talk to her. I'll take care of this."

"You don't *want* me to talk to her?"

Not in this lifetime, he thought, but Roxane's tone of voice wasn't allowing any latitude in that regard. "Talk to her if you wish, but she's a volatile woman."

"Should I go armed?"

In a full suit of armor, more like; he still had scars from the lady's nails to remind him. "We'll go together. That should prove daunting enough for her."

"Whatever did you see in her?"

It wasn't a question that could be answered in polite company. "I was bored," he said, pushing away from the table, standing, wanting to get the ordeal over with as quickly as possible.

"And *I'm* assuaging your boredom now?"

"No, Lord, no," he protested. "It's not the same, and you know it. I'm sorry she's here. I can't imagine what she wants."

They weren't long kept in the dark about the reason for Mrs. Barrett's visit. As soon as they entered the room, she spun around from the window where she was agitatedly tapping her finger on the pane and hotly said, "I'm pregnant with your child, Robbie. Now what are you going to do about it?"

Roxane gasped and turned to go.

Robbie's fingers closed around her wrist and, ignoring Roxane's struggles to escape his hold, he mildly asked their visitor, "Why did you come *here*?"

"Because you weren't at home, and gossip had you at the countess's house. I didn't want to wait."

"When is this child due?"

"Your child."

"When?"

"November."

"Really. Why come to me? You're married."

"You heartless cur," Roxane spat.

"He'll do the same to you, my lady," Katharine Barrett said. "He's an infamous rogue."

"The child isn't mine, Roxane. Believe me."

"How original."

"Let me talk to her," he said softly to Roxane, not wanting the scene to escalate into a melodrama. "There's no need for you to be party to this. I'll explain later."

"Fine," Roxane crisply replied.

"I'll be upstairs shortly."

"Don't hurry." She shook her hand free.

He let her go, understanding her anger. But he sighed inwardly, knowing whatever his explanation, her response would be stormy.

Once the door closed on Roxane, he gazed at his ex-lover. She was out of character in her demure gray gown, although her warm smile was familiar. "My compliments on your staging and that gown. The Countess Kilmarnock's drawing room was a nice touch. Dramatic, likely to have the gossip mills in full swing within the hour."

"I rather thought the setting was good," the small blond woman agreed. "Your new true love seemed aggrieved. You'll have to soothe her temper in your usual way."

"Tell me why you're here, as if I didn't know." Robbie was not about to discuss Roxane with her. "And tell me whose child it is. It's not mine. You and I both know that."

"But then think how hard it will be to prove, darling Robbie, with so many red-haired men in Scotland."

"Mackenzie won't pay?" Robbie had never asked nor expected exclusivity in their liaison, and she'd been seeing Ian Mackenzie intermittently for years.

"His wife holds the purse strings. As an heiress, she has that prerogative."

"And I'm supposed to pay for Ian's child? Has your husband cut your allowance?"

She snorted. "As if that old miser even understands what it costs to live my life. And you've plenty of money, darling. You won't miss a little. If you indulge me, I'd be more than willing to tell the countess it was all a mistake."

"*That* I want you to do."

"For a price, my sweet."

"You should have been a shopkeeper."

"Or a lawyer, like you. Where would you like to begin?"

"Does Ian like the apartment I gave you?" Robbie sardonically asked.

"He finds it ever so cozy, and you know as well as I do that the price was no more than a wealthy man like you wagers on a hand of cards. Poor Ian has to beg his penurious wife for every shilling."

"I should add him to my tenant list."

"I'd be more than happy to oblige you—in other ways, if you wish," she murmured.

"I don't wish. Look, I'd rather not haggle about this

with the countess in a pet upstairs. Go and talk to
Coutts at White Horse Close and tell him what you
want. But I *will* require a written disavowal of my paternity. And it's not November, is it?" he blandly said,
his gaze drifting over her plump form.

"I don't intend to give away all my secrets without
payment, darling. I'll tell you later."

His liaison with Mrs. Barrett had been brief—six
weeks at most in the period before he left for Holland.
It wasn't possible for a pregnancy relating to his affair
with her to be so obvious yet. And he'd known better
than to take the risk of ejaculating into so mercenary a
womb. "Give Ian my congratulations. He must be
pleased."

"Since his wife is barren, he *is* rather excited."

"I want the countess informed of this deceit as soon
as possible."

"She won't listen to you, I presume, my bonny stud.
It's the price you pay for your licentious reputation."
Her smile was open and innocent, as though she'd not
just extorted money from him.

"Just send the note."

"Of course, darling. And you tell your lawyer I want
cash."

"I'll tell him, and I hope you haven't fucked up my
life."

"Now, if you were a pious cleric, who would believe
me? So consider, dear Robbie, you may have done your
own fucking up."

"I hope like hell not," he softly said. "Or I might
have to come and exact a pound of your flesh."

"Any time, darling. Ian is out of town quite often."

"Acquit me," he bluntly said. "I'm not sure I can afford another child of yours."

"Of course you can. You could afford a dozen with your banks and fleet and trading posts." She stopped his protest with a wave of her hand. "Don't worry, darling. I'm not completely without scruple."

"Take my advice. Invest the money."

"I will, and thank you. You and your brother are terribly sweet."

"My brother?" His eyes flared wide at the disclosure. "Then why didn't you go to him?"

"Because he's in love. Who would believe me, when he's been head over heels for his wife for so long?"

Robbie laughed despite himself. "Who else is in the running for father?"

"No one as rich as the Carres, darling. Or as generous," she added with genuine sincerity. "I could name the baby after you."

"Lord, no. Although I'm flattered," he added with a smile. "And I wouldn't advise you to name the baby after Ian, either. His wife will make his life a living hell. Why not name it after your husband? Or isn't he that benevolent?"

"With luck, he'll die soon."

"I see. This is an awkward situation for you."

Her pretty mouth quirked into a smile. "I'll be visiting Holland soon, to give birth to the—awkwardness. And I *will* send the countess my apologies."

"Thank you. Make them very specific. I'm going to *need* your disavowal. I'll have my valet take a message to Coutts immediately." He wished her good fortune in her travail. Ian's wife kept him on a tight curb, and he wasn't so certain Katharine wouldn't tire of him if someone better came along. She was a self-indulgent little fortune hunter for all her cheerful, unabashed sexuality.

"Thank you, Robbie," she said, her gaze downcast like that of some undefiled, trembling virgin.

"Save that precious pose for Ian. He's more gullible. But you're welcome so long as the countess gets her explanation with all speed." And with a pointed look indicating he expected prompt compliance, he left the room.

*N*o, NO, NO, NO, NO!" ROXANE CRIED AS HE ENtered her apartments and began explaining. "No more excuses, no more explanations. I don't want to hear them. I don't want to hear a single one. Don't you see," she hotly insisted, "this won't ever change. The women aren't going to go away if you marry me. And I'm too selfish. I don't want that constant frustration in my life. I can't deal with it. I'm sorry."

"The child isn't mine. She's going to send you a note of explanation."

"How much did that cost you?"

"It's the truth. The child is Ian Mackenzie's."

"Or so she says, for a price. Don't look at me with that bland expression. I'm not stupid. That woman wouldn't leave without being paid. So any note from her really doesn't mean much."

She'd had time alone to consider whether she could face another disaster like this, and the painful realization was that she couldn't—or wouldn't. She knew from agonizing experience that no matter how fervent, love eventually faded. Because if it didn't, she never could have loved again after Jamie. So this, too, would pass, this tumult of loving Robbie. She particularly didn't want her children drawn into a relationship that might end in misery for everyone.

"You're not being reasonable."

"Maybe I don't want to be reasonable when my breakfast is interrupted by one of your paramours."

"I apologize for that."

"I wish an apology was enough, but this isn't going to work out for any of us. I'd like you to leave. I don't mean it in anger. I'm just not capable of dealing with any more friends of yours."

"Because you don't care enough."

"Because I care too much."

"It doesn't sound like it to me. If you cared, you'd try to understand."

"Don't put the onus on me," she retorted, unwilling to be put on the defensive because of the women he'd slept with.

"Why does it seem as though I'm spending my life apologizing to you," he said, chafing in his role as supplicant.

"Do you think it has something to do with the indiscretions of your life?"

"Roxane, don't go moral on me. You're hardly in a position to take on that virtuous pose."

"I beg your pardon?" she coolly pronounced.

"You know what the hell I mean. You've indulged your passions like the rest of us."

"Not quite like 'the rest of us,' if you're speaking of yourself. Acquit me of that style of dissipation."

"Are we arguing degrees now?"

"We're not arguing about anything. There's nothing to argue about. You live your life as you please, and I'll live mine."

"That's it? All because Mrs. Barrett came calling?"

"You don't understand, do you?" she incredulously murmured.

"No, I don't. I wasn't at fault."

"Maybe you never will be, and that's what worries me."

"So you'll throw away our love?"

"I'm just realistic about my ability to accept all the changes you'd bring to my life."

"You talk as though they're all horrendous."

"No, but too many are. Maybe I'm set in my ways. Maybe I'm too selfish. Blame me if you wish. But passion isn't enough to overcome all the other obstacles."

"Why not?"

"Because I don't have only myself to think about."

He strode away in disgust and stood at the windows overlooking the garden, his hands braced on the frame. "You want this to be over?"

"Yes."

"Fine." He pushed away from the window. "Thank you for your time. It was . . . pleasant." With a faint bow, he walked toward the door.

She watched him, already feeling the pain.

But then he turned at the threshold and said, "You're a damned good fuck, Roxane."

And her pain was engulfed by so monstrous a rage, she was glad no weapon was in sight. "You're not so bad yourself," she coolly replied.

It gave her pleasure to see the flaring anger in his eyes.

"We try," he softly said and, pulling the door open, he left.

The soft click of the latch felt like a knife to her heart. She forced herself not to cry, because she couldn't afford reddened eyes before her children. Finding her wrap, she composed her face and her thoughts as best she could and went to take them shopping.

Her explanation of Robbie's leaving was bland, and so fabricated even the children looked startled for a moment, but when she said, "If everyone wishes, we can go riding on the downs when we're finished shopping," the conversation immediately turned to everyone's favorite mount.

And her life went on.

Chapter 16

 $\mathcal{T}$HE VERY WORST TIMES WERE WHEN THEY MET
in public, at some social event—a ball or dinner, a
levee or political soiree. With Parliament in session
everyone was in town, and the social calendar was so
filled with events, some evenings required attendance
at several entertainments. And on the nights the sessions lasted late, the men would troop in at all hours,
still contesting their divergent views.

The Carre brothers always drew attention when
they arrived, not only for their physical splendor, but
for their provocative sensuality. They'd stand on the
threshold surveying the room, Johnnie looking for
Elizabeth, a graceful smile forming as he caught sight
of her, Robbie examining the array of ladies vying for
his favors with a shameless audacity, as if knowing they
were all his for the asking.

Of late, he'd been giving considerable attention to
young Miss Lauder of Fountainhall—a tall, dark,
slender girl from the country who liked to perform
in amateur theatricals. Rumor had it he was about to
propose.

He and Roxane met by chance one night, at a pro-
duction of *Love Makes the Man* held in the Countess of
Marischal's small theater. It was decorated by Grinling

Gibbons with such splendor, the carved ornament partially distracted from those on the stage. Although Miss Lauder played the young ingenue with considerable enthusiasm, she stood apart in terms of eagerness alone.

Less engaged in the performance than others, many of whom were Lauder relatives, Roxane had slipped away through a side door as the first act was coming to a close and, returning some time later, came upon Robbie in the unfrequented back corridor. She smiled with what she hoped would pass as civility.

Capping the flask from which he was drinking, he bowed, moving aside marginally to let her pass in the confined space, the skirt of her gown brushing his leg. "I wouldn't go in right now. You'll interrupt the soliloquy."

Stopping, she half turned. "You've seen this before?"

"Delphine's been rehearsing."

"She's very . . . good," Roxane said as pleasantly as possible, trying to picture Robbie listening to the young girl rehearse in her high, childish voice.

"No, she isn't, but thank you for your courtesy."

"She has other charming qualities, no doubt."

"Are you asking?" he lazily drawled, a touch of mockery in his voice.

"Not at all."

"Do your escorts have charming qualities?" His piercing gaze belied the languidness of his words.

"Some more than others."

"Callum, for instance."

Her lashes came up suddenly at his brusque tone,

her wide violet gaze fully revealed, and his stomach lurched for a moment at the haunting memories in that lush glance. "For instance," she agreed, her blasé tone forced. At such close quarters, his scent filled her nostrils, and she wondered with a twinge of regret whether Miss Lauder knew how warm his skin was to the touch and how his hair brushed your cheeks when he lay over you. How he smiled like no other man in the world so it seemed as though nothing could dispel your happiness.

"Where is he tonight?"

It took a moment for his question to penetrate her musing. "Callum's gone north on business."

"You're free, then."

"I'm always free. I understand, though, Miss Lauder has clipped your wings, of late."

"Hardly."

"Gossip errs?"

"Doesn't it always? Unless you're truly sleeping with Argyll."

"And *you've* taken up with his wife," she countered.

His head dipped in waggish acknowledgment. "When she's still in London, tucked away where she can't bother him. Have you?"

"Have I what?"

"Slept with him."

"After what he did to my children? You can't be serious."

"He came to call, though."

"Are you spying on me?"

"Don't flatter yourself. Amelia mentioned it."

"Well, then, she should have mentioned as well

that I threw him out, along with his fulsome apologies and false promises. As I did with another man of my acquaintance."

"If you're snidely referring to me, I resent being compared to that traitor. At least I earn my money honestly. So if not Argyll," he blandly drawled, "does Callum have your undivided attention?"

"You're drunk."

"Just beginning, darling. I won't be drunk till morning." But he had enough whiskey in him to ask the next question. "Is he keeping you satisfied?"

"Is *Miss Lauder* enough for your carnal appetites?"

"I can always make time for you." He glanced up and down the secluded hall. "We have a few minutes now, if you wish."

"I've never been interested in speed. You must be thinking of someone else."

"Would you like to go someplace where we can take our time?"

"Wouldn't you be missed by all the Lauders of Fountainhall? The audience is awash with them."

"I'm not particularly concerned."

"I suppose your wealth overcomes your iniquities."

"I suppose it does. Should we go?"

"I'm charmed, of course, by your gallantry," she sardonically replied, "but perhaps some other time, should I ever become desperate for a quick fuck."

He smiled. "I didn't say quick." A fleeting tenderness shone in his eyes. "Ours never was, was it?"

"But then that's your specialty, is it not?" she lightly noted, forcing herself to ignore his gentle gaze.

"I thought it was yours," he said, a roguish amusement replacing the transcient compassion. "What the hell," he added, cheeky and bold, "at least have a drink with me for old times' sake. That amateur performance is so damned boring, there's no point in going back until we have to." Opening his silver flask, he offered it to her with an unreserved grin. "It's your favorite blend."

"From your brewery at Inverness, you mean." She smiled back, unable to resist his simple candor. The play was unbelievably boring. "I suppose there's no point in feuding."

"None at all, my darling Roxie, when we've escaped from those insipid dilettantes for a moment and have half a flask yet to enjoy."

"You always were a man of insight." She took the small silver container from him and drank. The taste of his sweet tobacco mingled in her mouth along with the liquor. "You're smoking again?"

"I'm indulging in any number of vices to pass the time."

"And your sweet young miss doesn't disapprove?" She passed the flask back to him.

"The lure of the Carre fortune curtails her disapproval. She never argues with me. Unlike you."

"Which no doubt accounts for your boredom."

"Do you think so? Is that the problem?" He poured a generous portion into his mouth.

"How should I know? I was never a sweet young miss."

"No, you weren't." His dark gaze took in the splendor of her voluptuous form, elegantly displayed tonight in embroidered plum-colored silk that set off her glowing skin to advantage. And he felt an overwhelming urge to touch her. When he handed her the whiskey instead, their fingers lightly brushed, and he sucked in his breath as though he'd been burned.

She tried to take a step back, but the narrow hall restricted her movement.

"You're caught," he whispered, pocketing the flask.

"No," she breathed, flustered, alarmed, trying to shift away to the side.

He moved swiftly, planting his palms firmly on the wall on either side of her head, capturing her between his arms. "Now you're caught." He leaned forward until his face was only inches from hers. His lower body swayed lightly against hers, and they both felt the familiar wild thrill. Maybe he was drunk or simply more impulsive, but he moved a step closer, his hands slipping downward, closing on her hips, pulling her hard against his body so she could feel his arousal. Then he bent his head low and took her mouth in a fierce, invasive kiss that reminded them both of the glorious pleasures they'd shared, and made them forget all but riveting sensation.

"Oh, there you are!" a light, high voice cried.

Roxane wrenched her mouth away and pushed against Robbie's solid weight. "Let me go."

For the briefest moment she wasn't sure he'd release her.

Nor was he.

"I've been looking all over for you!" Miss Lauder cheerfully exclaimed.

The candlelight in the narrow passage was dim enough to partially conceal the activities taking place. "Let go," Roxane ordered Robbie. "Are you actually *looking* for scandal?"

He shot a quick glance at his advancing inamorata,

and while she may not have deterred him, when he saw her formidable mother turn the corner of the doorway into the corridor, he stepped back.

"Thank God someone can intimidate you," Roxane murmured, taking in the large-boned woman in magenta crepe striding toward them like a hunter stalking her prey.

"I think she outweighs me." His voice was sportive. "And I wouldn't want you to get hurt if she starts swinging."

"Don't worry about me. I can handle Caroline Lauder. The question is, can you?"

He rolled his eyes and grinned. "It's a toss-up."

Roxane had a moment more to straighten her bodice before Miss Lauder and her mother, eyes flashing, descended upon them.

"You missed my soliloquy, darling," Delphine chided, taking Robbie's hand in hers and lightly rapping his knuckles.

"The countess and I were discussing our racers," he said, tactfully easing his hand from hers. "She and I both have thoroughbreds running tomorrow in the stakes."

"And that's more important than my performance?" the young girl inquired with a dramatic lift of her brows.

"Roxie and I haven't seen each other for some time."

Caroline Lauder didn't like the intimate sound of his reply, and like a general intervening when the outcome of a battle begins to look dicey, she immediately said, "I'm afraid everyone is going in for dinner now, and Lady Marischal is waiting. You'll excuse us, won't you, Countess?" She backed against the wall so she could shoo her daughter past her. "Are you coming, my lord?" she pointedly inquired.

Robbie glanced at Roxane, Lady Lauder noted with displeasure.

"Please go," Roxane quietly said to him. "I'll be along later."

"There, you see," Caroline promptly asserted. "Delphine, take my lord Greenlaw's hand. It's so very dark in here."

But my lord Greenlaw didn't so easily comply; he kept his hand to himself, and on the way into dinner he fell into a moody silence.

Roxane joined her friends shortly after, and found if she didn't look at the company at the duchess's table and if she listened carefully to the conversation going on around her she could pretend for even minutes at a time that Robbie Carre meant nothing to her. But she wasn't able to maintain that studied equilibrium once the dancing began, because the young girl in Robbie's arms looked up at him with such innocent yearning, she was eaten with jealousy.

She excused herself early, allowing Lord Crosbie to escort her home because if she didn't he was likely to make a scene. But once they were away from the party, she made it clear to him that his advances were unwelcome.

He wasn't a complete gentleman with two bottles of wine in him, but then she wasn't completely a lady in her current surly mood. While her protests weren't enough to deter him from trying to seduce her, her carefully placed kick left him prostrate on his coach seat and fully aware of her feelings.

She entered her house in high dudgeon, wishing for a moment Callum was back from his trip north. Although she had no strong attachment to him, he was entertaining, and he indulged her capricious moods. They rode, they hunted; he played chess with her, and they both were ardent farmers. A widower with children of his own, he understood the demands of her family.

In the following weeks, she and Callum enjoyed each other's company, while Robbie seriously diminished his supply of Inverness whiskey and continued to elude Caroline Lauder's marriage net. He and Roxane met occasionally at social functions, but never again in private.

Just as well, Roxane thought, aware of her susceptibility.

And while Robbie considered approaching her on occasion, Callum was always by her side. Like a husband, he grimly thought.

Then, abruptly, Roxane disappeared from the social whirl. Her children wanted to be in the country for the rest of the summer, rumor had it. Or she'd slipped away with Callum, others said. But she was gone.

And Robbie's black mood darkened.

Chapter 17

⊷∞∞⊶

JOHNNIE AND LORD CARBERRY, BREAKFASTING together prior to the September first session, were discussing the day's agenda for Parliament. It was early, the sun barely risen when Robbie walked into Amelia's breakfast parlor, his evening attire causing mildly raised eyebrows.

"I'll change later," Robbie said, responding to their examining glances. "Right now I need some food." He walked over to the covered dishes on the sideboard and, taking a plate, filled it to overflowing. Nodding at a servant pouring coffee for David, he said, "Bring some brandy." And sitting, he murmured, "The Duncan sisters wouldn't take no for an answer. I'm exhausted."

He ate in silence while Johnnie and David resumed their conversation concerning the issue of treaty commissioners and the number of votes they hoped to carry. They'd written down the names of those who could be counted on to oppose the queen's right to nominate, and those who would not, as well as those lairds still evasive or looking for payment for their votes. And last but not least, the direction of the equivocating Duke of Hamilton was discussed.

"Fletcher says last he spoke to Hamilton, he promised to vote for our proposal," David said.

"And when was that?" Johnnie asked. "He changes by the minute."

"Last night."

"We'll have to keep someone at his side today to prod his good judgment, especially now that he lost the appointment for the Council of Trade." Johnnie grimaced. "The Douglases have a history of selling out for personal gain. It's a defect in their breed."

"Why not pay him more than the English," Robbie murmured, taking the proffered bottle from the servant and pouring a generous portion of brandy into his coffee.

"He's angling for more than money. The court is luring him with titles we can't deliver."

"Ah, the enticements of the fashionable world and all its vanities," Robbie returned. "Another failing of the Douglases." He drank his heavily laced coffee and, pouring another considerable amount of liquor into his cup, indicated with a nod to a servant that he desired more coffee.

"Slow down on your drinking," his brother cautioned. "Everything could turn on this vote. We need you thinking clearly."

Robbie looked up from cutting his beefsteak. "Words of counsel from you, dear brother, who, rumor has it, rarely drew a sober breath until you married."

"Rarely is perhaps better than never," Johnnie retorted. "If Miss Lauder is causing you to drink so much, send her away."

"Actually, she's my curb on excess. In the boredom of her company, I find transient relief from my dissipation."

"You *could* go and see Roxane," Johnnie bluntly said.

Robbie's head came up like a shot, and the look he sent his brother was malevolent. "No, I could not."

David's gaze moved from brother to brother, and he spoke first, breaking the tense silence. "I wonder if it would be possible to get a definitive promise of support from Hamilton? And if so, could we depend on his word?"

He received no answer for what seemed a long time, and then Johnnie's gaze swung around to him and he softly said, "We'll talk to him again before the session. At least it's worth a try."

"What's worth a try?" Amelia queried, coming into the room on a cloud of perfume, her rose silk morning gown sweeping the floor behind her.

"We're debating Hamilton's degree of deceit," her husband explained.

"An unending debate." She sat at the table and poured herself a cup of tea. "You look devilish fine this morning, Robbie. You needn't have dressed for us." A minute sharpness underscored her banter.

"And you look devilish fine as always, Amelia," Robbie pleasantly returned, offering her a smile.

"Who entertained you last night?" She didn't disguise her pique this time.

"Did I offend you somehow?" Robbie set his cup down and gazed at her across the table.

Amelia opened her mouth as though to speak, then shut it.

A small silence descended on the breakfast group.

"Tell me and I'll apologize," Robbie finally said.

It was obvious Amelia was wrestling with some issue as she twisted her teacup between her hands. Seconds passed, the sounds of the street outside the window suddenly intrusive. Then her hands went still and her gaze came up, chill and piercing. "Roxane's pregnant."

Robbie surveyed the three pair of accusing eyes trained on him. "Don't look at me. I haven't seen her for weeks."

"She's three months pregnant." Amelia's voice was soft.

Robbie leaned back in his chair and regarded them with a bland look. "And she doesn't want anything to do with me." Logical words, temperately delivered, but even as he spoke with constraint, he felt as though someone had gutted him, and his life was draining from his body. "Don't look at me as though I were the black-hearted miscreant. I did everything but beg her not to leave me. And she told me to go to hell. Where I've been, by the way, ever since."

"Do you want me to talk to her?" Johnnie asked.

"And say what? Are all the previous impossibilities suddenly irrelevant? Will true love prevail now that she has a child in her belly?" The stinging, caustic words matched his cynical mood. Was Callum the father? he sullenly wondered. "Look, I don't care what you do," he muttered, coming to his feet. "I'm going home to bed." Suddenly achingly weary, he didn't know if he could make his way from the room. He felt empty, depleted, sick at heart.

Both Carberrys looked at Johnnie when the door

shut on Robbie. "I'll let him sleep for a few hours." Johnnie sighed. "But we need him for the vote. Now tell me what you know of Roxane's feelings, Amelia, and then we'll see what we can do to make everyone in this mess reasonably happy."

Amelia shook her head. "*Roxane* never confided in me. Her maid told my maid. You know how servants are. They know more than we do."

"Is Callum with her at Glenroth?"

"Apparently not. She and the children are alone. She's planting two new orchards, she told me in her last letter. Nothing more."

"At least this situation takes care of Miss Lauder," Johnnie said with a grin. "Wouldn't that have been a disaster."

"He would have drunk himself to death," David astutely observed.

"Roxane won't let him do that." Johnnie's tone was assured.

"Are you that hopeful about a reconciliation?" Amelia cast him a questioning glance. "They're both more stubborn than most. And she has a long list of what she considers practical assessments of their future, none of which have merit in my view. Love is love. You discovered that, didn't you," she said with a meaningful glance at Johnnie.

"Oh, yes," he replied. "And I had considered myself the man least likely to succumb."

"So there's hope for them."

"I'm in my bludgeoning mood, and they're both behaving like sullen children. So after the session today, I'll see if Robbie will ride down to see Roxane. And if he won't go, I will."

"And do what?" Amelia wasn't as sure as he that either party would be easily bludgeoned.

"See that my brother does the right thing," Johnnie rapped out.

"Regardless of the paternity?" David looked at them both. "Has anyone considered that possibility?"

Amelia shook her head. "She'd know. Roxane was always careful."

"I'll attest to that," Johnnie said.

But Robbie wasn't so sure, and the vile possibility that the child might not be his plagued his thoughts. As did the worse possibility that Roxane might marry someone else even if the child *were* his. Utterly fatigued, he still found it impossible to sleep, and he spent the morning sequestered in his bedroom, drinking—a habit he'd acquired of late when the woman he loved had walked out of his life.

Slouched in his chair, a bottle close at hand, he alternately cursed and coveted her, one moment contemplating the exaltation of his child growing inside her, the next irritably recalling her on Callum's arm, as she'd been so often of late. He'd swear again at that point and lift the bottle to his mouth. As his mood turned more benighted and his resentments grew, he finally realized there wasn't, nor would there be, enough liquor in the world to completely purge Roxane from his thoughts. So once this vote was over today, he sullenly decided, he'd ride to Glenroth and see if the child was his.

The Carres had never bred saints; benevolence had nothing to do with his visit.

To that purpose, and fully aware of the importance of the vote that day, he heaved himself out of his chair, called for his valet, and saw to his toilette. By noon, he was bathed, shaved, dressed, and waiting when his brother came to fetch him.

"You'll go to see her?" Johnnie was scarcely through the bedroom door when he spoke, his expression grave.

"When the vote's over."

"What exactly are your intentions?"

Bristling at the tone, Robbie coolly said, "You sound like her father."

"And I'll act like her father if you don't treat her properly."

"What precisely does that mean?" Even sober he took orders poorly, and he was far from sober.

"Cross me and you'll find out," Johnnie replied, contemplating his brother with an irate gaze.

"You should have married her yourself."

"I'll let that pass. You're three parts drunk."

"Did you ever consider it?" Robbie pugnaciously asked, jealous of every man Roxane had ever known.

"No, nor did she. Look," Johnnie said, "I'm not your rival. We were friends. She didn't love me. Satisfied?"

"Sorry." Robbie's response was rueful. "I've never been jealous before, and now I can't stand to have a man within a mile of her."

"Then you'll have to convince her to marry you."

Robbie softly swore, a fleeting grimace crossing his face. "Or someone will."

Sensible of the effects of jealousy, his brother didn't extend the argument. Time enough for coercion later, should it be necessary. "You look presentable,"

Johnnie declared, his gaze drifting over Robbie's well-cut bottle-green coat and tan breeches. "Now, if you were only sober."

"Don't need to be sober to vote against the bloody English. I could do that in my sleep."

THE SESSION WAS PARTICULARLY BITTER THAT DAY, the opposition trying to impose restrictions on treating for union, the court pressing hard to block those measures. The level of debate reached tinder point. But the various opposition factions couldn't agree and by late afternoon, the court was finally successful in winning acceptance for a treaty. But all wasn't lost for those wanting independence for Scotland; considerable maneuvering was still required before acceptance advanced to a conclusive settlement. Those wishing to retain Scotland's liberty could insist that Parliament elect the commissioners. If they could triumph on that vote and the nominations were left to the Scottish Parliament, then any negotiations would prove abortive. The opposition had more than enough votes, even if Argyll and Queensberry mustered every bought and bribed man. Above the raucous debate, Johnnie and Robbie exchanged a satisfied glance. They were gleeful, anticipating a stalemate to the Parliament of 1705, just like those of the previous two years.

With evening approaching, Hamilton, the ostensible leader of the opposition, assured his followers that the question of appointing the treaty commissioners would not come to a vote that day and many left to go home to their families or clubs to dine. But no sooner had they departed Parliament House than

Hamilton called to be heard, and after making a speech that shifted disturbingly from conciliatory to ingratiating, he ended by moving that the nomination for treaty commissioners be left to the queen.

The Carres and all who had been fighting for Scotland's liberty for so long were struck dumb. Not only had none of them expected the proposal to be moved that night, but never at any time by His Grace, the Duke, who had from the beginning of Parliament to that day roared and exclaimed against it on every occasion. Twelve or fifteen men ran out of the house in rage and despair, crying aloud that there was no purpose in staying any longer when the Duke of Hamilton had so basely betrayed them. Those more sensible scrambled to recall their colleagues from their dinners, or hurriedly rose in the assembly to make sharp, angry speeches against the duke. But the government ministry, apparently prepared for this remarkable perfidy, seized the chance and called a hurried vote before the absent members could be recalled from their homes and lodgings. The resolution was carried by a mere four votes.

The irascible Fletcher nearly burst a blood vessel, and Lockhart spoke for all who stood shocked and speechless at the vile treachery of their leader. "From this day," he said, "may we date the commencement of Scotland's ruin."

Now there would be no real negotiation for union, but simply an arrangement between two groups, each nominated and controlled by the queen's English ministers.

It was over.

Scotland was lost.

❧

THE LONG STRUGGLE FOR INDEPENDENCE HAD been sacrificed for the most ignoble greed, and all those who gathered at Patrick Steil's that night talked of nothing else. Some spoke in whispers as though at a wake, others cried for vengeance, many were left speechless—so awful, so horrendous their desolation.

A small cadre tried to suggest parliamentary obstructions to the terrible consequences of the vote, but even they knew it would be little more than delaying tactics. What was done was done, and Scotland was to be swallowed up by England without hope of reprieve. [19]

Robbie had been silent during the postmortem in Steil's, too wretched and disenchanted to muster a response. Not only had his country been crushed under the heel of England, but his personal life was as afflicted.

Men like Queensberry and Argyll would be dominant in the affairs of Scotland now, appropriating whatever government funds were available, giving out offices and places in return for favors, legally raping the country.

While Callum Murray, possible father to Roxane's child, was definitely in favor with the Countess of Kilmarnock. Probably wooing her right now—despicable thought.

The baleful state of his affairs, both public and private, made Robbie seriously consider the life of a hermit. And while, by turns, the caustic and mournful discussion continued around him, he contemplated moving to one of his remote estates, far away from the ruinous events in his life.

When he finally rose toward morning to take his leave, Johnnie glanced up. "When are you traveling north?"

Cryptic as was the question, Robbie understood. "Later," he evasively said.

"When later?"

"I'm not sure."

"It requires a solution."

David looked up at Johnnie's tone, as did several others.

"But perhaps not *my* solution," Robbie murmured, an acerbic edge to his words.

Johnnie's glance flickered in the minutest warning, but when he spoke, his voice was mild. "If I don't see you before you go, I offer you Godspeed."

"I'm going home to bed," Robbie murmured, "but thank you for your good wishes."

But he didn't go home directly; his thoughts were too disordered, too intense for repose. He walked instead, up and down the streets and byways of the city, trying to sort out the chaos, or at least separate the possible from the impossible, no longer sure he wanted to see her, debating his options—whether he had options. Would she even see him if he went to her? Did he want to? Did he wish to prostrate himself again? And if he did—an uncertainty at the moment—what guarantee did he have that Roxane would respond favorably? If he were to ride north as ordered by his brother, make his proposal of marriage to save her from scandal, would she accept?

In the weeks of their separation, she'd appeared in society in her usual fashion, on the arm of one man or another, Callum more than most, but not exclusively. She'd not looked particularly distressed or broken-hearted. And how miserable was he without her? *Merde.* He wished he was more sober to deal with some unfathomable scale of emotion—or perhaps more drunk. That was it, he decided, as he had so often of late. He needed a drink.

Directing his path toward his lodgings, he proceeded up High Street as the sun began lightening the sky, still as irresolute as when he'd left Steil's tavern. Not sure what to do. Not sure what his brother would do if he did nothing.

Not sure he cared.

HE LET HIMSELF IN, QUIETLY WALKING PAST THE porter asleep in his chair, picking up a fresh bottle of whiskey from his study before ascending the stairs to his bedchamber.

Opening the door to his apartments, he stood arrested on the threshold for a moment, his grip tightening on the whiskey bottle. A pulse beat later, he quietly closed the door behind him and, leaning against the paneled oak, uncorked the bottle and took a much-needed drink.

The liquor burned down his throat while a similar heat ignited his temper. What the hell did the little bitch think she was doing? he wondered, gazing at the nude, nubile Delphine Lauder asleep in his bed. The white-on-white embroidered linen quilt partially covered only her legs in the warmth of the late summer morning. If he was interested, he would have appreciated the fulsome beauty of her blushing nakedness.

But he wasn't.

Nor had he ever been.

The question now was how to extricate himself from this unprincipled trap.

First he locked the door. He wanted no witnesses to the scene. Or at least no further witnessess. Then he moved to the foot of the bed and, lightly running a finger down her ankle, waited for her to wake.

Her lashes fluttered open and when she saw him, she smiled.

When he didn't smile back, she pouted prettily. "Aren't you happy to see me?" Rolling on her back, she offered him an unobstructed view, stretching lazily, like a practiced courtesan.

"Who saw you come in?" he brusquely asked, ignoring her coquetry. He had no intention of joining the Lauder family.

She shrugged slightly. "I don't know, some of your servants. I didn't think to ask their names," she pettishly replied. "Mama said you'd be *pleased* to see me."

Warning bells had immediately sounded when he'd walked into his room, but her "Mama said" signaled a more foreboding menace. He wasn't dealing solely with a naive young girl; Caroline Lauder had set out to capture him as a husband for her daughter.

"I'm never pleased to find a young virgin in my bed," he softly said.

"What if I *wasn't* a virgin?" she murmured, offering him a seductive smile. "Would you like it better?"

A chill ran down his spine at Caroline Lauder's duplicity. "What I'd like is for you to quietly leave."

"That's not very friendly."

"I'm not feeling very friendly at the moment."

"You'll have to marry me, anyway. Mama said so. I spent the night in your bed, and you're obliged to do the respectable thing." She sat up, lifted her chin, and regarded him with an open gaze. "Everyone knows that."

"Except me," he bluntly noted.

"You won't marry me?" she gasped, her blue eyes wide with shock.

"Never."

"I'll tell Mama," she threatened, pursing her lips in displeasure, "and she'll make you marry me."

"She can't." The Carres had been wealthy too long; they did as they pleased. "Now, as I see it you have two choices," Robbie offered, wanting her out of his house as quickly as possible. "You can leave, or I can throw you out. It makes no difference to me."

"You wouldn't!"

"In a minute."

"Think of the scandal!"

He almost laughed. "Only for you, Delphine. Scandal is common to my life. Now be a good girl, put your clothes back on, go home, and tell your mother to find someone else to marry you."

"You're not very nice," she grumbled.

"I'm surprised your mother thought I might be." And then, feeling a twinge of sympathy for the young girl manipulated by her mother, he offered a small recompense in lieu of his hand in marriage. "Pick out some jewelry from that box over there." He indicated a rosewood-and-ebony box on his bureau. "As a parting gift."

Her expression brightened and she scrambled from the bed. Watching her walk across the room without regard for her nudity, he decided Delphine had had considerable experience in the bedroom. Not that he cared. Strangely, for a man of libertine habits, she had no effect on him.

The array of jewels in the large box drew a cry of delight from her and, turning to him, she slyly said, "Are you sure you won't marry me? I'd love a very rich man for a husband."

"Sorry, you'll have to settle for jewelry. I'm not inclined to marry. But take what you like," he generously added, just wanting her to leave.

Avaricious by nature, she took advantage of his magnanimity and selected the most expensive items— a diamond necklace and earrings sumptuous enough for a queen, two rings of emeralds, a ruby bracelet of great value. She displayed the jewels on her pink flesh for him to admire. "I'm *ever* so grateful," she purred.

He smiled at her attempt to seduce. "And I'd be grateful if you'd get dressed. I'll have a footman see you home."

"Mama's going to be angry," she warned.

He shrugged. "This wasn't very original."

"I *told* her it wouldn't work," Delphine frankly admitted. "You never even tried to kiss me."

"She should have listened to you. Now, if you don't mind, I'm in a hurry."

He kept his distance while she dressed, but once Miss Lauder was fully clothed, she came up to him, stood very close, lifted her doelike eyes, and whispered, "Kiss me once before I leave."

"I'd rather not." Wary of the Caroline Lauders of

the world, he didn't want to give her the slightest excuse.

But Delphine kissed him anyway, and moments later as she untwined her arms from around his neck, she murmured, "If you should ever tire of Roxane, remember me, darling Robbie. . . ."

How DID SHE KNOW? HE THOUGHT. HOW DID SHE know when he didn't? But the sound of her words echoed in his ears after she'd gone, and images of Roxane filled his mind—all tempting and lush, imbued with desire and memories. And abruptly, he decided to travel north.

Exactly why was unclear, nor did he give himself time to further ruminate on the capricious motives impelling him. He promptly called for his valet, gave instructions for his journey, scooped the jewelry box under his arm and, bounding down the stairs, paced curbside, waiting for his carriage to be brought round.

Chapter 18

$\mathscr{H}$E SLEPT IN HIS TRAVELING COACH, TOSSING and turning on the cramped seats for the greater part of the journey, waking intermittently, at the rough patches, at a post stop or inn, for food, for whiskey once. But after he had the whiskey, he found he'd taken a dislike for liquor and tucked the bottle away.

Although when his driver shouted, "Glenroth in sight!" he wondered if he might need fortification for the meeting with Roxane.

A prescient consideration as it turned out. For he found Roxane entertaining a house party—with Callum Murray playing host.

The large, fair-haired man immediately rose from his seat beside Roxane and came up to Robbie, who stood in the doorway surveying the vast number of people surrounding the woman he'd come a great distance to see.

The two men took measure of each other as though they were calibrating the exact length of each other's coffins.

"You're a long way from Edinburgh." Callum's gaze was chill.

"And you're a long way from Cardhu," Robbie countered with the same bad intent.

"I came down for the race meet."

"So did I," Robbie lied.

"Without stopping, from the look of you." Callum glanced at Robbie's rumpled attire.

"I thought I'd wait for Roxane's . . . hospitality," Robbie insolently replied, "before refreshing myself."

"I'm not sure her hospitality extends to you."

Robbie's brows rose in challenge. "Are you going to try to throw me out in front of all these people? I wouldn't recommend it."

"Not everyone has your penchant for scandal." There was a bulldog truculence to the set of Callum's mouth.

"Least of all you." Robbie knew how Callum Murray prided himself on respectability. And without waiting for further leave, he moved around him and strode into the room.

He looked out of place in the summery room filled with vases of colorful asters and dahlias, the furniture covered in white linen, the floor bleached pale; even the ladies' beribboned frocks were pastel in tone. He looked intensely masculine, tanned a deep brown, his disheveled red hair tumbling on the shoulders of his tobacco-colored coat, the dust of the road evident on his boots and his formfitting chamois breeches.

"Good afternoon, Countess," he said, his bow well-bred and polite. "I was in the neighborhood, and thought I'd stop by to visit."

The blatant audacity if such cool deceit drew everyone's attention.

"Would you like tea?" She forced the ceremonial response, steeling herself against his powerful masculinity, the shock of his arrival posing a danger to the particular reason she'd come to the country.

"I'd prefer whiskey." He moved around the small table and seated himself beside her on the settee before she could protest or take issue, before Callum could. "Is everyone enjoying the delightful weather?" he blandly inquired, his gaze taking in the group at large.

Lady Balfour found her voice first; the presence of Robbie Carre at the countess's tea table was titillating in the extreme. "At this time of year, each warm day is fully appreciated. Have you come for the fishing?" she archly inquired.

"Among other things," Robbie pleasantly replied. "I thought Roxane might like the news from the city." As if his long trip from Edinburgh was casually undertaken to bring the latest gossip.

A messenger had preceded him, so the basic elements of Hamilton's betrayal were known, but numerous questions were directed at him concerning the details. He explained at length the events of that night, a hush descending on the room as the nefarious drama unfolded. "So we all might as well repair to our country homes and see to our gardens," he finished, pouring himself another drink from the bottle brought for him. "The politicians from London will be orchestrating everything from now on. Queensberry and Argyll will have their English dukedoms, and all will be right with the world," he sarcastically finished.

"Will it be so different from Johnstone's reign?" Callum asked. "He, too, ruled Scotland under the court's instructions."

"Not so different, perhaps, just more galling, since there was hope at last that liberty might be ours."

"A pipe dream."

Robbie's gaze struck Callum with the full force of his patriotic zeal. "A real possibility, if not for men who would sell their country for gold."

"You sound as radical as Andrew Fletcher of Saltoun."

"I'm *more* radical than Andrew Fletcher. While the Murrays chose to hedge their bets and wait to see who would win." The remark was pointed and rude. And he waited—*wished*—for Callum to defend his position so he could escalate their disagreement, and by extension establish his right to the Countess of Kilmarnock by armed combat.

"I'm not hotheaded," Callum judiciously noted. "Nor eighteen, nor foolish. And the Murrays will survive this administration, as they've survived all those in the past."

"Without convictions."

"With prudence and a care for the future of our family," Callum fastidiously returned.

"You mean no guts," Robbie baited.

"Enough of politics," Roxane commanded, not about to allow the clash of swords in her drawing room, nor so unequal a match.

"Tell us of your brother's new heir," Lady Balfour interposed, following Roxane's lead. "I hear the Laird of Ravensby is thoroughly besotted by his wife and child to the exclusion of all else."

With one last scathing look at Callum, Robbie obediently directed his attention to Lady Balfour. "He was fortunate to fall in love with a woman of passion and feeling." His insolent gaze flickered briefly to Roxane.

"And yet his wife's English."

"But deeply loyal to her husband." Another disparaging glance at Roxane.

"Who no doubt deserves her loyalty," she snapped.

His eyes burned flame-hot, but his voice was mannered. "Elizabeth's a reasonable woman."

"A prerequisite in a wife, my lord?" a matron with a marriageable daughter coyly inquired.

"It would be highly beneficial," he murmured, the double entendre blatant.

"Is it only women who must fit some standard of conduct? Why not men, too?" Roxane caustically observed. "There should be prerequisites for a husband as well, Lady Tennant."

Lady Tennant's courage failed her for a moment under Roxane's unflinching regard. She was a country lady of simple ways, and had always understood that a woman's place was to lure the most exalted husband possible. And then submit. "I'm . . . sure, that is—possibly—" she stammered, not wishing to disagree with the countess but uncertain how to answer, when everyone knew husbands were under no obligation to meet any standards save that of appearing for their wedding.

"Lady Tennant isn't familiar with our city ways," Lady Balfour politely interjected. "Although I wonder, my dear Roxane, if only a rare few ladies can afford the luxury of requiring male standards."

"Then it's high time for such a change," Roxane submitted, her mouth set. "Independence isn't only a male preserve—or a political cause."

"Or a matter of melodramatic histrionics," Robbie sharply countered. "We all have certain responsibilities."

"Really, my lord," Roxane said with dulcet mockery. "But then how would I know about responsibilities, with only five children to raise?"

And so the conversation over tea continued, waspish, strained, uncomfortably personal, until, thoroughly out of patience, Roxane said, "If you'll excuse me, my children are about to begin their French lessons and I promised to listen to their exercises. Please, continue with tea."

Robbie immediately rose. "You can show me to my room," he said, offering her his hand.

She wished to slap it away, but knew she couldn't. Always unpredictable, Robbie was capable of most anything in his current reckless temper. "In lieu of bloodshed?"

"Something like that," he murmured, glancing down at his hand, palm out before her.

Callum surged to his feet, his face flushed with anger. "If he wants a confrontation, Roxane, I'm in the mood to oblige him."

"Don't even consider it, Callum." She cast him a grateful smile. "I'll take care of this myself." Ignoring Robbie's hand, she came to her feet.

"Are you sure?" Thoroughly enraged, Callum moved to block their departure.

"She's sure," Robbie growled.

Roxane's heated gaze swung toward him for a moment, but she said, "Really, Callum, I'm fine. He often acts like a child Don't take notice."

No one watching the confrontation would have

mistaken Robbie for a child, his powerful maleness striking, his fame as one of the finest swordsmen in Scotland universally recognized, the charged, edgy set of his shoulders blatant invitation to disaster. "We'll see everyone at dinner, won't we, darling," he silkily murmured, taking her hand in a harsh grip, his glance sweeping over her guests wholly innocent.

"If you'll excuse us," Roxane said, thinking he'd missed his calling for the stage. But her fingernails dug into the flesh of his palm as he escorted her from the room, and, once they were outside in the corridor, she jerked her hand from his and slapped him so hard her fingers left marks on his face. "How dare you embarrass me like that! How dare you attempt to draw Callum into a fight!"

"Spare me your impassioned piety," he retorted, suppressed violence in his tone, his cheek stinging from her blow. "I want to know about the child you're carrying."

The color drained from her face and, thinking she might faint, he reached for her.

But she slapped his hands away in a vicious flurry. "It's none of your business."

"I'm making it my business. So we can scream about it here within earshot of your guests, or we can go somewhere private and scream about it."

He meant it, she knew; heedless and hotheaded, he'd never cared about public opinion. Brushing past him, she stalked down the corridor, not looking to see if he was following her, half running in her agitation, her thoughts racing. How did he know? Who'd told him? How could the rumor have reached Edinburgh so soon? *How* was she going to deal with him?"

Breathless when she reached her rooms at the top of the staircase, unaware her children had seen Robbie arrive, she didn't notice them seated on the third-floor stairway, watching through the banister. Waving her maid out of the room as she entered, she turned at the windows and waited for Robbie's assault.

Quietly shutting the door, he surveyed the room, took note of her defensive posture. "I'm not going to attack you. Relax."

"Pardon me if I find that difficult to believe after your reckless provocation before my guests."

"I just wanted to make sure I talked to you."

"And you accomplished your desire with a noticeable lack of finesse."

"Callum's an ass," he brusquely muttered.

"In contrast to you, he's a veritable angel."

"Is that why you like him?" His voice was scornful. "For his angelic qualities?"

"Did you ride so far to query me on my friends?"

At the reminder of why he'd ridden so far, his expression turned forbidding. "Whose child are you carrying?"

"I don't have to tell you."

"Yes, you do."

"You forget I'm not one of your minions or one of your bedazzled ladyloves." Her voice was as determined as his. "And whether I'm pregnant or not is my concern alone, not yours. Don't you already have Mrs. Barrett on your hands? She should be more than enough to keep you busy."

"Don't start," he growled. "Coutts said she sent you a note. So that argument is over."

"Not for me," she tartly replied.

"You don't really want a doormat like Callum, do you?" If rivals were the topic of conversation, the man downstairs currently playing host was certainly more germane than Mrs. Barrett.

"He's preferable to someone like you, who has no concept of faithfulness. I also received a gloating note from the Duncan sisters." Her withering glance raked his tall form. "You've all become good friends of late, it seems."

He shut his eyes briefly and swore under his breath. But when he spoke, his voice stung with annoyance. "I'm getting fucking tired of explaining my actions to you. We aren't married or engaged. In fact, you let me know with unequivocal clarity that you never wished to see me again. And while we're on this perpetual subject of fidelity, tell me, is Callum merely a platonic acquaintance?"

She had the grace to look disconcerted.

"So don't crucify me," he said, "unless you're chastely pure. And if it matters, although I'm not obliged to explain to you, it was only the Duncan sisters."

Her surprise showed.

"I'm telling you because it seems to matter. And notice, I'm not asking for an accounting from you."

"They're the most persistent, I suppose." She couldn't curb the caustic comment.

"Persistent is too mild a term for them. They're both—"

"Don't explain."

"I wasn't planning to," he said. "Jesus, Roxie, I'm sick of this argument. Could we please abandon this subject? I'm so tired of it. I'm tired, period. I don't think I've actually slept in weeks—except on the ride down here, and a lurching coach doesn't exactly lull you to sleep." He walked over to the bed and sprawled on it without asking her leave. When he turned to look at her, his weariness was apparent.

"I hope this child is mine. I pray this child is mine," he confessed. "And if you'll let me try to set things right between us, I'd very much like you to be my wife. Don't answer right away," he quickly added, curtailing her response. "Let me finish. Even if the child isn't mine, I'd like you to marry me and I'd raise the child as ours. I had plenty of time to think about this on the ride from Edinburgh, and I'm sure of my feelings." He smiled. "Or I'm sure of my feelings now that I've seen you again." His brows arched. "Now that I've seen that ass Callum. Don't marry him. He'll make you miserable."

"And you won't?"

"I'll really try not to. And consider how your children feel. They can't like him much—be honest." His smile was beguiling. "He's so damned righteous."

"Maybe I like that stolid righteousness."

He groaned and shook his head. "Sweetheart, he'd drive you crazy in a month. And don't tell me you've been with him a month, because I know you haven't."

Her brows rose in query.

"Coutts had men watching you for me," he explained. "I was drunk for a week after Callum spent that first night with you in Edinburgh." He brushed a hand over his eyes as though exorcising the thought. "Could we please come to some agreement? I can't live without you—and you can't live without me, if you ignore all those logical considerations of yours."

"How exactly am I supposed to do that?"

"Come lie down beside me and we'll talk about it."

She didn't move. "What if this child isn't yours?"

It took him longer to answer than she would have wished. "I don't care," he finally replied. "I hope it's mine, but if it isn't"—his gaze went blank for a moment—"we'll manage."

"A little more feeling, if you please."

He sat up, swung his legs over the side of the bed and opened his arms wide. "I don't care if it's *Argyll's* child," he quietly said. "I think you'll have to agree, that's conciliatory in the extreme." His smile, tempting and intemperate, cajoled. "Come here now. . . ."

"I'm not fifteen. I'm not going to fall into your arms. We're not going to kiss and make up because you drove down here to harass my guests."

"And you."

"Most of all for that. You can't take over my life, not today, not ever. I won't allow it."

He let his arms drop. "Do we need lawyers here to negotiate a settlement? After all the legal maneuvering in Edinburgh the last few years, I'm about out of negotiating impulses."

"Lawyers can't speak for you."

"We're back on familiar ground," he said on a small sigh, rising from the bed and walking to the window. "I'm supposed to apologize and repent and you'll decide whether my atonement is sufficient." He looked outside for a moment before turning back to her. "Do you ever figure in any way in these events? Callum, the baby, maybe even Argyll?"

"Don't you dare accuse me of Argyll." But she had the grace to blush. "In terms of the rest, of course I'm involved."

"Thank you at least for that."

"You shouldn't have come down. We're managing very well without you."

"I'm not managing well without you. And be honest, Roxie, you're not actually happy with Callum, are you?"

She should lie and send him on his way. How simple it would be if she could.

When the silence lengthened, he said, "I've always liked your honesty best, darling. Along with a thousand other qualities that make me love you. Can we at least start with the premise that we love each other in this negotiation?"

"Loving you is easy. All the rest is hard."

He stood very still and let her words wash over him, heal and comfort him, make all the misery of his days past melt away. Then, cautioning himself to move slowly, he said, "Why not take the difficulties point by point and solve them?"

She smiled ruefully. "You're dealing with this very maturely."

"Are you saying I usually don't?" But his voice was teasing.

"Perhaps we both have tempers."

"I want to marry you today, and to hell with the problems. We'll solve them, with the children's help," he added, grinning. "They seem extremely sensible."

"Because they love you?"

"Of course."

She laughed.

"That's better." He crossed the room in three long strides and swept her into his arms before she could protest. "I like you laughing. Although I like you any way at all," he said, moving toward the bed.

"Don't, Robbie," she warned, slanting a glance at the bed.

He hesitated fractionally and then, turning, walked to a chair and sat down, placing her on his lap.

"I don't know if this is much better." She could feel his arousal instantly spring to life.

"Call it a compromise." A new huskiness infused his voice.

"I'm serious," she said, leaning back enough to direct a stern glance at him. "Making love isn't the solution to all our problems."

He didn't think it wise to disagree. "May I kiss you at least?"

"No."

She *was* serious, he realized, so he put aside his levity. "Tell me about the baby. How have you been feeling?"

"I'm fine," she replied, because she'd recognized the stricture in his voice and she didn't want to fight anymore or again . . . or at all. The epiphany struck her with such intensity, she felt the sudden jolt of realization. "I'm fine now that you're here."

"I know. I find that I care whether the sun rises, now that it's going to rise over your carrottop curls," he murmured with a smile.

She giggled, liking the sensation of happiness. "Titian-colored, I'll have you know."

"Of course," he agreed. "Titian-colored carrots."

Her laughter trilled into the sunlit room, and midway, Robbie stopped the silvery sound with a kiss.

"Mama! What are you laughing about?" Angus's high-pitched cry penetrated through the door, piercing the silence.

Robbie's mouth abruptly lifted from hers and, with a wry grin, he said, "Does this mean we're finished making up?"

"Unless you can make love while overlooking the clamor coming through that door. I'm not sure who to bet on in that contest."

"No contest there," he pleasantly replied, lifting her from his lap. Angus's deafening assault of queries were now augmented by the shushing sounds of his siblings.

Smoothing her skirt, Roxie cast him a searching glance. "Are you sure you want to take on all of this? Last chance to escape."

"I am escaping." Rising, he towered over her. "For your information, I'm escaping into a paradise of your making." His smile lit up the room, her life, her world. "And I'll see that you're happy, that *we're* happy," he whispered, dropping a light kiss on the tip of her nose. "My word as a Carre."

She felt for a moment as though she had her own knight-errant, who would slay all the dragons that threatened her. "I should call you Tristan," she said, smiling.

He shrugged. "There are still a few dragons . . . here and there."

"We'll stay out of their way."

He smiled, but knew better than to verbally agree. Argyll and Queensberry would be a force to be reckoned with in the future. "Come, my mama-to-be," he said instead, taking her hand, "let's see what the children think of our marriage plans."

When they opened the door, the children screamed their welcome for Robbie.

Glancing at Roxane, Robbie grinned. "I told you to ask them." Bending down, he scooped Angus into one arm, hugged the other children in turn, and responded to their greetings with smiling good cheer.

"We votedded!" Angus shouted over the noisy exchange of greetings and questions, his high-pitched voice filled with irrepressible elation.

"Shush," Jeanne murmured, a blush coloring her fair skin.

"But we did!" Undeterred, the young boy happily declared, "And no one likes Callum, 'cuz he always tells us what to do."

"Voted for what?" Robbie queried, a smile playing over his handsome face.

"Angus talks too much," James asserted.

"You have to marry Mama 'cuz we voted and so there," Angus proclaimed, safe in Robbie's arms, assured of the untainted goodness of the world at age five. "Don't he?" he inquired of his embarrassed siblings.

"If you say so," Robbie agreed, his smile broadening as he gazed at Roxane. "And I think this marriage better be really quick."

"Yippee!" Angus exclaimed. "Did you bring all your rapiers?"

"I'll send for them, if it's all right with your mother," Robbie replied, regarding Roxane with amusement.

"Say yes, Mama!" Angus cried.

"Do say yes, Mama," Robbie murmured, putting his hand out to draw her near.

She surveyed her children and the hopeful expectation alive on their faces. "Is this what you want?" she asked, feeling a happiness so delicious she reveled in the sensation.

"If you do, Mama," Jeanne solemnly replied.

"And you all agree?" She gazed at the older boys, who all nodded, their cheeks pink with embarrassment.

"Only if you're happy, Mama," James said in a grown-up tone.

"Are you happy, Mama?" Robbie asked, squeezing her fingers lightly.

Tears came to her eyes; her children's pleasure was so apparent. "I think we all are."

"We're going to need fireworks to celebrate," Robbie observed, winking at her.

"Fireworks!" The children's voices rose in a loud chorus of approval.

"I think we should be married tomorrow."

"Tomorrow!" The screams of delight brought the servants down from the nursery. And once the staff was assured of everyone's safety, Robbie suggested they all repair to the nursery to plan the wedding.

Roxane lost complete control of her festivities. The children were so filled with ideas, their excitement was contagious. "Do you mind?" Robbie murmured when Angus was suggesting clowns and acrobats for the entertainment.

"As long as they're happy," she quietly said. "Thank you for including them."

"I may draw the line at our honeymoon, although I'm not sure either one of us has much control over your delightful brood."

"At least the baby will be well entertained."

His expression turned grave for a moment before he composed his features. "No doubt," he said.

"It's your child." Her violet eyes were filled with tenderness. "I'm sure."

He exhaled as though the weight of the world had been taken from his shoulders. "I didn't think I was so territorial, so reactionary. I thought I could be blasé." He half rose from his chair, lifted her from where she sat, and placed her on his lap. "I find I'm completely proprietary. I hope you'll tolerate an outrageously jealous husband. And thank you for my child," he said with such profound feeling he found himself looking away for a moment to compose himself.

She touched his cheek, and drew his face around so she could see his eyes, shiny with emotion. "Thank you for our child. You've made us all very happy."

"For a thousand years," he murmured.

"At least."

"And I *will* make you happy."

"You always have, even—" She smiled.

"Even when you wanted to kill me," he murmured. "But then I know exactly how to put you in a better mood."

"Don't you, now," she whispered.

"So we should get rid of all those guests downstairs, so I can devote more time to your . . . pleasure."

"And how, exactly, are we to do that? Lady Balfour is here for a fortnight."

"Let me handle it."

"You won't insult anyone."

"No one but Callum," he replied with a grin.

He accomplished the remarkable feat in record time. The carriages bowled down the drive before the sun had begun to set, none of the guests disconcerted, save Callum Murray.

"How did you do it?" Roxane marveled, watching the procession of vehicles drive away, standing hand in hand with Robbie on the porticoed porch.

"I invited them all to the christening."

"You didn't!" Her face turned three shades of pink.

"No," he said grinning. "I invited them all to our wedding reception next month. That will give us plenty of time for a honeymoon."

"Lady Balfour will have her coachman drive hell for leather to Edinburgh to spread the news."

"As will the others in their local neighborhoods. So you see, no one's left unhappy, with such scandalous gossip to disperse."

"They'll all be counting the days. You know that."

"Do I care? And if anyone dares to question the *premature* birth of our child, I'll call them out," he pleasantly noted.

"Good God, promise me you won't, or half the country will be decimated by your sword."

"Let me threaten them, anyway."

He looked so hopeful, she laughed.

"As if I could stop you from doing anything you pleased."

"Only *you* can.'

She understood, looking into his eyes, that he meant exactly what he said. "Thank you."

"The pleasure is mine, my lady. And now that I've

emptied the house of tedious guests, I suggest we entertain the children at dinner. Once they're safely tucked into bed, I'll turn my attentions exclusively to your entertainment."

"A delightful prospect."

"I had a feeling you'd like it."

"But then I have since that first night."

"I know."

He always had, and now she understood as well that love was love without regard for circumstances, locale, personal idiosyncracies, or acts of God. It transcended practicalities and boundaries. It couldn't be contained, repulsed, or curtailed.

It was the triumphant, unequivocal exaltation of the spirit.

It was simply love.

Chapter 19

$\mathcal{T}$HE WEDDING HAD TO WAIT FOR FOUR DAYS, though, to give time for Johnnie, Elizabeth, Amelia, David, and their families to travel from Edinburgh. Roxane's children were impatient, saying, "Are they here yet?" so many times, Roxane threatened them with a month of stable duty if they didn't show some restraint. Her warning served to diminish the queries to only a hundred times a day. Manageable, Robbie said with a grin, for everyone with nerves of steel.

But he empathized with the children, as impatient as they, and when he said on the morning of the fourth day, "Let's ride out to meet them," he was greeted with cheers.

So their guests were met many miles short of their destination and escorted to Glenroth by a cavalcade of riotous children. Once the carriages reached the house, the Carberry children tumbled out of their vehicle and immediately ran off with their friends, leaving the latest addition to the Carre family to be cooed over.

"How beautiful he is," Roxane said, admiring baby Thomas, gazing up at her from his mother's arms. "Look, Robbie, he has Johnnie's eyes."

"And his coloring and size as well," Amelia noted. "He's a big baby."

"How much did he weigh?" Roxane asked, and the women compared notes on newborns as they walked into the house and sat down to visit in the sunny drawing room. The men's discussion centered on the machinations of the treaty commission, a conversation everyone joined in over tea and drinks. Dinner that night was a family affair, with the children included, and toasts were offered to the happy couple.

"I'm not sure it gets any better than this," Roxane said as she and Robbie came down from tucking the children into their beds. "Dinner was wonderful. I haven't seen the children so happy in a long time. Thank you," she murmured, touching Robbie's arm.

"I've never heard such creative toasts," he said, grinning. "Or bizarre ones."

"Their youthful ideas of pleasure are different."

"Apparently. Not that I consider a wish for happiness that includes elephants and tigers anything but an act of kindness."

"Good." Her sidelong glance was playful. "At least we don't have to produce an elephant for tomorrow."

"Truly a blessing," he murmured.

"Are you sure now?" She stopped abruptly in the middle of the hallway and scrutinized his face.

"I've always been sure."

"And we're doing the right thing?"

"The rightest." He didn't belittle her nerves; he knew her uncertainties, and while they weren't his, he understood her concern for her children. "They do like me, you know."

"I know." She sighed. "Sometimes I think Kilmarnock ruined my sense of spontaneity."

"We'll resurrect it."

"Starting tomorrow."

"Starting now. You'll always have my blessing to do as you wish. I'll never stand in your way."

"How brave of you," she teased.

He shook his head. "How lucky for me."

THEY WERE MARRIED IN ROXANE'S SMALL CHAPEL, set amidst a thicket of wild plum, the sound of birdsong heard occasionally over the harpsichord music that accompanied the ceremony. Her minister was a family retainer, as had been his father before him, and even while the law gave no allowance for patronage, Reverend Thomson was already training his son to take his place some day on the Forrestor estate.

Johnnie stood as groomsman to his brother, and Amelia was matron of honor for Roxane. The children were involved as well, strewing flower petals down the aisle, James giving his mother away, all of them singing a hymn of thanksgiving for the occasion. And when the ceremony came to the point where the question was asked: "Is there anyone who opposes this marriage?" Angus shouted, "No, no, no," so loudly, he startled the minister. Robbie signaled the flustered man to continue, while Roxane cast a restraining glance at her youngest. In short order—Jeanne now holding on to Angus's hand with an iron grip—the ceremony was over, and Roxane had become the tenth Countess of Greenlaw.

"Finally," Robbie said under his breath, and, sweeping his bride into his arms, he kissed her thoroughly. Cheers erupted and followed them as he carried her down the aisle and out into the sunshine of the fall afternoon. "Now you're truly mine," he whispered, smiling down at her.

"Now *we're* yours." Her joyful smile matched his.

"We're going to need a bigger house, aren't we?" he murmured, brushing her lips with his.

She laughed. "No. Bransley Hill's eighty rooms will do just nicely."

"A bigger nursery, then." A twinkle shone in his eye.

"We'll see about that."

"I'll see about that."

"If I allow it."

"As I recall, you're not too hard to persuade," he said, grinning.

"A charming quality in a husband." She smiled back.

"But then it's so much fun making you happy."

"I truly am."

"*We* are," he reminded her, and as if on cue, the children poured through the chapel door and surrounded them in a tumultuous throng.

At the wedding luncheon, more toasts were proposed, and high good spirits prevailed throughout the day. That evening the promised fireworks capped the festivities, the elaborate spectacle a colorful equivalent of everyone's joy and gladness.

And much later, when the house had quieted, when the last child had been tucked in and had fallen asleep, when the final guests had retired to their rooms, Robbie and Roxane entered their bedchamber and, turning to each other, smiled, a secret, sly smile of deliverance and tantalizing excitement.

Taking her hand, Robbie gently traced his finger around her wrist. "While our wedding day was perfect, it was *very* long."

She knew what he meant. "But we're finally alone."

Lacing his fingers through hers, he lifted her hand palm to palm with his as if determining some esoteric standard. "It feels different, doesn't it?"

She mutely nodded, intangible emotions tumbling through her mind.

"We're one life now," he murmured, his simple phrase miraculously making tangible the intangible.

"Not me here and you there . . ."

"But us."

Her heart filled with tenderness and passion, all her quiet and unquiet needs fulfilled by this beautiful young man.

"Are you tired?" His tone was solicitous, oddly grave.

"Not *that* tired, if you're asking." Her mouth curved into a faint smile.

Curved to kiss, he thought, and leaning forward he delicately touched her lips with his.

"A husband's kiss," she whispered when his mouth lifted from hers. "When I want a lover's kiss."

His dark brows rose in speculation, his gaze drifting over her moist lips, rosy pink, damp from his kiss.

"I want you even more than before, if that's possible," she breathed, slipping her hand from his, sliding her arms around his waist, molding her body against his tall, muscled form.

"And you want different kisses," he teased.

"Kisses and more."

"I'll give you a thousand kisses and then a hundred more and whatever else you want."

She could feel him hard against her, his arousal rising, swelling. "And if I become demanding?"

"So long as I can breathe," he said with a smile.

"How nice," she said, contented, beguiled, "for I find myself obsessed with making love to you, as though I've lost all sense of proportion. Elizabeth noticed at dinner tonight whenever I looked at you."

"Is not wifely adoration your duty?" he playfully observed.

"While you have husbandly duties, no doubt."

"To keep you properly fucked, you mean." His voice was lush and low.

"An astute man," she purred, "although I've been waiting for at least—"

"Five minutes?"

"Five minutes too long, my bonny husband."

He chuckled. "You understand, there *will* be times when I have to attend to matters outside the bedroom."

Her pout was delicious. "You didn't say that *before* we were married."

"But everything is quite different after marriage. You know the rules," he silkily murmured. "*I'm* lord and master now."

"Lord and master . . ." Her voice dropped a seductive octave and, stepping away, she curtsied prettily, gazing up at him from under her lashes. "Pray tell, will I like your sovereignty?"

He observed her from under half-lowered lashes, his

glance amused. "So long as you do what's required of you."

"You have requirements?"

"Only that you be biddable," he blandly said.

"And if I am, you'll reward me?" Her voice was velvety soft, the focus of her gaze on his breeches, stretched taut over his erection.

"I could be generous, I think." One brow lazily arched upward.

An immediate quivering response rippled through her. "If you but indicate what's required of me," she whispered, desire flaring in her eyes.

"Such eagerness . . ."

"You're not exactly uninterested, my lord."

He glanced downward, as though he'd not taken notice before, and lightly brushed his fingertips down the length of his arousal. "You'd like this?"

"Very much." She trembled as the size swelled larger; her fingers clenched hard against an overwhelming urge to touch him.

"Then you must have it," he gently replied. "As soon as you indulge my whims."

"Anything," she whispered, wanting to feel him, needing to feel him, her body pulsing, wet with desire. For the briefest second, she chastised herself for such abject submission, but the impulse quickly passed, inundated by more compelling urgencies.

"Such gratifying compliance," he murmured, moving forward to take her hand. "I look forward to my husbandly role."

"As do I," she replied.

AN INTERVAL LATER, STILL PANTING, ROBBIE MUR-
mured, "This . . . must be . . . heaven."

Eyes shut, Roxane smiled.

Bending his head, he licked the tip of her nose. "Or
my heaven."

Her lashes slowly rose. "One of blissful contentment, because of you."

Propped above her, he offered her a shameless grin.
"Because of me?"

"Of course. That's why I chose you."

"*You* chose *me*?" His laughter exploded, swirling
around them in the canopied bed. "As if I would have
let you get away."

"Are you saying you caught me?"

"And don't forget it."

"Am I caught literally or figuratively?" she seductively murmured.

His dark brows flickered in ribald amusement.
"Ready again, are you?"

"Do you mind?"

He shook his head. "Not this side of death."

"What a charming man," she whispered, tracing a
delicately placed finger down his chest.

"A charming *husband*."

"Yes, yes. And mine . . ."

Her smile gladdened his heart and he gave her all
his love, that delectable first night of their marriage
when the world was fresh and new.

Epilogue

———◆◆◆———

ℛOXANE WENT INTO LABOR TWO MONTHS early, and even though four midwives had been brought into residence at Bransley Hill, no one was fully prepared. The delivery turned out to be difficult, and as the desperate hours lengthened, all Robbie could think of was the scores of women he'd know who'd died in childbirth. It was all too common. Sitting beside Roxane's bed with her hand in his, he watched his wife's strength wane with a terror he'd never before experienced.

"Someone do something," he said, his voice tight with fear.

Unwilling to bear responsibility for the countess's death, the women suggested the two local doctors be called in. When Robbie took issue with the doctors' competence, they recommended a woman healer as well.

After the three were swiftly fetched and interviewed, Robbie was more prone to put his faith in the young woman. Unlike the doctors, she hadn't advised bleeding.

"The countess will slip away if they bleed her," the woman warned, and when Robbie had visibly paled, she calmed him. "Don't worry, my lord, your lady is strong yet. And the babies can be moved."

"Babies?" His astonishment was unmistakable.

"Two, my lord."

It took him a moment to come to terms with the surprising news. "Are you sure?" The woman looked too young to be so confident, her small, slender stature and braided dark hair only adding to her adolescent image.

"I'm certain, my lord."

A small silence ensued while he studied her, wishing he felt as assured, wanting surety for his wife's survival. But when he finally spoke, his tone was brisk, his judgment made. "Tell me what you need and I'll see that you have it."

While Robbie held Roxane's hand and prayed to any god who would listen, the young woman set to work with quiet authority. The babies were presenting abnormally, she explained. Moving the first baby into position with slow deliberation and neat-handed skill, she soon delivered a tiny baby girl, so small she fit into the cradle of Robbie's palms. When a boy was born shortly after, fragile and precious like his sister, the babies were put into baskets heated with hot, wrapped bricks.

Roxane's lashes fluttered open as Robbie kissed her cheek. "It's over," he whispered, stroking her hand with exquisite tenderness. "Rest now. I'm here."

Her eyes closed before he'd finished speaking. He glanced across the bed at young Margaret, who had performed such miracles. "You must stay until my lady is well again."

She nodded. "The next forty-eight hours will be critical, my lord, with the risk of childbed fever."

"We'll have to see that the countess is spared," he said, as if he could ward off the evil by sheer will. And for the next two days, Robbie left the room only briefly, to assure the children of their mother's health and to introduce them to their new siblings, who were being cared for by the nursery staff and wet nurses.

As the third day dawned, he came awake with a start when Roxane moved. Raising his head from the bed, he looked into her eyes and smiled before pushing away and dropping back into his chair.

"You look terrible," Roxane whispered.

Three days' growth of russet stubble covered his jaw, and dark shadows rimmed his eyes. "You look wonderful," he breathed.

"The babies—"

"Are doing well."

"The children?"

"Impatient to see you, whenever you feel strong enough."

"I feel awake, at least."

"Good." Not wishing to tempt fate, he didn't say more, but he surveyed her with the vigilant exactness he'd acquired in the last few days, looking for any sign of fever. Her cheeks were rosy, not flushed, and he felt a measure of relief. "Would you like something to eat or drink?"

"I *am* hungry."

Leaning over, he delicately patted Roxane's hand. "I'll get us some breakfast."

After Roxane ate, the children were allowed a visit.

Having been warned their mother was still weak, they hugged her gently and spoke in rarely heard hushed tones. Until their new brother and sister were brought in. Excited to tell their mother of all the babies' feats, the children returned to their normal levels of clamorous noise.

In the months that followed, the earl's large family settled into a peaceful country life, far from the political machinations in London and Edinburgh. And in the succeeding years, the Carre brothers concentrated on their shipping trade, reaping extravagant profits from the lucrative markets in the American colonies. Their economic success marked a personal freedom from British rule, and in some small measure served as recompense for England's domination.

With determination and resolve, the Carre families cultivated their estates and businesses while studiously avoiding any political entanglements. Away from the world dominated by the English court, their families grew and prospered, their happiness increasing in equal measure. Home and family became the source of their greatest pleasures, fortune smiled on them, and the magical wonder of love, once found, endured. . . .

---⊸≋≋≋⊸---

NOTES

SOME READERS MAY HAVE NOTICED THE CHANGE IN ROBBIE'S title from Master of Graden in *Outlaw* to the Earl of Greenlaw in *To Please a Lady*. As Johnnie Carre's heir, Robbie was Master of Graden—the Scottish designation "master" connoting an heir to a peerage. Once Johnnie's son, Thomas, was born, *he* became Master of Graden. Johnnie's larger properties, inherited from his father, were now passed on to his son. But in Scotland, peerages can descend through the female line as well, so Robbie had inherited, through his mother, the titles of Earl of Greenlaw, Viscount Kintire, Laird of Tron. Her properties in East Lothian passed to him with the titles.

1. See page 17. As chief of the Campbells, the Duke of Argyll had more men at his command than there were regular troops in Scotland, and better fighting men at that. At the time, the Scots army consisted of three thousand men. With a large Campbell fighting force loyal to him, the Duke of Argyll's influence extended beyond the political arena.

2. See page 19. The Duke of Hamilton, leader of the Scottish party for independence, was, after the Parliament of 1704, increasingly erratic in his behavior. Reports of his willingness to negotiate with the queen were already in the air by the fall of 1704. Roxburgh wrote from London to Baillie of Jerviswood on December 12, 1704: "I have been told by a

friend of Duke Hamilton's, and one that knows him well, within this eight and forty hours, that if the Queen has a mind for this business, Duke Hamilton was vain and necessitous." And James Johnstone, who as Lord Register was a key figure in the conduct of Scottish affairs in London, also wrote to Jerviswood on January 13, 1705: "I have had suspicions, but now I am certain, that Duke Hamilton is tampering by the means of Harley with the Lord Treasurer. . . . He must have his debts payed." And again, on February 15, 1705, he addressed Jerviswood: "Duke Hamilton's friends are so gross as to intimate to great men here that he is *Chambre à Louer* (Room for Hire). But for all that's to be done now, I find it's thought scarcely worth the while to make the Purchase." Before the 1705 session was over, however, Hamilton apparently found a way to prove that his support was worth the purchase.

3. See page 36. Condoms were referred to as French *lettres* because they were tied at the open end with a ribbon. The French, though, referred to condoms as *redingotes des Anglais* (English riding coats). The earliest published description of a condom used to prevent conception appears in Gabriel Fallopio's *De Morbo Gallico* (Padua, 1563). In English, it was named for a Dr. Condom, physician at the court of Charles II, who ruled from 1660 to 1685. In the Argyll Papers, Myln says: "John, Duke of Argyll, was made Commissioner to the Parliament 6th March 1705. He brought along with him a certaine instrument called a Quondam, which occasioned the debauching of a great number of ladies of quality, and other young gentlewomen." John Campbell regarded women as available for his pleasure, and he came to Edinburgh prepared.

4. See page 66. A Scottish peerage didn't necessarily allow a Scottish noble to sit in the English House of Lords, whereas

an English peerage automatically bestowed that privilege. Also, an English peerage was more likely to offer the recipient an opportunity to share in the numerous highly lucrative government offices, positions, and pensions. For his part in passing the Union treaty, the Duke of Argyll was rewarded with the English titles of Baron Chatham and Earl of Greenwich. Since he had no son to inherit, only five daughters by his second marriage, he arranged for his eldest daughter, Lady Caroline, to have the rights of a male heir to those titles. Otherwise they would have passed to his younger brother, whom he disliked.

5. See page 76. The property rights of married women in Scotland were strong in some respects and weak in others. A wife's moveable property was under her husband's control, although marriage contracts could be used to enlarge or restrict the wife's rights. In the case of heritable or immoveable property, the married woman had stronger rights. She could not dispose of this without consent, but neither could the husband sell his wife's land without her permission, and he could not arbitrarily deny his wife permission to dispose of her separate estate without good cause.

Unmarried women, however, enjoyed superior legal rights, and widows were effectively on a par with men. Widowhood was the only stage of the female life cycle in which women could be truly economically and legally independent. Widows not only controlled their own wealth, but they were entitled by law to at least a third of their husband's moveable estate and could also take over his business.

6. See page 77. For Hamilton's treachery, he was rewarded by the English with an English dukedom, The Order of the Thistle and the Garter, and the appointment as ambassador

to Paris. Generous monetary rewards accompanied each of these honors.

In terms of Argyll's compensations, he was both arrogant and self-confident in his dealings with the English. He wrote to the Earl of Mar during his negotiations with the English court: "My Lord, it is surprising to me that my Lord Treasurer, who is a man of sense, should think of sending me up and down like a footman from one country to another without ever offering me any reward. Thier is indeed a sairtain service due from every subject to his Prince, and that I shall pay to the Queen as faithfully as anybody can doe; but if her ministers thinks it for her services to imploy me any forder I doe think the proposal should be attended with an offer of a reward."

Lord Treasurer Godolphin eventually agreed. Argyll was created Baron Chatham and Earl of Greenwich—later Duke—and given the rank of Brigadier General in the English army—later commander in chief of the English forces in Spain. His emoluments for the last position alone amounted to close to 100,000 pounds per year. Argyll's younger brother, Archibald Campbell, only twenty-three at the time of the Union, was made Viscount of Islay, Lord Oransay, Dunoon, and Arrase.

7. See page 87. In traditional Scottish society, a married woman retained her father's surname. Among the Edinburgh middle classes, however, the convention of adopting the husband's surname began in the late seventeenth century and became the norm by the late eighteenth. The late-seventeenth-century observer Thomas Morer believed that retention of the maiden name implied that Scottish women were more independent of their husbands than was the case in England. . Wormald agreed, and argued further that the wife

and her relatives were not fully joined to her husband and his family since descent in Scotland was reckoned agnatically (through the male line) rather than cognatically (female line) as in England.

8. See page 103. Daniel Defoe led a checkered life. Although the son of a tallow-chandler, he was determined to claim for himself the status of a gentleman. His quest for position and wealth began with his decision to become a London merchant. By 1706, when he came to Edinburgh (I've taken literary license and placed him in Scotland a year earlier), he'd been educated for the ministry, had a failure of faith, married a lady from a family of means, become a prosperous merchant, gone bankrupt twice, and been imprisoned, pilloried, and saved from the hell of Newgate Prison by Robert Harley, Speaker of the House of Commons. From that point on, he became "Robert Harley's man," and both his writings and activities were for the greater good of the moderate Tory position as represented by Robert Harley. He was sent to Scotland as an English agent to write pro-Union propaganda and send back information on the state of the Union negotiations. Serving ostensibly as a merchant conducting business in Scotland, he used that role to acquire information to report back to his masters. Just for fun, I added him to Queensberry's spies.

9. See page 157. The Covenanters were a powerful Presbyterian influence on Scottish history for 150 years after the Reformation. They regarded their spiritual kingdom as superior to the state, and promulgated the ideology that each person made his or her own direct and individual covenant with God. At various levels of zealotry, they pledged to be good examples to others of Godliness, Soberness, and Righteousness;

to fight against the Popish Tyranny; and to defend true religion all the days of their lives. As with so many zealots, they had no tolerance for other religions.

10. See page 152. When William of Orange landed in England to take the throne from James II, Archibald Campbell was at his side, ready to repair his fortunes. For Argyll's help in putting William on the throne, the new king restored his estates and elevated him to Duke of Argyll, Marquess of Kintyre and Lorne, Earl of Campbell and Cowal, Viscount of Lochow and Glenila, Lord Inveraray, Mull, Morven, and Tiry

When it came to the game of political chess, the first duke (John Campbell's father) spoke plainly: "When I come to speak, even with those I am best with, of making a model to carry the King's business, by buying some, purchasing others, and making places void for others, tho' these be but of the smaller sort, nor is it yet advisable; many other I meet with, this tutor has this friend to protect, the other has another, which does confound affairs. . . . However . . . I will send for you, for your satisfaction and mine, a schedule, by which I'd carry thirty members of parliament off, and so carry the affair." Argyll's sons owed as much to nature as to nurture.

11. See page 163. The landed families of Scotland, whatever rank or extent, were united by a complicated tangle of relationships. There was a kinship of feeling, a realization of common interest, a sense of loyalty that arose partly from the feudal relationship that bound the laird's Jock' to the laird as it bound lesser noble to magnate and magnate to king. Heads of noble families had to provide for substantial establishments and large kinship groups, so their need for funds was predicated on the size and number of their dependencies.

12. See page 181. A Scot's pound equaled one-twelfth sterling (English pound).

13. See page 181. When Argyll was twenty-one (then Lord Lorne) he met Mary Browne, and the gossip of the day reported that the young lord was strongly drawn to her. His passionate, impetuous wooing led to a speedy marriage. On December 30, 1701, the contract was signed. Unfortunately, in the early days of their marriage they discovered they were unsuited to each other. The disillusion affected John more severely than Mary, who was even then in delicate health. They immediately separated, but she didn't die until January 1717. He remarried in June of that year.

14. See page 188. One of the more blatant instances of the Campbells' using children as pawns took place in 1498. John Cawdor's daughter, Muriel, born after his death, was left without a protector. And there was more than one powerful leader ready to move in and act as guardian to the girl for the sake of her fortune. However, Archibald Campbell, second Earl of Argyll, who was Lord High Chancellor at the time, had political priority and moved first.

For about four years Muriel was left with her maternal relatives, the Roses. Then one day the Campbells came to take her under their guardianship. They gave as an excuse that it was time for her to start school, and they proposed to take her to the Argyll country. In the ensuing disagreement there were casualties on both sides, with seven Campbells lost. As the fight progressed some of the Campbells seized the girl and rushed her away with a guard. Everyone knew there was much more than the girl at stake, for when she rode south with the Campbells, the Cawdor inheritance rode with her.

When Campbell of Inverliver, who led the sortie, was

asked if he didn't consider seven men a high price to pay for the custody of a four-year-old girl who might die before her inheritance could be impounded, he replied: "The lassie can never die sae long as there is a red-headed lass on the shores of Loch Awe."

15. See page 193. Many young men of good family became lawyers, simply for the value of legal training in politics or in estate management, or merely for a broadening of their education. In 1720, Professor Alexander Bayne had addressed his first-year students (students began university much younger in those days—between 13 and 16) in the class of Municipal Law at Edinburgh University with the argument: "But besides, gentlemen, you will consider what an ornament it is to know the law of your country. . . . Let us but consider, then, the knowledge of our law, as the proper embellishment of a gentleman, without regard to the useful part; and does it not even in that abstracted light deserve your application?"

16. See page 204. Since wealth and landed estates were kept in the family whenever possible, marriage between cousins was common. The following anecdote is an example of a variation on that custom: In the late sixteenth century, Thomas Craufurd's fortune fell to his granddaughter, who became "the heiress of Crosbie." But the title and land would pass to a male relative. In order to retain her property and grandfather's title, Jean Craufurd was determined to marry her second cousin Patrick. The problem was that Patrick was, in the words of the song, "ower young to marry yet," since he was ten years younger than Jean. However, she "reserved herself" for her cousin and married him in 1606, when he was eighteen and she was twenty-eight. Thus the two families of Craufurd of Crosbie and Craufurd of Auchenames were once more conjoined. Patrick and Jean settled down to a long and

happy married life at Crosbie. They had six sons and two daughters.

17. See page 213. It was an age of heavy drinking. At dinner, the lady of the house did the first honors—the toast given without delay. French wines were the drink of choice, and both sexes drank heartily. English visitors always remarked on the conviviality of the social occasions in Scotland, and how differences of rank weren't regarded as an impassable barrier, as they were in England. Social gatherings always encompassed an interesting mix of guests. The eighteenth century was also the age of the tavern clubs, most situated in the thoroughfare leading from the Castle to the Watergate. They were open round the clock—"from the gillbells to the drum." From well-known clergy to esteemed judges, the habitués of the taverns ran the whole gamut of society. Even society women would on occasion join a party at a tavern, particularly in the winter, when the Firth of Forth oysters were best. Raw oysters and porter were set in huge dishes on the table, and everyone would indulge without restraint. Hospitality and conviviality were a particular characteristic of Scottish society, with women participating in equal measure.

18. See page 213. In England the ladies left the table directly after dessert and retired to the drawing room for tea. In Scotland the ladies stayed to share the gaiety after dessert. The cloth was taken up and the table was covered with decanters of port, sherry, Madeira, and pitchers of punch, along with the profusion of small glasses. The health of each lady was drunk, and then the guests', each in turn by name. A much more open socialization between men and women was practiced. However, by the middle of the nineteenth century, English customs had infiltrated the Scottish dinner

table, and ladies would often adjourn for tea when the table was cleared.

19. See page 276. Political management, the spoils system, and the use of influence were indispensable to the government. And all were employed to see that the Union proposal passed the Scottish Parliament. What's astonishing are the small sums necessary to buy those votes needed for passage. With the exception of the prominent magnates who demanded and generally received generous sums, the rank-and-file members of Parliament who were paid for their votes realized modest returns. Seafield writes: "Culloden has been with me; and I think, if his pension be continued to him, we will have his assistance." Seafield continues, "I think also that Bracco will be assisting; I have agreed with him for two hundred pounds a year." Queensberry writes to the court that the Earl Marischal might be detached from the opposition for a pension of three hundred pounds—in this case he's referring to Scots pounds—a very small amount. The court managers received more munificent rewards. Seafield was made a viscount with a thousand pound pension each year. Queensberry was given an English Dukedom and an annual pension of three thousand pounds for life. Argyll and his brother Archibald's compensation was of course the most distinguished in terms of titles, wealth, and power. The brothers dominated Scottish politics after Queensberry died in 1711. At John's death in 1743, Archibald succeeded to his title as third Duke of Argyll, and continued as the uncrowned ruler of Scotland until 1761.

**Look for Susan Johnson's
next sensual novel**

**Available summer 2000
from Bantam Books**

Here's a sneak preview.

The Marquis of Redvers caught sight of the Honorable Sarah Palmer and her aunt Lady Tallien before they saw him, and quickly slipped away down the nearest aisle. The crowds at the Great Exhibition offered him refuge, the daily attendance of forty thousand—a veritable crush beneath the glass barrel vaults of Paxton's brilliant design. Taking no notice of the exhibits, he moved swiftly through the throng, concerned only with putting distance between himself and the two ladies. Sarah, newly out, had set her cap for him—always reason for evasion—while her aunt Bella, one of his many lovers, had begun making demands of him of late. Definitely time to move on, now *and* in the future.

Quickly glancing over his shoulder, he detected no tell-tale bobbing pink bonnet feathers in the mass of humanity behind him and gratified, he determined to make his un-availability crystal clear next time he met the Palmer ladies. But not today, not after two nights of women and carouse; he was damned tired. And if Sarah Palmer didn't under-stand he wasn't in the market for a wife, her aunt certainly should, as did anyone in the ton with half a brain.

Swiveling around a second too late, he crashed into a lady reading a brochure. She began to pitch backward, her astonished cry swallowed up in the din of the crowd. Re-acting instinctively, he caught her arms, pulled her hard against him to keep them both from falling. Her eyes flared wide at the impress of his muscled chest against her breasts, his powerful thighs braced against hers and stunned, she looked up into dark eyes suddenly regarding her with interest.

She was exquisite—golden-haired, dazzling, graphically voluptuous—and even after two sleepless nights of de-bauch, the marquis's senses instantly came alert. "Pardon me," he murmured in a deep, low, fascinated tone.

"You're pardoned." A modicum of reserve underlay her words.

But he didn't let her go. Her lavish breasts, shapely thighs, and wide-eyed beauty were too intriguing. "You're French," he said.

"Unhand me, please." Her voice was cool now, her arms held out wide.

A gentleman despite all his profligate ways, he released her and stepped away. But he took note of the brochure in her hand, the machine on the cover a vast conglomeration of gas lights and mirrors. The exact one, he reflected, gazing over her shoulder, on display in the booth behind her—the apparatus set at the head and foot of an operating table. "I've been thinking of buying a dozen of those," he remarked, pointing at her brochure, his smile gracious.

Her surprise showed.

"For my tenants' hospital," he mendaciously added.

"You must have a very large establishment." She was wary. He'd never seen that look before in a woman, his reputation for pleasing women well-known.

"Just a small one at each estate," he improvised.

The caution left her eyes, replaced by a spark of interest. "Do you employ doctors or just nurses? I've found that nurses often . . ."

Her conversation became quite animated at that point and guiding her to one side of the stream of traffic, he replied to her questions with answers that further encouraged her passionate interest in the very odd field of patient care. He was infinitely charming but then he'd had enormous practice.

Was she equally animated in bed? he wondered, debating how best to discover that fact for himself. And if the purchase of a dozen of those light contraptions might entice this dazzling woman into his bed, he decided it would be money well spent.

He invited her to dinner—just a small party of relatives, he spontaneously devised—and her hesitation was rather that of propriety than disinterest.

"You may know my aunt Lady Markham," he offered. Her dress and manner were of his world, so they both understood the requirements of protocol.

"My father does," she replied. "Her husband brokered the treaty between Greece and Turkey."

"Your father?"

"Pasha Duras."

"Ah . . . the freedom fighter." Pasha Duras had served in the Greek government for a time; his name was well-known in Europe. "I could send a carriage for you at nine."

"Will your aunt be there?"

If he had to drag her from her bed. "Yes," he said.

"Well, then . . . I'd like that." She finished with a smile that outshone the room lights. "My name is Venus."

Perfect casting, he reflected, wondering if she'd inherited her namesake's amorous persona as well. "I'm Jack Fitz-James."

"The Marquis of Redvers," she said with distaste. "I'm afraid I'm busy tonight. If you'll excuse me." And turning abruptly, she walked away.

But the marquis never withdrew from a challenge. Apparently she was planning on staying in London for another fortnight at least. Plenty of time, he mused, watching her disappear into the crowd, for a leisurely seduction.

"Found a new woman?" Ned Darlington quirked his brow in sardonic query as the marquis approached the Turkish exhibit. Pushing away from the glass display case filled with the weapons they'd come to see, he added, "Is she blonde or blonde?"

Jack's gaze narrowed in mild scrutiny. "How the hell can you tell?"

Baron Darlington's tone was indulgent. "How long have I known you?"

"Long enough apparently." The marquis slowly smiled. "But this one's utterly gorgeous."

"Aren't they all?"

Jack's smile only broadened. "So cynical, Ned, when I'm enchanted."

"No doubt that single-minded fascination accounts in no small measure for your success with the ladies."

"I do like 'em. That's no secret." The marquis's dark brows flickered with pithy import. "The lady calls herself Venus."

"How appropriate considering your reputation for fucking."

"I rather thought it auspicious."

"So when are you joining her in bed?"

"Since she cut me cold, it might be a few days."

The baron chuckled. "Losing your edge, my fine stud?"

"She's French."

"And obviously doesn't know of your special talents for pleasing the ladies."

Jack's perfect white teeth flashed in a grin. "Apparently she does and that's the rub."

"So you'll have to change her mind."

"My thought exactly."

"French ladies know what they want. Maybe you're not her style. Have you thought of that?"

"We were having a very pleasant conversation until she discovered my name."

"Along with your propensity for vice." Ned shrugged. "If she's prudish, don't waste your time."

"But I want to."

"You want to assail the impregnable citadel? Since when?"

"Nothing's impregnable," the marquis softly murmured.

The baron cast his friend a speculative look. "That

comment almost calls for a wager . . . and if I didn't know your unerring seductive skills, I'd hazard my money."

"She just has to come to know me better," Jack Fitz-James said with a disarming grin.

"I expect she will. Have you ever been refused?"

"Not until today."

But regardless Ned's wisdom in not betting on the outcome of the marquis's seduction, he related the story of the lady's refusal with droll merriment to some friends and many of them were less prudent or perhaps less discerning. Or maybe simply ripe for any scandalous wager. By the time the marquis entered Brookes that evening, gossip apropos Venus Duras had preceded him and the betting book was filled with an array of wildly extravagant wagers. Understanding the speed with which gossip swept through the ton, he received all the ribald and licentious comment with equanimity. But he took notice, as well, that there were those who had put money on the lady—on her ability to deter his advances.

He spent most of the evening gambling and won as usual, drank with his renowned and notable capacity, and adroitly deflected most of the conversational gambits having to do with his interest in Miss Duras. Until later that night when everyone was well into their cups and discretion vanished along with tact.

"She's at the Duchess of Groveland's ball tonight," one of his gambling companions remarked with a waggish arch of his brow. "Why aren't you there?"

"You already missed the dinner," another noted with a grin, for the marquis's disinterest in society dinners was well-known.

"Are we gambling or discussing my sex life?" Jack drawled, looking up from his cards, surveying his companions with an open gaze.

"Both," the young Viscount Talmont cheerfully retorted, signaling the dealer for another card. "Did you know the untouchable Miss Duras has turned down two dukes and a passel of earls in the last fortnight?" Undeterred despite Jack's blank look, the viscount remarked, "Think you can do better?"

"I'm not offering her my title, Alastair. I hope that's clear to everyone."

"Don't have to be clear to us, Redvers. Although I don't suggest you mention the transience of your interest to the lady straight away." Lord Halverstam cast a sportive look around the table.

"I'm also not in the market for advice," the marquis murmured, "although I'll take some of your money if that's the best you can do." He nodded at the man's cards spread out on the green baize.

"Damn, Redvers," Charles Givens muttered. "How the hell do you do it hand after hand?"

"Just lucky," Jack pleasantly replied, scooping in the markers from the center of the table. "Or maybe you're paying too much attention to my love life and not enough to your cards."

And for the next several hands with varying degrees of inebriation, everyone concentrated on their cards. Without any better results. The marquis won another twenty thousand by the end of the hour and after glancing at the clock on the wall, he waved a footman over and ordered a bottle of brandy. Gathering his winnings, he handed them to another servant, bid his adieus and rose from the table without explanation. Taking the brandy from the footman just short of the door, he raced down the stairs.

He'd promised the Duchess of Groveland he'd come and dance with her before midnight and he had only ten minutes to make good on his promise.

The marquetry case clock in the cavernous entrance hall of Groveland House was striking midnight when the Marquis of Redvers strolled through the opened doors. He handed his brandy bottle to Peggy's majordomo, whom he greeted with genial familiarity. "Don't bother announcing me, Jerrold," he added. "I'll cut in on the Duchess."

"As you wish, my Lord," the august butler replied, his mouth twitching into a restrained smile. "She didn't think you'd arrive on time."

"Don't I always?"

"My words exactly, my Lord. Lord Redvers is to be depended on, I told her."

"How much did she lose?"

"Ten guineas, my lord," the majordomo replied with obvious pleasure.

"Only women are always late, eh, Jerrold?"

"It rather seems the case, Sir. Would you like some of your usual vintage?"

"In a few minutes perhaps. And I forgot my damned gloves again."

"I could procure some for you, Sir."

Jack shook his head. "Hate those damned things. Peggy won't mind."

"I'm sure she won't, my Lord. Since the Duchess considers you the finest dancer in the ton, she'll be pleased to dance with you, gloves or not."

"Well, then," the marquis said, "I'm off to do my duty by my godmother."

"Very good, sir." Offering the young marquis an impeccable bow, he watched the object of his employer's affection stroll to the staircase and ascend to the floor above. Then snapping his fingers for an underling, he saw that the marquis's favorite champagne was sent up to him.

The Marquis of Redvers stood in the doorway to the ballroom, surveying the numerous guests twirling to the strains of a waltz, the crystal chandeliers illuminating the gilded room, the glittering light contending with the sparkle of jewels, the shimmer of silken ball gowns and gleaming coiffeurs ornamented with flowers and feathers, the satiny glow of bared shoulders and décolletages—all the grandeur and brilliance of the fashionable beau monde assembled under the duchess's splendid Tiepolo ceiling.

And one by one, those guests took notice of the gloriously handsome young marquis standing in the doorway. His splendid height was attributed to the Fitz-James connection with Charles II, as were his excesses, although his dark good looks, everyone agreed, came from his mother's family. The DeLanceys had contributed beauty to England's bloodlines since the time of the Norman invasion. The faultless hand of his tailor was evident in the fit of his evening rig, the fine wool smoothly flowing over his lean, muscled form, his damask waistcoat subtle in tone, eggshell rather than white, calling attention even in its understatement to his taut, honed torso. Eschewing the hirsute fashions of the time, he was clean-shaven, his bronzed skin evidence of his devotion to the sporting life. But what most attracted attention and gave him his special cachet beyond his notoriety were his eyes. He had gypsy eyes, black as ebony, sensual, magnetic; some said it seemed as though he could see right through you. But those who knew him best saw the laughter and mischievous sparkle more often than not.

"Darling! You've come!" The duchess's jubilant voice rose above the diminishing hum of conversation as everyone regarded the infamous young lord who was here tonight, they hoped, to make good on their wagers. Arms outstretched, Peggy Hexton crossed the large ballroom with a beaming smile on her heavily rouged face. The duchess had been a great beauty in her day and retained the less subtle cosmetics of her generation. Her hair was brightly hennaed and she wasn't svelte anymore, but she was cheerfully enamored of life and embraced each day with enthusiasm.

"Would I stay away from you?" Jack replied, taking her hands in his and offering her a warm smile. "When my favorite waltz is playing?"

"Every waltz is your favorite, you sweet boy," she lightly retorted, pulling him onto the dance floor. "And now that you're here, I'll have someone decent to dance with."

The duchess had been on the stage before she captured the duke's heart and while he was long dead and she could have any man with her fortune, she'd never remarried. She preferred her freedom, she always said, but Jack knew hers had been a love match and while he didn't precisely understand the concept, he envied her the obvious bliss she'd enjoyed.

"I intend to keep you by my side for a good long while," she warned as they moved into their first turn.

"I'm here as your cicisbeo, darling." The marquis winked wickedly. "You may order me about at your will."

"What if I order you to make amends to Miss Duras?" she archly said.

"I would, of course. But for what do I need to make amends?"

"She seems angry with you."

"She's here?" He'd not seen her, but then the crowded ballroom limited visibility.

"I had her beside me at dinner. She's a very remarkable woman."

"I'm not sure I like that particular tone of voice."

"What tone?"

"That matchmaking tone. I'd recognize it in the roar of a hurricane." Or on the last day of the apocalypse, he reflected, any inference to matrimony having the same effect on him as a vision of hell.

"Good God, Jack, she's more than a match for you. She doesn't want to be married either. You should have heard her at dinner. Although she was completely charming, there was no doubt of her disinterest in marriage."

"Are you humbugging me?" he said, swinging them in a double twirl with flawless precision. "There isn't a woman born who doesn't want to be married."

"She wouldn't agree with you."

More than intrigued, for he'd not stopped thinking of Miss Duras since their meeting, he debated the possibility that she might be available for a liaison outside the normal courting rituals. Not that he hadn't perfected evasion of those rituals to a fine art, but were her disinterest in marriage true, how much more pleasant their relationship could be.

He didn't question his ability to persuade her to become closer friends. Only the timetable was in debate.

"You'll have to introduce me then." His smile lit up his face, for he knew his godmother's propensity for gambling. "I suppose you have some money riding on this."

"Perhaps a little." Gazing up at him, she lifted one hennaed brow with a dramatic flare reminiscent of her days on the stage.

"I hope it's not more than a pony," he challenged. "I can't guarantee swift results."

"Or any results, some are saying," she murmured, playfully tapping his shoulder with her fan.

He scrutinized her for a moment. "Did you bet on the lady?"

"What if I did?"

"Traitor." But he was grinning.

She made a small moue. "I didn't, of course. Knowing you so well." She refrained from saying the beautiful, intelligent Miss Duras would give him a merry chase though. He'd find that out soon enough. It was about time someone resisted the young boy's surfeit of charm. And on the obverse side, the young lady might find Jack's unconventional attitudes refreshing.

At base, of course, she really couldn't resist a bit of matchmaking.

While all the guests at the duchess's ball waited with bated breath for the marquis and the Frenchwoman to meet, the lady in question, unaware of the speculation rife in the air, was enjoying the evening. She loved dancing and the duchess, so warmhearted and cordial, had become a comrade of sorts at dinner. She seemed to understand what so many nobles didn't—that the poor deserved respect, compassion and, rather than moralizing, a decent chance to earn a living. The duchess had also donated a generous sum to Venus's latest charity hospital being built in Paris.

Additionally, she'd offered her men to relay the new hospital equipment Venus had ordered at the Great Exhibition from the warehouse to the docks, saving on dray fees.

During dinner, too, when a female guest had rudely asked Venus about her lack of a husband, the duchess had come to her defense. "Don't mind Clara," the duchess had said, sotto voce. "She's green with envy over your looks." And for some time they'd spoken quietly about the advantages and liabilities of marriage, agreeing that if a woman had her own fortune, there was little reason to marry simply to be married.

"Wait until you're swept off your feet," the duchess had counseled, and when Venus had remarked that that was highly unlikely considering the men she'd met and known, her hostess had winked and said, "Sometimes it happens when you least expect it."

When the dancing began, Venus was besieged with partners and while all the men she danced with were solicitous and affable, some gallant to the extreme, none touched her emotions. But then no man ever had. On occasion over the years, she'd questioned her lack of interest, concerned she was some aberration of womanhood. Not tonight, however. She was having a marvelous time dancing and if her suitors didn't spark her fancy, they certainly were offering her immense pleasure.

Shortly after one, her escort conducted her into the supper room where buffet tables had been set up for the guests' refreshment. After seating her at a small table, he left to bring them chilled champagne. Leaning back against a gilded chair, Venus gently fanned her heated cheeks, her gaze surveying the extravagant display of colorful ices on the nearest buffet table.

"Darling, bring us all some of that pineapple ice."

Hearing the duchess's voice, Venus turned around with a smile that froze on her face when she saw the man beside her hostess.

"Go now, Jack, and do my bidding as you so gallantly promised you would." Peggy Hexton shooed him away with her ivory and silk fan. "You look as warm as I feel," she went on, dropping gracefully into a chair beside Venus. "Are you enjoying yourself?"

She wanted to say, *Until now,* but in the interests of courtesy, answered instead, "Yes, very much. Your musicians are wonderful."

"You dance well."

"I like to dance."

"Then you should dance with Jack. He's the very best."

"I'd rather not."

"He's really quite harmless, my dear. And you'll enjoy his skill immensely. I always insist he come to squire me at my balls."

"I'm afraid I generally avoid men of Redvers' ilk."

"I doubt you've known a man like Jack. Come, darling, it's only a dance."

How rude would she be if she continued to resist her

hostess's coaxing? Would she be thought unduly rigid? Could the marquis really be as notorious as gossip attested? "We'll see," Venus evasively replied, taking note of the duchess's piloting away of her returning escort with a stern look and a wave of her hand. She realized it wouldn't be easy to withstand her wilful hostess.

Satisfied with her maneuvering, the duchess was in good spirits, regaling Venus with humorous descriptions of some of her guests. When Jack returned with their ice she said, "I was telling Miss Duras about Lady Clara's prim daughter, who, thank god, couldn't come tonight."

"Amen to that," Jack lightly replied.

"Lady Clara has set her sights on Jack for her daughter, you see." The duchess shot a facetious glance at her godson.

"Peggy finds humor in my misery," the marquis observed, pulling up a chair beside his godmother.

"Surely you have to marry someday," the duchess playfully said.

He cast her an oblique glance. "I see you're bent on torturing me. I'm sure Miss Duras would prefer some other amusements."

"Not necessarily."

He found her sardonic smile captivating, but then everything about her was extremely fine, like a magnificent work of art. "Then consider me at your disposal, ladies," he offered.

"I'm donating some money to Miss Duras's hospital," the duchess abruptly said, as though having seen the incipient rapport between the two young people, she wished to further put the lady at ease. "You've plenty, Jack. Give her some for her charity."

He smiled. "That sounds very like an order, Peggy."

"Damned right it is. You're as rich as Croesus. Tell him how much you need," she directed, nodding at Venus.

"That's not necessary, really, but thank you, Lady Groveland."

"Stuff and nonsense," she snorted. "You needn't be polite

with Jack. He likes plainspoken people—like me," she added with a grin that creased the rouge on her cheeks. "And you need cash for that hospital."

"Why don't I send you a bank draft in the morning," the marquis suggested, rescuing Venus from his godmother's commanding enterprise.

"Make sure it's sizeable." The duchess struck his hand with her sorbet spoon.

"Yes, Peggy. Now are you through ordering us about?"

"Take Miss Duras for a dance and I'll be silent the rest of the night."

"There's an offer we can't refuse," the marquis said, turning a beguiling smile on Venus. "Once around the floor, Miss Duras, and we're free of Peggy's interference."

"Not forever, mind you," the duchess quickly interposed.

"For tonight at least," he countered with a piercing look meant to arrest her persistence. He didn't need help enticing a woman.

"For tonight," she reluctantly agreed, clearly in her element when ordering others' lives.

"Would you mind, Miss Duras?" Rising from his chair, he offered his hand to Venus. "In the interests of calm and tranquility for the remainder of the night, I remind you." An impudent light sparkled in his eyes.

Understanding her hostess wouldn't be gainsaid, Venus capitulated. The beauty of the man was truly breathtaking at close range; dancing with him would be far from an ordeal. "A laudable reason, Lord Redvers," she said, "I'm a proponent of calm and tranquility."

But when her hand touched his, any probability of maintaining calm and tranquility vanished.

They both felt the same inexplicable thrill and his fingers closed over hers with more force than he intended. "Excuse me," he instantly said, but he didn't release his grip. Instead, he placed his other hand under her arm and drew her from her chair as though she were more fragile than moonbeams.

They stood very close for the briefest of moments before his better judgment roused itself, before he remembered where they were, before he moved back a half-step and said in a normal voice that took enormous effort to produce, "Come dance with me."

The duchess was smiling as they walked away.

Venus wasn't aware of walking into the ballroom.

Lord Redvers was particularly aware of the hush that descended on the room when they moved out onto the floor.

But a second later, all the gawkers and voyeurs and gamblers who were counting their winnings disappeared from his perception. She was smiling up at him, a temptress in flowered yellow mousseline and he felt it in more than the obvious places. He felt it like a jolt, a primal hammer of arousal and excitement and if Peggy wouldn't be so smug, he'd tell her she was right tomorrow.

ABOUT THE AUTHOR

SUSAN JOHNSON, award-winning author of nationally bestselling novels, lives in the country near North Branch, Minnesota. A former art historian, she considers the life of a writer the best of all possible worlds.

Researching her novels takes her to past and distant places, and bringing characters to life allows her imagination full rein, while the creative process offers occasional fascinating glimpses into complicated machinery of the mind.

But perhaps most important . . . writing stories is fun.

Romance Readers Never Go to Bed Alone!

SWEEPSTAKES

GREAT READING MEANS YOU NEVER GO TO BED ALONE AGAIN!

**You could be one of 100 lucky readers
to win this limited-edition "Romance Readers
Never Go To Bed Alone!" nightshirt
<u>ABSOLUTELY FREE</u> from Bantam Books!**

To be eligible for a free nightshirt submit your entry to:
**ROMANCE READERS NEVER GO TO BED ALONE! Sweepstakes,
2 Accradata Drive, P.O. Box 5812, Dept. TP, Unionville, CT 06085-5812**

100 winners will be chosen in a random drawing from all eligible and completed entries.
Your entry must be received by November 2, 1999.

Have you read this author before?
☐ Yes   ☐ No

What format books do you buy?
☐ Paperback   ☐ Hardcover
☐ Trade Paperback

What other kinds of books do you buy?
☐ Mystery   ☐ New Age
☐ Scifi/Fantasy   ☐ Nonfiction
☐ Thrillers/Suspense

How did you choose this book?
☐ Author   ☐ Title   ☐ Cover
☐ Advertisement   ☐ Recommendation

How many books do you read a month?
☐ Less than one   ☐ 1-2
☐ 3-5   ☐ More than 5

How many of the books you read are romances?
☐ Less than one   ☐ 1-2
☐ 3-5   ☐ more than 5

Where did you buy this book?_____

NAME _____AGE _____

ADDRESS _____

CITY _____STATE _____ZIP _____

E-MAIL ADDRESS _____

NO PURCHASE NECESSARY.
Be sure to get your entry in by November 2, 1999!
See reverse for Official Entry Rules.

Bantam

Romance Readers Never Go to Bed Alone!

Official Entry Rules:

1. NO PURCHASE NECESSARY.

2. Enter by completing the official entry coupon, or by printing your name, address, age, and answers to the questions on the previous page on a 3"x 5" card and mail the coupon or card to:

ROMANCE READERS NEVER GO TO BED ALONE! Sweepstakes,
2 Accradata Drive
P.O. Box 5812, Dept. TP
Unionville, CT 06085-5812

Entries must be received by November 2, 1999. No mechanically reproduced entries allowed. Entries are limited to one per person. Not responsible for late, lost, stolen, illegible, incomplete, postage due or misdirected entries or mail.

3. One Hundred (100) Prizes will be awarded: The Prize is a free "Romance Readers Never Go To Bed Alone" nightshirt (100% cotton; one size only). Estimated value of prize: Approximately $18.00. No transfer or substitution of the prize will be permitted, except by Bantam Books, a division of Random House, Inc. ("Sponsor") in its sole discretion, in which case a prize of equal or greater value will be awarded.

4. On or about November 16, 1999, the winners will be chosen in a random drawing conducted by Sponsor's marketing department from all eligible and completed entries received by the entry deadline, and the winners will receive their prizes by mail. Odds of winning depend upon the number of eligible entries received, which is anticipated to be approximately 10,000.

5. Entrants must be residents of the United States and Canada (excluding Quebec). Limit one entry per person. Void in Puerto Rico, Quebec and where otherwise prohibited or restricted by law. All federal, state and local regulations apply. Employees of Bantam Books, Random House, Inc., its parent, subsidiaries, affiliates, suppliers and agencies and their immediate family members and persons living in their household are not eligible to enter this sweepstakes. All federal and local taxes, if any, are the sole responsibility of the prize winner. By accepting the prize, winner releases Bantam Books, Random House, Inc., and their parent companies, subsidiaries, affiliates, suppliers and agents from any and all liability for any loss, harm, damages, cost or expense, including without limitation, property damages, personal injury and/or deaths arising out of participation in this sweepstakes or the acceptance and use of the prize.

6. By entering, entrants agree to abide by these Official Rules and the decision of the judges, which shall be final.

7. For the names of the prize winners, available after November 30, 1999, send a stamped, self-addressed envelope, separate from your entry, to Romance Readers Never Go To Bed Alone! Sweepstakes Winners, Bantam Books, Dept. DS2, 1540 Broadway, New York, New York, 10036 by December 31, 1999.

8. Sponsor: Bantam Books, a division of Random House, Inc., 1540 Broadway, New York, New York, 10036.